Wen

VLG – Book Six

Vampires, Lycans, Gargoyles

By Laurann Dohner

Wen by Laurann Dohner

When Gerri's VampLycan stepfather died, her mother moved them far from his clan. As a teen, it was the most devastating day of her life, because it took Gerri away from Wen, the boy she'd loved since childhood. Fifteen years later, that boy has become a gorgeous man straight out of her wildest fantasies — and when he requests to meet her, Gerri suspects just seeing him will set her up for heartbreak all over again.

The petite blonde he fell for as a young VampLycan is still beautiful — and all human. Though Gerri's always been the one he longs to be with, Wen can't mate her. After the death of his brother, Wen was forced to assume the duties of firstborn, which include mating another VampLycan. But he needs a human to pull off his current mission for his clan, hunting a rogue Vampire in a human city. And he'll take any stolen moments with Gerri he can get.

As the danger surrounding the mission mounts, so does their passion, until it's equally perilous. It will take everything in him to keep Wen from claiming his mate…because doing so could mean her death.

VLG Series List

Drantos

Kraven

Lorn

Veso

Lavos

Wen

Wen - VLG - Book Six

By Laurann Dohner

Chapter One

There was no mistaking that the tall biker-looking dude in the leather jacket had to be Wen. His hair was shorter these days though, no longer flowing down to the middle of his back. It was dark brown, a bit shaggy, and fell to his broad shoulders. His father towered above other men at six feet seven, and his son inherited more than just his height. He had the same bodybuilder frame, with broad shoulders and thick biceps that stretched out the material covering them. The graceful, predatory way he stalked down the sidewalk in the opposite direction also assured her she had the right guy. Men moved out of his way, giving a wide berth, but women turned their heads, taking second looks.

Gerri sighed, stepping out of the shadows of the building across the street. Her blonde curly hair, falling almost to her waist, might as well have been a flag waving to say hello. The strong breeze whipped it into her face from behind now that she'd left the shelter of the doorway. She'd tried keeping it short but the tight curls drove her insane after a few weeks. The weight of having it long left it wavy instead. There was also the drawback of resembling a blonde version of a famous fictional orphan after she cut it off—and the jokes that went along with that. So she just let it grow, usually kept in a single braid down her back, but she hadn't had time to do that earlier. She'd hit snooze on her alarm clock too many times.

It had been hard to fall asleep the night before, knowing she'd see him again.

The wind blew down the street in his direction and he spun around, now striding her way, eyes hidden by the dark sunglasses he wore. She resisted cursing in case his hearing was as good as she imagined. It was a hot day, and she'd begun to sweat. He'd clearly picked up her scent. She could have gone bald or had facial surgery and Wen would still be able to locate her with his eyes closed...something she should have remembered. They'd grown up together. It didn't matter what hair products or laundry detergent she used. It had been a game to try to fool him when they were kids. Wen could always track her.

He made a beeline toward her, crossing the street.

The urge to run struck but she held still. He'd catch her before she made it half a block, and the results could get messy. They were no longer kids. A game of chase could easily turn deadly if she triggered him to go into hunt mode. She wasn't willing to risk it. They weren't friends anymore.

He stopped two feet away, and she hated having to lift her chin to stare up. The size difference between them had always been drastic but now it seemed ridiculous. He was well over a foot taller than her five-foot-five frame, and he had to have about a hundred and fifty pounds on her.

"You didn't grow much."

His deep baritone voice was just a reminder of what he really was. It gave her chills down her spine. He appeared to be human, a large one, but he wasn't. "You reached out to me and I came." She loathed the reality she called her life at that moment. He'd have hunted her down if she'd have refused a meeting. Seeing him again was painful and something she'd wanted to avoid. "As if you really gave me a choice. Your message on my voicemail was a bit threatening. I didn't appreciate that."

He tilted his head, and she was grateful that the sunglasses resting on the bridge of his nose were too dark to glimpse his eyes. She had a feeling they probably weren't as human-looking as his face at that moment. The soft growl that rumbled from him hinted that she'd pissed him off.

"Sorry." She lowered her gaze to his immense chest. "You have to admit this is a bad idea. We said our goodbyes and they should have stuck." She refused to step back and bow a little at the waist to show regret. The verbal apology would have to be enough. His customs weren't hers anymore. "It's too dangerous for me to be anywhere near you. It was rude to make threats toward me if I didn't text you back and meet with you today." She didn't add the part about how she realized he wouldn't be concerned if he got her killed by association. "What do you need?"

"We have to talk. Why did you pick this place? It's too public. What are we doing here?"

She wasn't surprised that he knew where she lived, since he'd somehow gotten her cell number. "I rented a room upstairs. I figured you'd want privacy." She backed up, turned, and prayed he wouldn't do something to get even for her rudeness. The boy he used to be wouldn't be so easily offended but he'd grown into a man she didn't know. "Follow me."

He didn't snarl a warning that she was being too pushy, so she breathed easier as she entered the cheap motel. The desk clerk wasn't there, probably in the back watching porn. Two drug addicts hung out in the corner of the small lobby and she guessed they were waiting for their dealer to show. The place was a hive of undesirable criminals but it didn't have any security cameras. They also accepted cash, rented rooms by the hour, and never asked questions.

"You don't trust me inside your den?"

She waited to answer until they reached the elevator and the doors closed them inside. "It's called an apartment out here in the real world, and it wasn't about trust. I figured that it was best if I could just say I'm a hooker doing a john if we're seen together. I have no idea why you're in Reno or who you're hunting."

"What makes you think I'm looking for someone?"

She sighed as the elevator doors opened, then dug out the plastic key and strode forward. The room was between the stairs and elevator. She unlocked it and pushed open the door, waiting for him to pass. He took a few steps inside, sniffed, and frowned.

"Hooker would be correct. This place reeks of sex."

She closed the door and locked it. "Sorry. I did a visual and it appeared okay. I even sprayed some scented stuff around."

"So I smell. Flowers and unwashed bodies don't mix."

Gerri leaned against the door and lifted her gaze, peering at his sunglasses. "What's up, Wen? I figure it has to be pretty dire for you to go to the trouble to reach out to me. I'm not easy to find."

9

"You didn't answer my question."

"You're hunting for someone. You wouldn't leave Alaska otherwise. It's what you guys do. Is he a bloodsucker, a Were, or a combo?"

He paused. "It's complicated."

"A fur bat? Shit."

His generous mouth curved upward. "You know they find that term offensive."

"I learned it from you. I'll make sure I share that fact if you tattle and a GarLycan comes after me to extract a little payback." The past blurred with the present for a second. It was a teasing conversation they may have had as kids. "Why call me? I don't know shit. I avoid anything that I think isn't what it appears to be."

"The city is full of bloodsuckers. How do you avoid them?"

"I don't go out after dark." She forced a smile and clasped her hands together over her stomach. "It's pretty simple. There are bars over my windows on my brick-exterior apartment. They would have to make a lot of racket, waste too much time and energy to break in. There's easier prey to go after. I keep the curtains closed, don't display myself as a snack, and I own a few poison-tipped crossbows bolts, just in case." She paused, a memory flashing. "Plus a really sharp ax. I've only ever had one come after me."

"I take it he won't do it again?"

"Nope. It was before I learned to live behind bars and thicker walls. I shot him full of arrows, kind of pinned him to a wall so I had time to take his head off, and used my ax to do it."

"His nest didn't come after you?"

"He was rogue. You should have smelled him. He probably hadn't bathed in months or changed his clothes. No master would ever allow one of his to stink that bad." She cleared her throat. "I also moved the next day without a forwarding address, just in case he had banded together with a few others. I'm good at getting lost."

"What did you do about the blood? It sounds as if it was messy. Humans have police and crime techs, if you left what they would have viewed as a murder scene."

"UV lamp, and I opened the curtains to let in a lot of sun. Vamp blood just goes away when you expose it to both. I remembered that. I had to patch the walls though. Good thing hardware stores open so early."

"How is your mother?"

It hurt to think about her, even after four years. "I have no clue. She hooked up with a Were, so I split. I know you don't like that term but I live in the human world, and they called themselves Werewolves. Some of his pack began sniffing after me. Becoming a human version of a bitch in a pack isn't in my life plans."

"None of them interested you as a mate?"

She hesitated, glanced around before staring at his dark glasses. "They weren't traditional. I'm not one to judge but that sickened even me. Let's leave it at that."

He leaned in, one hand flattening on the door near her face. "Let's not. Explain."

Anger stirred but she wasn't going to test his patience. He'd never had much as a kid, and she figured he'd have none at all now, since he'd become an adult. "They had a sharing-is-caring motto, okay? They don't believe in mates. I wouldn't bend over and take it from any guy who wanted me, even if huge sums of money were involved, so I sure as hell wasn't going to do it for free just because my mother was with their alpha. Any woman was viewed as community property by the men. Not my thing."

"The alpha allowed anyone in his pack to fuck your mother?"

"Didn't I just tell you their pack motto?"

"I don't understand. How many men shared your mother?"

"I really didn't want to know who Mom was getting it on with or how many it involved. She ordered me to stay but that wasn't going to happen."

"Damn. I liked Carol."

"Then join their pack and you can nail her too, since they're into that."

He growled low, sounding his irritation. "I didn't mean it that way and you know it. I assumed she avoided all the other races after her mate died."

"I think she missed the type, you know? Domineering, total control freak, with a bonus side of worship-me mentality." She ducked under his arm and quickly got past him, not comfortable feeling pinned in. "She's different now."

"Obviously. What changed her?"

12

"The whole slower-aging thing finally wore off and she kind of flipped when she got her first gray hair. I think it made her feel human and she didn't want that."

"But she is."

"Tell *her* that and see how much she rants. Been there and done that." She walked to the other side of the room and turned. "I think she joined up with that pack hoping they'd turn her. They aren't into claiming a mate, so it could only happen with a shitload of biting, bleeding, and hoping she survived long enough to become one. I wasn't going to stick around to watch. You know the success rate is so low because it's too brutal. While I was there, she was just drinking some of the blood they shared with her. That's dangerous too, when you're not mated, but she was willing to risk her body rejecting the blood. I hear that's a horrible way to go. I didn't want to be there to see if that nightmare happened.

"Now let's stop playing catch-up and just get to the point. What do you need from me, Wen? I don't know the right people if you're looking for contacts. I have a human-only policy on friends now."

"Okay." He stalked closer, invading her personal space again. "I need a human, and you fit the bill."

"Why me?"

"You know what I really am."

"Just pick someone else and tell them, then."

"They might not handle the truth well, and I couldn't trust a stranger."

"You can't trust me. It's been fifteen years since I left."

13

"You're still alive. You never told anyone about your life in Alaska."

"I know better. I don't need a big target on my back with everyone nonhuman tracking me to make sure I can't blab. Plus, even if no one in your world considered me a real threat, humans shove people ranting about Vampires, Werewolves, and Gargoyles into straitjackets. I hear the meds are excellent in mental hospitals but that's not my thing. I don't do drugs." She backed up. "Why are you so close?"

"I don't smell a man on you."

"And you won't. I'm not dating anyone right now. It ended poorly with the last boyfriend."

"Why?"

"I dump guys who cheat and play head games." She stared up at him. "Are there any boundaries you won't cross? I'm not asking about *your* sex life."

"I'm single."

"This week. I know too much about your kind. You obviously haven't found your mate, or you wouldn't be tracking someone without her on your heels."

"I wouldn't have left Alaska. Mated males don't hunt this far from home."

She nodded, hating the tiny bit of relief she felt. There had been a time when she'd daydreamed about becoming his other half. *I was just a stupid kid.*

Yeah, keep thinking that, and maybe I'll even buy that excuse one day.

She chewed on her bottom lip. "What do you need me to do? Is this going to take more than a day? I have a job."

"Not anymore."

"Damn it, Wen! What does that mean? I can't afford to lose my paycheck. It keeps me fed and a roof over my head. You have to pay for those things out here in the human world."

He said nothing, but she could feel him staring at her.

"What? Your leader deals with shit like taxes, paying any human bills the clan incurs and all that. I'm on my own."

He reached inside his front jacket pocket and withdrew a thick wade of cash. "For your time. I'm not sure how many days it will take, but you aren't to leave my side until the bastard is dealt with."

"What is he and why do you need me?" A sinking feeling settled in the pit of her stomach. She refused to take the money, despite the fact it was probably more than she made in six months working her job. "Shit. I'm bait, aren't I?"

"No."

She still didn't reach for the money. "Then what do you need me to do? Just cut the crap. Don't sugarcoat it."

"Fine. Sit."

She studied the bed. "No way. Do you know how many germs and tiny bugs are probably crawling all over that thing?" She glanced at him. "I'm not the weak-kneed type."

He grinned as he returned the bills to his pocket. "That's why I want you. You've always been tough, Gerri. You're the strongest human I've ever met."

"Knock off the false flattery. Just spit it out."

"I'm tracking a ghoul maker."

"Those don't exist."

His dark eyebrow lifted above the sunglasses. "Are you sure?"

"Shit. What are they exactly? Give me the highlights."

"It's what we call a master Vampire who's creating an army of soldiers."

"What the hell does that mean?"

He reached for his sunglasses, removing them. The sight of those beautiful blue eyes made her feel like an idiot for believing she'd be impervious to him after all the years they'd been apart. She'd never forgotten they were mesmerizing, but the memory of their sheer magnificence had faded over the years. He had the kind of eyes that someone could get lost in. A brilliant blue that reminded her of sapphires. Her gaze dropped to his mouth, avoiding looking directly into his eyes again.

He shoved his sunglasses into his shirt pocket. "Think slowly rotting corpse with the Vamp hunger, but they go insane within a few months, tops. Faster if the Vamp abandons them and doesn't feed them his or her blood to help them survive that long. Soldiers are brutal killers, harder to take out than a regular Vamp, since they heal faster. They tend to cannibalize their own bodies doing it, hence the rotting corpse. We just found out they can turn their victims into the same thing. This asshole Vamp dropped off one of them on the edge of VampLycan territory and it made more. Five soldiers wiped out a small town. There were dozens of deaths."

"For real? How did that go over with the clan? I bet Trayis is fit to be tied that this happened on his doorstep."

"It wasn't outside of our clan, but another."

"So why are *you* here? It sounds like it should be that clan's problem, not yours."

"It's a long story, but Decker isn't in charge there anymore. The new leader, Lorn, asked other clans to help solve this mess because he has his hands full with a few internal problems. I volunteered to track and kill this bastard. He left a mess behind and it could have exposed our kind. It's a problem for all VampLycans."

She let all that sink in. "Someone challenged Decker?" That surprised her.

"Forget that part. Focus on why I'm here."

It was none of her business. That's what he should have said. She wasn't offended that Wen didn't want to share news from her old home. They liked to keep clan business private and she wasn't a part of that world anymore. "Fine. So you're tracking some jerk making amped-up Vampire zombies on speed."

"He needs to be stopped."

She decided Wen's chin was good to look at, safe. "The master is endangering everyone by leaving behind big enough messes that it could draw attention to your kind and others. An entire town being wiped out had to be a nightmare to hide."

"Exactly."

"So you've become Wen, the Vampire hunter."

He grinned, flashing perfect white teeth, minus the noticeably sharper points. "I think you've watched too many movies."

"You got the reference, so I'm not the only one."

"Guilty."

She still liked Wen. That wasn't good. They were no longer friends and he had become an adult. Those were the most dangerous of his kind and he'd had years to grow out of the sweet person he used to be. With maturity came responsibility. She knew what that meant to a VampLycan. The males were trained to fight, to effectively take out threats and do anything to protect the clan. They wouldn't kill innocent people for the hell of it but anyone who knew too much was considered expendable.

"What do you need me for, specifically? Am I tasty enough to catch his eye? Or maybe you think he'd want to turn me into an amped-up zombie Vamp? Am I his type or something?"

"We got Intel that he hangs with a group of rogue Lycans and Vamps who've joined forces. They're working together for once. This ghoul maker wants to start a war."

"Is this ghoul maker trying to breed? Is he a moron? It's against the law for a Vampire to create more VampLyans. That was in the treaty."

"I'm surprised you remember our laws."

Whoops. It would be smarter to pretend she'd forgotten all about her childhood. It was out of the bag though. "That one just kind of stuck with me. You don't want Vampires breeding more VampLycans unless it's a love match. You protect all of your race, even if someone isn't born into your clan."

"He's not attempting to breed with any of the Lycans that we know about. He's trying to convince them that we want to wipe out all Vampires and Lycans."

"That doesn't even make sense."

"Obviously. This asshole is stirring fear in hopes they'll join forces to wipe us out first."

"Why? I mean, it's not as though he wants to take your territory. It's too remote. There aren't enough blood sources up there, and they sure don't want to feed off animals."

"His master was killed after they invaded clan territory and kidnapped a VampLycan. It's a long story. Bottom line, he fucked up and pissed us off. It's a given that we'd retaliate. He fled Alaska, joined with those rogues, and now is trying to make it seem as though we're going to start a war with the packs and nests."

She considered that. "Every nest and pack would attack you guys if they saw a large group of VampLycans enter a city. They'd believe him, and think you've declared war on them."

He inclined his head, growing somber. "Exactly. He's manipulating the situation to make it seem as if we're the aggressors. I'm here to end that."

"I'm still not clear on why you called me."

Wen reached out and wrapped his warm palm under her chin, forcing her to look into his eyes. "He left this mess on our doorstep so I was sent to end him. It will raise a little suspicion when they discover I'm here, but I plan to give them the impression I've gone against the clans. As for you, what's more rogue than someone like me choosing to be with a human over my own people? I need them to believe I've fled my clan because I refused to give you up. I can track, get the information I need, and then kill this son of a bitch without anyone being the wiser until it's done."

Her mouth parted. "What?" She ignored the implied insult that he was too good for her. "But Trayis has allowed some of his clan to mate with humans."

"The nest who invaded VampLycan territory is more familiar with Decker's laws. He would have killed for that offense."

"Shit." If that was the case, she could understand how some crazy Vamp would buy into the ruse. Decker hated humans. That was no secret.

He grinned and his eyes glowed brighter bluer.

She squeezed her eyes closed. "Don't pull that Vampy thing. Don't manipulate me."

"I wasn't going to."

"Liar."

He growled.

She peeked up at him. "Your irises are glowing. That only happens when you're about to pull that mind-control shit, Wen. I got older, but I'm not senile. I remember."

20

He smiled. "They also glow when I think about sex."

"Is the smell in here is getting to you? Breathe through your mouth."

"You wish, golden locks." He wrapped his arm around her waist, hooking her, and she gasped when he tugged her against the hard, long length of his body. "I'm going to have to convince them we're lovers...and you know what that means. They aren't clueless humans."

Her knees buckled from the shock of what he was implying. He held her up though as she softly cursed, recovering. Her gaze locked with his.

"They need to smell me all over you. Inside you." His voice turned raspy and way too sexy. "It's a good thing you turned out so pretty, Gerri. It won't be a hardship fucking you."

"No!" Her hands flattened on his chest. "No, Wen."

His eyes narrowed and his low snarl was a warning.

"That means let me go, because it's not happening. Did you hear me about not wanting a big target put on my back?"

"There will be no consequences."

"Bullshit. My mom had a lot of flaws once she lost her mate, but being dishonest wasn't one of them. I know about the birds and bees when it comes to humans and nons. She never went anywhere without at least one member of the pack to guard her ass. Anything with a hyper-acute sense of smell knew it, because she was carrying their scent from getting it on with them. It's one thing for me to come here willing to *say* I was a hooker if anyone saw me with you. What you're talking about is something totally different; you want to *flaunt* that you're fucking me. I'd have to carry your scent but without the protection the pack gave my mom. That's like telling every Werewolf and Vamp that I'm available for whatever they want. I'll be a walking advertisement that I'm already tainted by your world and open season could commence. *No!*"

"Tainted?" he snarled.

"Knock it off. Maybe that was a poor choice of a word, but you know what I mean. Your scent will draw attention and they'll be much more likely to go after me because humans and others don't cross lines by getting intimately involved in a relationship. The ones who don't want to kill me outright will think it's fine to take sex or blood from me. I'll be considered a stray pet they can just grab and keep." She paused. "Abuse at will? No way."

He blew out a breath and seemed to calm. "I'll protect you."

"What happens when you catch this ghoul maker guy and split town? How long will the scent of you linger? I'm not a whore; you can take your money and shove it where the sun doesn't shine. And others don't know the meaning of the word no, either. I don't want to be passed around to anyone who decides to attack me because I smell like a doggy sex treat or a willing blood donor. Don't do this to me, Wen! *Please.* For old time's sake. We used to be close."

"I promise that won't happen."

"Bullshit. You won't be around to stop any hybrid dogs or Vamps from taking what they want from me. It will get me killed because I'll fight."

"You have my word that I won't leave your side until my scent is gone."

"What is your word worth to a mere human? Come on. I know the rules VampLycans live by. You'd die before breaking a promise to your own kind but to someone like me? We're here to step on if the need arises. It's what's best for the clan, always."

"You're not just any human, Gerri. You used to be *part* of my clan."

"I was the kid everyone put up with because my mother was mated to one of you. It wasn't all roses and pretty words. Some of the clan detested me. At least a dozen of them viewed me as an idiot who would betray them one day. The only reason I survived was because you protected me from having any so-called 'accidents'. Trayis would have punished them but only after he was shown my dead body."

"I will still protect you."

She dropped her chin, resting her forehead against his chest. "Please, Wen. Find another woman. Brainwash her with your eyes and force her to heed your commands. Anytime she starts to get curious about you, just wipe her memory."

"They'd know I was inside her head. No one would believe I'd abandon my clan for a woman I had to hold by force. They're hollow shells if you repeatedly mess with their minds." He pressed against her, effectively pinning her to the wall. "Pretty but brainless isn't my type. I need you."

The sexy way he growled those last words did things to Gerri. She tried hard to ignore it. Her nipples still reacted by aching and her stomach clenched. She'd fallen for Wen as strongly as any young, clueless girl could. The L word came to mind but it just brought back the pain. Part of her had wished he'd stopped her from leaving when her stepfather had died and her mother had packed them up.

Wen had arrived—but he'd come to say goodbye instead. He'd just let her mother take her away.

"You're fifteen years too late, buddy," she got out, pushing against him. "Let go and back off."

"What does that mean?" He refused to move or allow her to wiggle away when she tried.

Gerri warred with herself. It burned to have to admit the truth to him but maybe he'd have a heart. She doubted it, but they'd once been close. The fact that she didn't have to look at him while speaking helped.

"I can't fuck you, Wen. Don't ask me for the impossible. I'm sorry you've been sent on some shit secret-assassin kind of mission, but I can't help out."

"You admitted you like men." He pushed her against the wall harder, almost crushing her. He was all around her, his firm body pressed tight against hers. "Tell me you don't find me attractive. I won't believe it and could prove you wrong. You'll enjoy it."

"Son of a bitch." She stopped shoving since it was like trying to move a boulder. "You totally grew up to be an asshole, didn't you? I know the shit you guys can do to a woman. Pheromones make you smell so good it turns chicks on. You're also horny as hell and could seduce a tree if you set your mind to it. Just don't do it to me, Wen. Please? I don't want to be hurt."

He bent his head and backed off a little. She breathed easier—until he pressed his face against her neck. His hot breath fanned the sensitive skin under her ear and he softly growled when he spoke. It was sexy as hell and caused awareness of him to course through her body. She made the mistake of breathing through her nose. The smell of him hit and she barely managed to stifle a groan. He was definitely using his ability to scent like pure sin against her.

"I'll be gentle."

She pushed at him again but couldn't budge his body. "You're not hearing me."

He brushed his lips over her earlobe. "Very gentle."

She knew he would be, and that he could get her naked on the bed within a few minutes or less. She'd seen a VampLycan or two in action going after women. That scared her enough to be blunt. "I don't want you to break my heart a second time, damn it! Let go and stop, Wen!"

He stiffened and his mouth stopped touching her. She opened her eyes when he jerked his body far enough away to put space between them. His chin was where she should have looked but instead she peered up into his eyes. The surprise she saw there was evident. He hadn't expected her to say that.

"You always thought you were so smart when we were growing up. Guess what? You were an idiot!" She paused but the anger wouldn't be denied. "You have no right to show up and blow apart the life I worked so hard to put together for myself. It was tough forgetting about you."

He actually paled. That was something, since he was a golden tan from all the time he obviously spent in the sun. "What?"

"I was in love with you." The words were whispered but it felt good to finally get them off her chest. "It broke my heart when I left the clan because I had to leave *you*. You didn't have that problem. I'm not going to play the role of your lover because it will mean nothing to you once you're gone. But my life will be a mess again, if I even manage to survive and not let you get me killed. I can't take that kind of heartache again, Wen. No thanks. Find another woman. I'll say the same thing to you that you said to me the last time we parted. Bye. Have a good life!"

She moved fast, darting under one of his arms still pressed against the wall. She rushed toward the door and exited, happy when he didn't stop her.

The elevator wasn't there, so she had to wait. The sound of heavy footfalls coming down the hallway made her tense and turn. Wen stormed toward her with his sunglasses back on his face and a stern frown twisting his lips.

"You were just a girl at the time. That's bullshit. You didn't love me."

"Whatever. Keep playing stupid. You were always so good at it." She turned her back on him. "Find someone else. It won't be me."

The elevator doors opened and she entered the lift. It was a relief when he didn't join her. The doors closed and she pushed the button, then leaned heavily against the wall. It was for the best that he'd finally been clued in. He'd find someone else to help him. Another woman could be his bed partner, playing the happy couple to catch his ghoul. The idiot who agreed to be Wen's lover would end up with the broken heart, dealing with smelling like a walking advertisement for "come and get me" to any bloodsucker or Lycan who figured she was a fan of dangerous men—or a threat to be eliminated.

26

She breathed easier when she left the motel and returned to her car parked two blocks over. One glance behind her assured that he hadn't followed. In seconds, she was behind the wheel and on her way home.

Wen knew the score. It bothered her pride, but it would be worse to nurse her heartbreak while dodging predators after he returned to Alaska. Her life wasn't the greatest but it beat that. Her dead-end, boring job was welcome. Getting involved in VampLycan politics wasn't.

Chapter Two

Gerri towel-dried her hair and smiled at the computer screen. "No way, Ann. You know I don't go to clubs."

Her friend frowned across the live feed. "Please? Ben will be there but I'm playing hard to get. I blew him off two weeks ago when he invited me to his birthday bash but I want to go. I'll look desperate and sad if I show up alone. We go together and it's just a coincidence. We'll accidentally run into him."

"That's the lamest thing ever. You realize that, don't you? He's not a moron. He'll see through your ruse as soon as you walk into that club. You don't hang out with his crowd. Did you get an official invite like his friends did?"

"No, but it's a nightclub, open to the public. You think it would be that obvious I was there to run into him?"

Gerri tossed the towel over the handlebars of her stationary bike in the corner of the guestroom she'd turned into a computer/exercise room. "Totally. Find out where he eats lunch near your office and show up there one day. That's way smoother and more believable. I don't know why you want to play games though. Just say yes when he asks you out."

"That's why you're single. Men like a challenge. I don't want him to think I'm easy."

"Then don't sleep with him on the first date."

"You've seen him. Who would say no?"

"Me." Gerri leaned closer to the screen. "Just go to the club and tell him you changed your mind. Or don't. I'm not going with you. My plans tonight consist of watching a movie and being in bed before ten. I need clean clothes and I had to take off work today, so I promised Robert I'd come in tomorrow to make up the time. You're lucky you have a washer and dryer inside your condo. I have to put the first load in by the crack of dawn when our Laundromat opens or it never gets done because my neighbors hog the machines until closing time. Now—grow a set of balls and call Ben if you don't want to show up unannounced. It's just after seven, and you said it starts at nine. Get him while he's still at home so he can swing by your place to pick you up. Problem solved."

"What if he asked someone else? That would be awkward to hear over the phone."

"It would be more awkward being introduced to his date at the club. Just call him. I'm out." Gerri clicked off the connection, shaking her head.

"Are human dating rituals that seriously messed up?"

Gerri jumped in her seat, her heart racing. She didn't turn around though, not needing to. "How in the hell did you get in?"

Wen was quiet, and she finally turned her head to the side, finding him leaning just inside the door. He looked as if he'd been there for a while, with his comfortable stance. The jacket was gone but he still wore the same clothes. His eyes were uncovered, and as she stared into them, she wished he still sported the sunglasses.

"I forgot to brace the door but I locked it. Did you break my locks?"

"You live in an apartment."

She pushed out of her chair, gripping her robe tighter. "The manager has a spare set of keys," she guessed. "You hypnotized poor Mrs. Wagnor into handing them over."

"It was easy."

"That's so rude and wrong. Just because you can, doesn't mean you should mess with people's heads. She's a sweet lady. You didn't do anything to her, did you?"

He scowled. "I don't harm innocents."

"You just force them to your will. What did you tell her?"

"I completely wiped her of meeting me. She won't remember a thing."

"Do you still have my key?"

He grinned. "Yes."

"What happens when she notices my set of keys are missing and thinks she's gone senile to have misplaced them?" She crossed the room but kept a good four feet of space between him. "Return them to her so that doesn't happen. You guys never think about the consequences of the crap you do. Leave now, Wen. We have nothing left to say."

"I disagree. I remember *your* parting words when you left our clan too. You told me to eat shit and called me dog face."

"I was mad!"

"I had come to say goodbye and wish you well."

"I thought you were coming to stop me from leaving."

He moved fast, and Gerri gasped when his hands gripped her around her waist, hoisting her right off her feet. She clutched at his arms as he stormed out of the guestroom and into her bedroom. He broke the connection between them by flinging her through the air. She landed on her back, bouncing when she hit the mattress. It took her a second to realize what he'd done.

"Damn you!" She struggled to sit upright.

"What was I supposed to do? Knock your mother on her ass and throw you over my shoulder? Rush into the woods to live out there with you while the entire clan hunted for us?"

Her mouth parted, but no words came out as she stared at one very angry Wen. His eye color had darkened to a deep midnight blue, a sure indication that he was close to changing shapes. She glanced down and spotted the telling sign of his fingernails lengthening. Hair seemed to darken and thicken along his arms, spreading upward to his biceps. He snarled, the sound loud in her apartment, and he flashed some sharp fangs.

His reaction killed her anger and made her wary instead. It wasn't like a VampLycan to easily lose their skin. She finally found something to say. "Calm down. Don't go all beasty in my apartment. I'd never get all the hair you'd shed out of my carpet."

"They would have caught us within two days—that's what I figured, anyway. Your humanness would have slowed us down, even with me carrying you on my back. I thought we could seek sanctuary with the GarLycans if we could make it that far, to give you time to mature. It was crazy, since they would have turned us back, but my mind went there anyway."

Astonishment silenced her.

"Your mother refused to stay. I begged her but she didn't want that kind of life for you. She said everything reminded her of her mate and it was breaking her heart. You were fifteen, so I had no right to claim you. The age of consent is eighteen unless both parents die. Then it's seventeen. I even considered killing your mother. It wasn't my best day."

"Wen...what are you saying?" She scooted down the bed to sit on the edge, not sure her legs would support her enough to stand.

He glanced at his hands, flexed them until all the extra hair faded from his arms, and then lifted one to brush his fingers through his hair. He turned away, giving her his back. "I had feelings too. I planned to track you down later...but things changed."

Her entire world felt as if it were crumbling around her. He'd once thought he was in love with her too. That's what he was saying. What he left unsaid hurt. "You found someone else you cared about more? Do you have a mate? Where is she, Wen? You wouldn't leave a mate for anything. It's against your nature."

He sighed and slowly faced her again. "There's no mate, Gerri. My older brother was killed and his responsibilities fell to me. My parents took it hard. He was their first son. My mother went a little insane too. She took his loss the worst. They knew how I felt about you, but made it clear they'd reject you as my mate. They've demanded I mate a full-blooded VampLycan. My offspring will carry our family name and position in the clan."

Part of her was relieved he wasn't mated but she was also sad. "I'm sorry about Gerbin."

"Thanks. I couldn't put you in danger. My mom really has lost her mind and my father is overly protective. She's mentally fragile, which makes *him* crazy too. I worried that she'd try to kill you if I ever brought you home—or he would do it to keep her happy."

"They think my being human would make for weak grandkids."

"Yes."

They stared at each other. He let his hand fall to his side, where it fisted. He took a step closer but then halted. "I'd hoped the attraction would be gone when I set out to find you." He glanced down her body. "You want the truth? I saw you...and all those feelings I used to have resurfaced. You're beautiful, G.L. You have no idea what you do to me still."

Gerri remained seated, sure her legs wouldn't support her now. The old nickname was a reminder of the past. He'd teased her about her golden locks and called himself the big bad wolf. She'd pointed out he had his fairy tales mixed up but he hadn't cared. "That's why you really came to me for help?"

"I *am* hunting a crazy Vamp, but I thought of you when I came to the lower forty-eight. My plan gives me an excuse to both spend time with you and accomplish my mission."

"Two birds with one stone, huh?"

He smiled, the blue of his eyes lightening. "Yes."

"So you lied about me needing to play the part of your lover because you were hoping if you got me into bed, you could rid yourself of the itch? Finally scratch it?"

All humor fled. "That was the truth. The only way I'm going to get close to him is if we go in together as a couple. He'll know I'm there for him otherwise, but my exit from the clan to be with a human is plausible. He's most familiar with Decker's clan, since he's the bastard who sent them to Alaska. I not only have to kill him, but I need to find out what kind of damage he's done before I do. That means spending at least a few days around him."

"Why would Decker do that? I deserve answers if you want me involved."

He hesitated, then sighed. "You're right. Decker wanted to rule all four clans, not just his own. He's been making sneak attacks on our clan and the others for years. Lord Aveoth forbid him to outright go to war with other VampLycans. The fear of having the GarLycans defend Trayis's, Velder's, and Crocker's clans kept him mostly in check. Then Decker thought he'd finally found a way to control Lord Aveoth and make him join forces to take out his enemies. It backfired. Instead, Lord Aveoth is furious and wants him dead, so Decker fled."

"Decker is insane. Never anger a fur bat. They're cold and mean." She shivered, remembering the few times she'd seen GarLycans from a distance when one would visit the clan to relay a message. They were terrifying. "Plus they fly. You can't even outrun them."

Wen grinned. "Very true. That's why Decker fled." His features turned grim. "The stupid bastard tried to blackmail Lord Aveoth. We're guessing Decker was furious when he learned that Lorn took leadership of the clan he left behind. He sent a nest of Vamps to fuck with them. Then that small human town suffered."

34

"The Vamps needed to eat."

"It was more than that. We took out that nest but one of them survived. He's the one I'm going after. We're guessing he's blaming Decker and all VampLycans for the loss of his beloved master. He has to be stopped before he causes us more trouble."

"So you're going after him. But you're a VampLycan. You can't hide that from this Vamp, can you?"

"He'll know what I am. He's collecting rogues, so I'll pretend to be one. It's a good cover to say being hunted by the same clan members tracking *him* because you and I are forbidden lovers. It has a touch of truth to it, since my family would be outraged if they knew I've come to you for help. I'm hoping he'll add me to his nest or whatever the hell he wants to call it. I'll get my information and then be able to kill him."

"Wen...I can't do this for you." But she was tempted.

Wen approached her and lowered to his knees, so close she could reach out and touch him. "I need your help. I don't trust any other human enough and a manipulated woman wouldn't convince them I'm not a threat. Even Vamps can't stomach mindless blood slaves for long and kill them. You know what I am, and I wouldn't have to worry about you turning on me. You know that some humans would think we're monsters if they learned the truth. I might end up with a knife in my back while I'm sleeping next to one, since I'd have to reveal what I am. I wouldn't die, but it would blow my cover if the woman tried to take me out. That doesn't sound real loving, does it?"

She swallowed.

"I need to not only get to him, but I have to find out what he's done. That means staying at least a few nights to gain information."

"What kind of information?"

"Whether or not any of the nests or packs have taken this dickhead's words as truth. I need to know if the Vampire Council is urging all the nests to attack us or if it's just the one this jerk belonged to."

She could understand why that would matter. One nest could be dealt with. The council ordering every nest to go after VampLycans would be seriously bad.

"Aren't you curious about what's between us?" He leaned closer, staring deeply into her eyes. "I am. I can't offer you forever, but don't you wonder what it would have been like if we'd had the chance to be together?"

"Wen…" He was so sexy, and she longed to touch him.

"Worst case scenario, we're going to realize what we had was real. Best case, we'll learn enough to never want to see each other again. We won't be certain either way unless we become lovers."

She closed her eyes, unable to stare into his anymore. "God, Wen. Don't do this."

"I'm not touching you yet."

Yet. "What happens if it was real and those feelings are still there? What if they deepen?" She forced herself to look at him again. "What if we both want forever?"

Wen looked away that time. "It can't happen. I have to return home and it wouldn't be safe for you." He returned his gaze to hers. "I'd be afraid my family might want to hurt you or our children."

Children. Her guts twisted just imagining having some with Wen. She'd stopped dreaming about that long ago. His family would see her as the enemy. He'd stated as much. She knew all about VampLycans and the importance of first sons. Wen had become just that after his older brother's death.

She hadn't met Wen's brother, Gerbin, too many times when she'd lived with the clan. He'd been born over twenty years before Wen. The elder sibling had traveled a lot, doing what Wen seemed to be doing now. He would leave the clan to track down and kill enemies. Wen's father was an elder, ranked high in the clan, so it would fall to his firstborn to carry on that legacy of being an enforcer for the clan leader. There was a real chance any children she and Wen would produce together might lose the ability to shift forms, therefore making them useless in that role. Even Trayis, the clan leader, wouldn't want that to happen to Wen's children. They were all about keeping the clan strong.

Her mother had been allowed to mate a VampLycan because he'd been a tradesman. He wasn't a fighter but instead artistic. Her stepfather had been a genius with a chainsaw and a large chuck of wood, selling his sculptures for big bucks that he'd shared with the clan. He'd actually met her mother while he'd been out in the human world at an art show to promote his work.

"It's too big of a risk to take," she managed to say.

"I don't see it that way." Wen shook his head.

Her anger returned. "You wouldn't. I was the one picked on and who lived in fear that someone would finally shove me over a cliff just to be rid of me. Some of those kids were mean, Wen. I don't ever want my child to suffer through that shit or to be seen as weak. I could get pregnant. Did you even think about that? Whoops! It happens. Then what? You'd have the option of killing me outright or taking me back to the clan, where our child would face prejudice. You said it yourself, your own parents would pose a threat. And even though some of your clan might be assholes to a half-human kid, they'd still keep our baby safer than I could. I wouldn't last two weeks out here on my own once my scent changed. Every freak with a nose would know I was carrying something not totally human. I might as well paint a sign that states 'kill me' and hang it around my neck."

A muscle in his jaw clenched and his eyes darkened. "I won't get you pregnant, Gerri."

"I'm not like you." She was stunned she had to remind *him*, of all people. "Your women can breed when they want to because they can control their ovulation. But you can totally get a full human pregnant. I don't have any freaky self-birth-control thing going on."

"I would smell it if you were ovulating."

She frowned back at him. "That's disturbing on so many levels. But what if we're in the middle of this mess you want to drag me into and I hit that time of the month? I'm not on anything."

Some of the tension left his features and his eye color lightened further. Humor glinted. "You've never heard of condoms? Do I need to explain what they are to you? Human men wear them to prevent pregnancies from occurring."

"Very funny. Those can break."

"It won't happen. You're hunting for excuses now."

"No. I'm using your own words against you. You said these rogues needed to smell you all over me." She paused. "Inside me. That means no condoms."

"I'll know when your ovulating, and if they say anything, I'll tell them I'm avoiding getting you pregnant because we're on the run."

He probably had a point, but so did she. "You can't guarantee I won't get pregnant by accident."

"You're not the first human I've touched, Gerri."

The stabbing sensation was jealousy, and she hated feeling it. "Oh, that's a selling point." She rolled her eyes. "So not hot."

"Sorry." He actually appeared to regret the words. "I don't want to hear about the men you've allowed access to your body. I was just stating a fact. I managed to not get them pregnant."

Them. She wanted to ask how many he'd slept with but resisted, not sure she'd like the answer. "That you know of. Did you stick around long enough to make sure?"

That muscle along his jaw jumped again. "Of course. I always used a condom and none of them broke."

"Into dating humans, huh? I bet your parents love that."

"I've been sent out into your world on many occasions to hunt others and do business for the clan. Sometimes I'm gone for a few months."

And VampLycan males are as horny as hell. He didn't need to state that. It also served as a reminder that he'd never contacted her before. "Why come see me now?"

"This time you don't smell of someone else."

His answer stunned her. "What?"

"This isn't the first time I've sought you out, Gerri." The blue color of his eyes darkened again. "I've never left my territory to travel into your world without having someone track you down first. The Lycan I hired reported you were involved in a relationship every other time. I didn't care anymore if I had to take you from someone. I need you, and I'm tired of waiting for it to be the right time to find out what's between us. Make your excuses, protest all you want, but you're not avoiding the inevitable." His gaze lowered to the waist of her robe. "I'm going to fuck you, Gerri." He stared back into her eyes. "Tonight."

Her heart rate spiked and so did her breathing. "Wen, please don't."

"You want me as much as I do you. Tell me otherwise and I'll call you a liar. You're not afraid of me. You should see how flushed your skin is right now. I can hear your heartbeat." His nose flared as he inhaled. "I can smell how wet and needy you are. You've been tormenting me since I walked in the door."

She clenched her thighs together, horrified because she knew what he was picking up with his super-nose. "That's not from you. I masturbated in the shower. Stop sniffing at me, damn it! That's so rude, and I hate having to admit something so personal. You damn VampLycans have no respect for privacy."

He smiled. "Were you thinking about me when you came?"

She wanted to punch him because he'd hit it dead on with his guess. She usually fantasized about him. "Get out, Wen. I was actually thinking about my ex-boyfriend."

The lie seemed to set him off. His features twisted with rage and a snarl burst from him. He lunged and knocked her onto her back. It didn't hurt, but she was so stunned that she didn't react quickly enough to stop him from shoving her robe up her legs and spreading them. His hands gripped her inner thighs, holding them wide open.

"I'll be the best you've ever had, Gerri. It will be my memory that fills your mind from now on when you touch yourself, wishing it were me instead."

"Goddamn you!" She knew he'd exposed her from the waist down. She wasn't wearing anything under her robe. "Let go." She was turned on, wanting him, but it was a bad idea. "Stop it!"

"I haven't even begun." Some of his temper faded from his harsh tone but he showed his fangs. They were intimidating as hell and a little scary to see. He actually opened his mouth more and ran his tongue over the sharp tips. "Be still. I don't want to cut you by accident."

Her mouth parted, wondering what the hell that meant, but then he bent, sitting on his ass on the floor to lower himself. His hold on her thighs tightened and he jerked her entire body closer to the edge of the mattress. It put her pussy right under his nose.

"Don't you dare," she whispered.

He had the nerve to wink. "I've wanted to do this forever."

She stiffened and stopped trying to squirm away the second he lowered his face and his hot breath fanned her lower region. It was something right out of one of the more sexual dreams she'd had about Wen. Of course, she hadn't expected to feel the front of his fangs pressed to either side of her clit, giving him easier access to it. The first lick of his raspy tongue over the sensitive bundle of nerves had her tightening her hold on his arms.

He growled and his tongue vibrated against the spot that was the most receptive to pleasure.

"I hate you," she moaned.

His response was to growl deeper and wiggle his tongue against her clit. She released his arms and clawed at the bed. It felt too good to fight. None of her ex-boyfriends could do what Wen was doing. Only he could pull off oral sex while doing an impression of a vibrator at the same time. She panted, trying to remember not to buck her hips in case he cut her with his fangs down there. It would probably hurt.

Her nipples beaded tight under the terrycloth robe, making them overly sensitive, and the soft material suddenly felt rough. Heat spread through her belly as pleasure shot from her clit directly to her brain. She was going to come hard and almost embarrassingly fast, since Wen wasn't wasting time with foreplay. Every muscle felt as though it was rigid and her back arched off the bed.

"Oh God," she moaned, then bit down on her lower lip to stop talking.

Wen growled deeper, probably loud enough for her neighbors to hear, but she didn't give a damn. The climax tore through her. It was brutal and fierce, so intense she couldn't think, just wonder if she'd survive because all the blood seemed to rush to her brain, almost blowing it.

It took her a moment to come down from the high, and she realized she was being flipped over. Material ripped as Wen stripped her of the robe in the process. She was sweating and the air felt chilly after being wrapped in the warm material. Her knees hit the carpet and she was bent over the bed until her hips were pushed tight against the side of the mattress. The distinct sound of his zipper mixed with the harsh breathing from both of them.

She should protest but she didn't. She wanted him. Gerri turned her head, flipping some of her damp hair out of her face. Wen was on his knees behind her. His eyes were bright blue and glowing. It was a reminder of what he'd said about them doing that when he was turned on. They were absolutely beautiful, and so was he.

Her gaze lowered as he shoved down his pants. It wasn't a surprise that he didn't wear underwear. The size of his cock was slightly scary. He was thick, long, and incredibly hard. The only thing that drew her attention from it was when he reached up and tugged his shirt off, tossing it aside. All that tan skin was revealed, and the sight of his eight-pack abs was stare worthy. Everything about Wen was big and intimidating. Sexy.

"I'll be gentle." His voice was gruff, more animalistic than human.

She faced forward and closed her eyes, trying to relax. "You better be," she got out. "You're huge."

"Flattery will get you everything with me."

His hand braced next to her shoulder and he pressed against her back. He was hot but it was skin, not fur, so he completely kept his human form. She was grateful for that because some VampLycans could beast out a bit during sex. She'd walked in on her mother and stepfather once, something she wished she could forget. He'd been mostly human but had a shitload of hair, along with some extended jawline action going on, and fangs. She didn't want that with Wen.

Wen used his knee to bump her inner thigh and she spread her legs more. "I wish you were bigger. You are so delicate, G.L."

He used his other hand to grab her hair, something she didn't expect, and bared one shoulder and the side of her neck. He leaned over and his lips brushed skin, kissing her. She relaxed even more, glad he wasn't just going to fuck her right off the bat. He used that same hand to reach between their hips and fondle her clit. She was wet, could feel how much so as he slid higher and one finger slowly breached her pussy.

She moaned in response; it felt incredibly good as he tested to see if she was ready to take him. He didn't immediately withdraw but instead seemed intent on exploring her by sinking the digit in deeper. He twisted his finger so the tip of it rubbed and she moaned when he found the right spot. He stilled and rubbed it again. Gerri arched her ass to give him better access.

"Got you, G.L."

She wondered what that meant, but then his finger withdrew and something far thicker rubbed against the seam of her sex. He found the entrance with the crown of his cock and pushed forward, breaching her pussy. It stretched to accommodate the girth of his shaft but she'd never taken someone his size before. It was a tight fit, and her head lowered until her forehead rested against her mattress. He was gentle, not going in fast, and allowed her to adjust to him until he was fully seated.

"Fuck," he growled, his mouth against her ear. "You're going to kill me."

"Ditto," she moaned.

He withdrew, but not totally, and pushed back in. He was rock hard and every nerve ending down there seemed to get hit as he filled her again. He stopped, growled low, and repeated the action a few more times until some of the tightness of their joining eased as her body grew familiar with him.

She moaned again when he nipped her with his teeth along the curve of her shoulder. It wasn't painful. She was sure he didn't break the skin, but that jolt of his fangs added to the pleasure. She'd never guessed she liked being bitten, but then again, it was Wen.

He did it again, a little to the right, closer to her throat as he picked up the pace of fucking her and adjusted the angle of his dick.

"Oh God," she moaned, understanding now why he'd said he got her. Every glide of his cock hit that spot he'd found with his finger. She'd heard about a G-spot but was suddenly a believer in its existence, if that intense feeling was any indication.

He fucked her faster, harder, and she frantically reached for his hand still braced on the bed, needing that contact. She clung to him, wanted to move with him, but he kept her pinned down with the weight of his chest along her back. She could only take him and feel.

Her vaginal muscles clamped around him right before she came. Her cries were muffled against the bed but Wen's snarl wasn't when he tore his mouth away from her shoulder, no longer nipping her skin. He gripped her hip in an almost bruising hold as he frantically fucked her. She felt it when he started coming. His dick throbbed strongly, almost a heartbeat pulsing against her vaginal walls, until he stilled. A slight feeling of pressure followed, small bursts of it, and then liquid heat spread inside her.

Wen collapsed mostly on top of her but then seemed to remember he could smother her with his weight. He lifted up enough to make sure she could still draw air into her lungs. They both suffered from ragged breathing and sweat tickled her from where their bodies were still pressed together. It wasn't a surprise that sex with Wen would be nothing less than hot, messy, and mind-blowing.

She waited for him to pull out when she felt his cock soften somewhat, but he didn't budge. Gerri finally lifted her head, opened her eyes, and looked at his face. He was turned away though, his hair hiding his features. Something on the wall across the room seemed to hold his full attention.

"Is my neighbor pressed up against the wall listening to us? I'm sure we put on quite an ear show for him."

Wen didn't respond.

"Hello to Wen? Did you fall asleep?"

"Shut up, Gerri," he rasped. "Just don't talk right now."

That pissed her off. She struggled to lift up, and he shifted his weight enough to allow her to raise her chest off the bed. She braced her hands and shoved her ass back, hoping to dislodge him from his position over her.

He hadn't been prepared for that. His dick slid out of her as he fell back, landing on his ass. She crawled up on the bed, ripping at the cover to twist it around her body as she rolled, glaring at him.

"You fucked me. I told you this was a mistake. Don't you dare tell me to shut up if you regret it. Did you have to come inside me? You know I was worried about getting pregnant. Would it have killed you to pull out first?"

She took in his features as she spoke, noticing the way he appeared a little worse for the wear. His jaw seemed off, a little too long, and his nose had a smashed appearance, wider than it should have been. The fangs were still present but his eyes weren't glowing anymore. They were pitch black. Hair had grown along his jawline and on parts of his cheeks.

"What the hell? You went beast on me? You asshole!"

He snarled and rolled, yanking up his pants as he struggled to his feet. He gave her his back as he tucked in his dick and zipped his fly closed. "Shut up, damn it. Give me a few minutes."

"I told you about my parents and the trauma I suffered after I caught them fucking. You thought it was funny but you agreed that was so wrong of him to go all half-shifted on her ass, literally. I can't believe you did that to me."

Wen tried again to force his body into submission. It wasn't listening. He'd never had that problem before and it made it worse, hearing Gerri rage at him. He didn't blame her for being upset. He closed his eyes and tried to ignore her. He centered his focus on his rapid heartbeat, slowing it.

A soft object hit his back. It felt like one of her pillows. He smiled, grateful it wasn't something more solid, like one of her bedside lamps. He realized the humor helped when his face tingled, assuring him that his jaw had shifted back into a human position and the hair on his face had receded. Only Gerri would dare assault him with harmless sleeping paraphernalia. He ran his tongue along the top of his teeth to make sure his fangs had retracted. He took one more deep breath, opened his eyes, and turned.

Gerri had most of her comforter hiding her body. She was on her knees, clutching the thick bedcover, and held another pillow she was about to pitch his way. Her hair was a mess of damp ringlets falling in disarray over both bared shoulders, even covering one of her eyes and half her face. She looked adorable and sexy as hell. His dick hardened.

"I'm sorry." He meant it.

"Go to hell!"

He was already there. Wondering what it would be like to take Gerri had always kept him awake at night, but the reality had been much better than anything he'd fantasized about. He was in deep shit, and man enough to admit it. He'd suspected she might be *the one* for him—but now he was pretty certain. He'd lost control of his body, and that was a first. It was also a sign, one that he desperately wanted to ignore.

"I'm sorry," he repeated.

"Get out, Wen. I'm totally serious. You got your itched scratched and you regret it. Thanks for fucking me over, just like I knew you would. Now out!" She let the pillow fly.

He dodged it by stepping sideways. His humor fled. "I don't regret it—and we're going to do it again."

He winced at her horrified expression. She'd enjoyed the sex as much as he had. He would never forget the sweet sounds she made while he fucked her and how good she felt, twitching as she came with his dick buried deep in that hot little pussy of hers. She could become his favorite addiction.

She recovered enough to glare at him. "Out, Wen. Bye. Have a good life!"

Gerri was never going to forgive him for those words he'd once spoken. That was the second time she'd thrown them in his face. He'd been young then and had no choice but to allow her to walk away. Times had changed. He couldn't exactly take her home with him but he had time before he had to return to Alaska. Every minute would be spent with her.

"I had to get control of my body. I didn't mean to partially change. The sex was that great. I needed silence to do it, needed to block you out." He wasn't going to elaborate more.

"So that was an accident? You accidently went all beastly on me and whoops, you couldn't pull out either? You had *me* pinned, not the other way around."

"You need to smell like me. I planned on the second part. I marked you from the inside."

She turned her head, looking for a weapon. The paperback book on her nightstand was her choice. She flung it at him. He threw up his hand to easily defect it. It bounced off his palm and hit the floor. That seemed to irritate her more as she huffed, searching for something else as she yanked open the nightstand drawer. He tensed, hoping she didn't have a gun. It wouldn't kill him but a bullet would hurt.

The object she withdrew stumped him. It was bright pink and plastic. "What the hell is that?"

"A rabbit." She pitched it at him.

He caught it and studied the strangely shaped object. He wasn't familiar with sex toys but it didn't take a genius to figure out what it was. A grin split his face as he arched his eyebrows. "Is this a hint?" He took a step closer as his thumb pressed against a button. It turned the thing on and the vibrations made him laugh. "Nice. I've never used one on someone before but I'm willing to give it a try."

"Oooooh!" she yelled, and almost fell off her bed when she tried to get out of it, still tangled with the comforter.

He was ready to lunge forward to prevent her from hitting the carpet, but she caught her own balance before the need arose. He kept back, turning off the sex toy so it went silent and still.

"I'll mark you," she muttered. "I wish I had a whip or a belt. You need your ass beaten."

He laughed, tossing the toy on the bed a safe distance from her. "That sounds kinky but I'm not into that. Are you?"

"You spank me and I'll rip off your nuts." She pointed a finger at him. "You're pissing me off. I don't think you're being charming."

He lifted his hands and schooled his features. "Calm down."

"I will once you leave."

"I missed how unreasonable you can be. It's cute."

"Oh, I've got cute for you." She suddenly dropped the comforter, streaking naked into the bathroom. The door slammed before he could react, a lock clicking into place.

He walked to it but didn't kick it open. The sound of water coming on had him clenching his teeth. She was showering to remove his scent. He'd bet she planned to wash all of him away too. He lifted a hand and fisted it, knocking. "Stop it, Gerri."

"Fuck off!"

He'd replace the doorknob. He gripped it firmly and twisted, applying enough strength that the cheap thing didn't stand a chance. He didn't want to damage the door or the frame.

He strode inside the bathroom and found Gerri about to step into the glass shower stall. The sight of her naked played hell with his already active libido. He wanted her again. The fact that she cursed, grabbing a towel to wrap around her to hide her body, wasn't lost on him.

"You're so rude."

"You're angry because what we experienced frightened you. I understand. I know you too well...but you know me too, G.L. You're panicking and acting this way trying to avoid the truth." He purposely used the nickname to remind her of the past. "I didn't mean to lose control. I wasn't prepared for that either. I damn near bit you. That's why I wanted you to be silent. The urge was still there. You have no idea how close I came to drawing blood."

She stumbled, taking a step back but forgetting about the lip of the shower stall behind her.

51

He moved fast, one arm wrapping around her waist and jerking her against his body to save her from slamming against tile. It put them flush together, and she stared into his eyes. He watched emotions flicker in hers, astonishment and then growing wariness. She shook her head but clutched at his biceps with both hands, clinging to him instead of attempting to push him away.

"I wanted to taste your blood in the worst way." He hated to admit it.

"Your kind only does that during sex to see if you found your mate. That urge is rare."

"You do remember."

She closed her eyes and he was surprised when she leaned her face forward, resting it against his chest. She felt right in his arms, despite their size difference. He tightened his hold by wrapping his other arm around her.

"You can't do that, Wen." Her soft voice was hard to hear over the shower, but he did.

"I know."

"Your family would never accept me. Maybe at one time, but not now."

The loss of his older brother had been heartbreaking, but so was the truth of her words. "I've mentioned that."

She turned her face, pressing her cheek against him. The feel of her warm tears wasn't expected. He reached out and turned off the water. The silence, with only their breathing in the small room, seemed amplified. He wrapped his arm around her waist again, wishing it would comfort them both.

"What if you had bitten me and discovered I tasted right?" She sniffed and released his arms, wrapping them around his waist instead.

"You know the answer."

"You would have to claim me."

"I'd have damned you into becoming a target of my family's wrath."

"This is all kinds of fucked up."

He smiled but it was with bitterness. "Yes, it is. I'm so sorry."

"Me too."

She sniffed again and wiggled, releasing him. He let her go as she turned away, hiding her face. She avoided looking at him in the mirror when she bent over the sink, splashing water on her face. She used a hand towel hanging next to it to pat all the water away. She finally straightened and turned, meeting his gaze again.

"You need to go, Wen. I really can't help you now."

"I disagree."

She gaped at him.

"I need you to pull this off."

"Are you insane?" She secured her towel a little more. "I don't have a death wish. We've had sex once. I can remove your scent if you get out of my way and let me in that shower."

"No. This ghoul maker is dangerous, and so are those rogues he's seeking shelter with, but I can handle them. I just need to get close

53

enough to take them out. You can help me do that. I'll be the target they come after if shit hits the fan, not you."

She shook her head, gazing at him with disbelief etched on her features. "I'm not talking about that. You want me to play lover to you as a cover to get in deep with those pricks, but that means we're going to have to keep having sex. I'm not naive, Wen. You have the urge to test a mating. I wish I could forget everything about my childhood but I was raised in your culture. Every time you touch me, that urge is going to grow stronger. Your scent on me will grow stronger too. Am I wrong?"

"No." He wouldn't lie to her about that.

"And if I taste right to you, if you have those strong feelings, you're going to mate me. Period. Nature is going to bitch-slap you so hard, you won't have a choice. Am I wrong about *that*?"

He frowned, saying nothing.

"I'll take that for a no. You're either damn sure I'm just going to be O positive with a little lack of iron in my bloodstream when you do bite me, or you already know someone else is your mate, so you feel safe enough to risk it. Which is the case?"

"I've never found someone else I wanted to test before. You're the only woman I've ever had feelings for."

"That makes it worse. What if you bite me and it's instant insanity time?"

"Then I'll know you're my mate."

"And what then? You'll find super VampLycan strength and be the first man ever to resist claiming a mate? Are you that delusional?"

54

He hesitated. "I'm sure I can control the urge to bite you. I also wouldn't be the first one to resist claiming a mate. It just doesn't happen often."

"I've never heard of that."

"You've been gone a long time and weren't privy to what was going on in other clans. Another VampLycan refused to claim a mostly human half-breed for his mate in Decker's clan. His love for her was strong enough to make sure she wasn't killed. Decker would have taken her out. Lorn knew it was a death sentence to his Kira if he made her his mate while Decker ruled."

She studied him. "Do you love me, Wen?"

He drew in a deep breath and released it. "I always have, Gerri. You will never know how close I came to killing the humans you dated. I wanted to rip them to shreds every time I read about one in a report. I would never endanger your life by taking you as a mate. I know it would be a death sentence for you in the long run. My clan leader would accept it but my parents wouldn't."

"Then walk away. It's too risky." She blinked rapidly. "Because I know I wouldn't be strong enough to say no if you asked me to go home with you."

"I'd rather have this time than none at all."

She glanced away and hugged her waist.

"We don't have forever, but I'll take whatever time I can get with you. The memories will be easier for you to live with than me."

Gerri whipped her head up and peered at him. "How do you figure that?"

"You have a much shorter lifespan, G.L. You're going to haunt me long after you're gone."

She closed her eyes and walked to him. "Goddamn you, Wen."

"Is that a yes?" He hugged her around her middle. "Will you come with me until my mission is completed?"

"This is so damn stupid...but count me in. I'll regret it otherwise. I already do," she admitted. "But I love you too."

He lifted her, determined to carry her to bed and make love. This time he'd take it slower, with her facing him, and be more prepared for the way he was going to respond to her. He'd keep his skin or put on a muzzle if he needed to, just to keep from biting her.

But the way his chest tightened and how strong his urge was to claim her told Wen more than a blood test ever could. She was his mate.

Chapter Three

Gerri woke with a big, warm body curled around her back. Memory was instant. Wen's hand cupped one of her breasts, his leg wedged between hers while they'd slept. The feeling that woke her was his stiff cock lightly tapping against her ass. She bit her lip and lifted her head off his other arm, which pillowed it.

One glance at the clock and she clenched her teeth. Her shift had started three hours before. Her boss would be pissed enough to fire her. She'd also lost her chance at getting laundry done.

"Go back to sleep or I will fuck you again," Wen rasped, his husky voice sexy.

"I'm going to be sore," she admitted, feeling tenderness between her legs. "Human, remember?"

He adjusted his body a little on the bed and nuzzled her shoulder with his face. The kiss he placed there was open-mouthed and he raked his teeth gently against her skin. "Sorry. We had a lot of time to make up for. I could bleed for you."

"No." She hated the way his offer had her stomach knotting.

"You can take my blood. That's safe and it will heal you."

"Pass. I'd rather feel a little pain than be hornier than hell. I know it's going to make me feel higher than a kite and give me an adrenaline rush, since I'm not hurt. Mom clued me in."

He chuckled. "That's not a bad thing."

She dropped her head back against his arm and closed her eyes. It was time to change the subject. "I'm shocked my phone isn't ringing. My boss should have called me."

"I turned your phone off after you fell asleep."

Anger surged. "You what?"

"You don't need that job. You're working for me now. I also returned the key to the old woman after you fell asleep, so she'd never miss it. I braced your door too. You should always put those bars across it. Some asshole could have gotten in the same way I did."

"Don't say that about the job thing when we're naked. It sounds obscene."

His hand on her breast gently squeezed. "You're worth every penny."

She jabbed him in his ribs with her elbow. "Not funny."

He laughed. "Was that supposed to hurt? It kind of tickled. You're going to have to work harder at it."

She wiggled and turned, facing him. He straightened his legs to allow it and rolled over onto his back. His hair was messy from sleep and his usually harsh expression was soft from him just waking up. The sight of him stretched out on her bed with the sheet low on his hips killed her urge to slap him. She reached out instead and ran her fingertips over the muscles along his stomach.

"I thought you didn't want me to fuck you." His hand gripped hers, stopping her from caressing him.

"Couldn't you have a pot belly?"

He grinned. "No."

She studied his chest and muscled arms. "You're beautiful."

"Couldn't you use the term studly or handsome?"

Gerri grinned. "I said I'd never sleep with a guy prettier than me. You blew that one out of the water."

He suddenly rolled, knocking her flat on her back and coming down over her. He pushed up with his arms, lifting his chest away from hers. He lowered his gaze and licked his lips. "You're the pretty one, G.L. All soft curves." He looked into her eyes, a glint of humor showing in his gaze. "You are a tiny powerhouse of sex appeal."

"Tiny powerhouse?"

He braced his weight with one arm to free the other. He gripped her hip with one hand. "You're short but you've got the best ass and breasts I've ever seen. Spread your legs."

"Anyone is short compared to you. And I want to but I'm really sore, Wen. We did it four times last night and you weren't exactly gentle those last two."

He opened his mouth and his fangs slid down.

Gerri's heart pounded. "What are you doing? Put the pointy teeth away."

It stunned her when he made sure she could see him bite his tongue. It had to hurt. Blood welled on both sides of it and he lowered himself. "Open to me." His gaze fixed on her mouth.

"No."

He released her hip and gently stroked her side. It tickled and she laughed. Wen's mouth covered hers and he instantly deepened the kiss.

The taste of his blood mingled on her tongue. She tried to turn her head but he reached up and captured her chin to hold her face steady. He was too good at it, and she started to kiss him back.

She reached up and wrapped her arms around his neck. He adjusted his body, rising up a little. She spread her legs, knowing what he wanted when his stiff cock nudged her thigh. She was wet and ready as he slowly entered her. She moaned against his lips.

The blood worked fast. She'd forgotten about that. It made her a little lightheaded and disoriented, but Wen kept her anchored to reality as he started to move, thrusting his pelvis in slow rolls, sending pleasure humming through her body. She moaned again, kicking at the tangled sheets to free her trapped foot and wrap her legs higher around his ass. He was gentle though, almost sensing her need for tenderness.

He broke the kiss and she opened her eyes. His were open too, glowing blue. He leaned a little to one side and raised his hand, biting his index finger. Blood welled from the tip and he offered it to her. She opened her mouth, sucking on it. He growled.

"That's so sexy." He tilted his head. "Give me your neck."

She released his finger. "You can't bite me."

He closed his eyes and stopped moving on her. "Fuck."

She unwound her arms from around him and tried to ignore the other symptoms of taking his blood. Her skin seemed oversensitive and warmth spread throughout her body. She clutched his shoulders and closed her eyes. Every second that passed made her more aware of him and her own body.

"Are you okay?"

"Yeah. I feel like I have a fever and it's spreading from my brain toward my feet. It's like taking the opposite of a sleeping pill."

He chuckled. "It's my blood hitting your bloodstream. It will pass in a minute or two. That's why I stopped. I'm waiting for you to recover."

"I'm glad this amuses you. I don't remember this happening the last time you gave me blood when I was nine."

"Don't remind me." He lowered his face and nuzzled her check with his. "I was so terrified that you were going to die."

She was certain she would too. An innocent stroll into the woods to sit by the stream had almost turned deadly. She hadn't seen the bear until only about six feet separated them. It had turned around about the same instant she'd spotted it.

She froze, praying it wouldn't attack. One roar later and it lunged.

The rest was kind of a blur. She's screamed and sprinted for her life. There was no safe place to go. The tree branches offered no help since it could climb after her. She just hoped to reach the village and safety. It hadn't turned out that way. She wasn't fast enough and the bear had nailed her with its massive claws, throwing her off balance. Pain assured her she lived when she found herself sprawled on the ground, but then the bear had come at her again. She held still, more out of hurting too bad than being smart by playing dead.

That's when Wen had shown up. She didn't see him at first but she heard his snarls. The bear roared and she managed to find the strength to lift her head. Wen had shifted to four legs and attacked the bear. He'd been much smaller, but a few well-placed swipes of his claws to the bear's face had it taking off in another direction.

Wen had shifted back and rushed to her side. He'd crouched down and she knew her injuries had to be bad, because he'd looked horrified. That's when some of the shock had worn off and she realized her side had been severely injured. She'd touched her ribs and her hand had come away covered in blood where it hurt the most. It had been a mistake to twist her head to get a look at what damage had been done. The bear's claws had torn through her shirt, ripping into her.

"G.L.!" The panic in his voice had been clear.

"Get help." It was all she could think to say.

He looked up. "It could come back. I'm not leaving you." He savagely bit into his arm and grabbed the back of her head. "Drink."

"It's against the law!"

"I don't care. Drink. I'm not letting you die." He shoved his arm against her lips, coating her lower face with his blood.

She'd been scared enough to swallow when it became hard to breathe. The bear had probably punctured her lung on that side. It had been gross to drink blood, it almost threatening to make her throw up, but she was desperate to survive.

Wen had finally pulled his arm away from her mouth and then tore the rest of her shirt to see the damage. He'd hovered his still dripping arm above her torn skin so his blood fell onto her wound.

He'd held her for a bit until she felt better, then scooped her up into his arms to run her back to the village. All hell had broken loose when they'd arrived. Her mother had cried when she'd seen all the blood but her injuries were healing. Wen's father had grabbed his arm and dragged

62

him away from her. She'd heard him yelling at Wen for bleeding for a human.

Her stepdad had promised to speak to the clan leader on Wen's behalf. Trayis had understood why Wen had saved her and hadn't whipped him for breaking the rules, but his father hadn't been as forgiving. Wen had suffered a week locked inside his room by his parents. It was a horrible punishment for a boy used to freedom. He'd assured her it was worth it, seeing her healed, and she hadn't even been left scarred.

Wen pulled her from her memories by running his fingertips over her ribs, letting her know he remembered too. "Does it ever hurt?"

"No. You totally healed it with your blood."

"You never listened to me. I told you to not go wandering around the woods without me by your side."

"I never did that again. Almost becoming a bear's breakfast wised me up."

He locked gazes with her. "How many times have you been hurt without me there to heal you?"

"A few."

He gripped her wrist, lifting her arm. "I noticed this scar. How did you get it?"

She glanced at the jagged, thin line on her forearm. "I told you I didn't want to stick with the pack my mom joined up with. That happened after I used pepper spray on one of the guys who decided not to take no for an answer, when he wanted me to bend over for him."

Wen's mouth flattened into an angry line. "Where is this pack?"

"Sacramento. Forget it. I have."

"Did any of them ever force you?"

"I was too smart and paranoid. Only one of them ever got me alone. He nailed me when he blindly lashed out with his claws after I'd sprayed him in the face, but it was only once. I was out of there before he could see again and I smashed a perfume bottle I kept in my purse, this real horrible shit, to confuse his nose and prevent him from tracking me while blind."

"What did Carol do?"

"Told me not to cause trouble. That's the day I packed up and left. She was more pissed that I'd upset her boyfriend than the fact that I was sporting a big bandage on my arm and was almost forced into being a pack bitch."

"What the hell happened to her? She used to be so protective of you."

"Losing her mate changed her. I told you that. She drank booze at first and had a hard time adjusting to life in the outside world. I'm pretty sure she was doing drugs too. She denied it, but yeah, she seemed high most of the time. She liked the alpha. I thought he was a pure asshole, and I had no respect for a guy who encouraged his girlfriend to fuck his pack."

"I can't imagine. I would shred any guy who put the moves on you."

"Well, VampLycans are possessive and you all have a god complex."

He grinned. "You called me a god a few times last night."

"I said 'Oh God'."

He chuckled. "You're feeling better." He moved his hips, slowing fucking her in shallow thrusts.

Gerri forgot about everything but the feel of him. She moaned and reached up, sliding her fingers into the hair at the base of his neck. She tugged and he lowered his mouth to hers. She kissed him. The pleasure mounted as he continued to ride her slow and steady until she climaxed. He pulled his mouth away and turned his head, hiding his expression from her when he came. They both stilled, Wen pinning her under him and Gerri clinging to him.

"Are you okay?" She was concerned when his head stayed tucked against his shoulder.

"Yes." His voice came out too gruff but she didn't feel any hair on the skin she caressed. He'd stayed in control.

"It's getting tougher not to bite me, isn't it?"

He looked at her then, and his eye color had changed to pure black. She was staring at his inner beast. It didn't frighten her. It was still Wen. She reached up and caressed his cheek. "Take some deep breaths. You're going to hurt yourself. You can't go that far over the line and stay in your skin. Do you need to shift?"

He gave a sharp nod.

"Ease out of me first because that would freak me out."

He withdrew his softening dick and rolled away from her. He was furry by the time he hit the floor on all fours. Gerri climbed out of bed and studied him.

"Damn. You're so much bigger now than you used to be." She put on a nightshirt.

He tracked her with his intense dark stare. She approached and ran her fingers through his fur. VampLycans in shift didn't look like wolves. They had a more human shape and the fur wasn't as thick. His limbs and shoulders were muscular, even in shifted form. She moved in front of him and crouched near his face, gently rubbing his muzzle. He curled his upper lip, flashing a row of sharp teeth instead of just two fangs.

"You're not pretty anymore." She fearlessly glided her hand over his extended snout to the side of his face and then scratched behind his ears. "Is this still your favorite spot?"

He dipped his head, allowing it.

She smiled. "You're still a puppy at times, aren't you?"

He growled and looked at her.

She met his stare and let him go, rising. "Stay off my bed. I remember how you can shed. I'm going to go make us breakfast. I just hope I have enough food. I bet you eat twice as much as you used to, and that was about six times more than I did back then."

He followed her into the kitchen and sprawled out on the vinyl tile near her dishwasher. The sight of her cell phone sitting on the counter reminded her that Wen must have gone inside her purse to find it. She picked it up and ran her thumb across the screen to turn it on. Six messages waited. She grimaced, identifying the same number displayed over and over. Each one had been from Robert, her boss.

"I'm so fired." She set it down and yanked open the fridge. "I haven't gone shopping so I hope you don't mind eggs and toast."

He growled low.

"I don't have bacon or ham. Sorry. I was waiting to get paid before I restocked the fridge. There are some hot dogs if you want meat."

He turned his face away.

She laughed. "You're such a snob. You should have brought groceries and a cook if you don't want to eat what's here or what I'm willing to make."

She went to work quickly, scrambling eggs and making half a loaf of buttered toast. It wasn't the best breakfast to offer a guy who could take down a large animal for a meal, but it would have to do. She loaded up his plate and set it on the table. He lifted his head, peering at her with those seemingly soulless dark eyes.

Her neighbors would scream in terror if they saw him. He wasn't cuddly or cute. The Vampire blood had mutated the Lycan in him, so shifted VampLycans looked more like hellish beasts with their more humanoid forms.

He rose up and tilted his head a little, staring at her in a way that conveyed his curiosity. Some emotion must have shown in her face.

"Do you want me to set the plate on the floor or can you shift back?"

He closed his eyes and she watched him start to change. The soft noises as bones shifted and popped had her wincing but she'd grown up with seeing shifters do their thing. The hair receded to smooth, tan skin, and one handsome guy emerged when he stood.

"Thank you. Why were you looking at me with a smirk on your face? I wasn't going to mess up your floor by getting food all over it."

"That wasn't it. I was just thinking about how fierce you look in shifted form. I'd forgotten."

He walked past her and entered her bedroom. She frowned. "The food is in here."

He returned in less than a minute with a towel wrapped around his waist. "I really should have brought a spare set of clothes with me when I visited you. I don't want to put on my pants and nothing of yours will fit me." He took a seat at the table. "This smells great. I'd kill for a steak though."

"Me too. It's not in my budget often."

He grimly regarded her and then glanced around her apartment. "I can tell."

"Don't insult my place."

"It's a dive." He held her gaze.

"It's affordable and it comes with bars over the windows. They don't have those in nice neighborhoods. The building is old too, and built more solid. New construction isn't as sturdy. These walls aren't as easy to tear through from one apartment into the next. I checked, and they have beams set apart every few feet. Some newer places build with cheap framing and only insulation between the walls."

"How do you know this?"

"Stud finders help me locate the beams behind the walls." She shrugged. "I use technology to help protect myself since I'm only human."

"Graves never told me how bad things were for you when he sent me reports."

"Who's Graves?"

"The Lycan I had checking on you from time to time. He's a relative of mine. My mom keeps in touch with some of her mother's people."

"Great. I take it that you trust him somewhat, since he probably knows I'm someone he could use against you if the need arises. You showed an interest in a human."

He frowned. "I've worked a lot with him and his brother Micah in the past, when I had to leave Alaska. They are both good guys. I knew neither of them would hurt you or tell anyone I keep tabs on you. They're family, and they honor the loyalty that goes with that." He glanced around the apartment again. "I wish Graves had told me you were struggling. I would have sent you money."

"It's kind of tough to get a decent-paying job in the human world when you come from a clan. I was taken to Alaska when I was almost a year old and didn't leave until I was fifteen. There were no records of my life during that time, and let's just say I never did the high school thing. Mom couldn't get me registered. Getting a driver's license was a bitch and a half. Mom told them I was homeschooled and we'd grown up in a hippie type community. She still had my birth certificate though, so we managed. Every employer asks for a high school diploma, which I don't have. It means shit jobs no one else wants. They just require a pulse and you showing up on time."

"You barely have any food."

"I was waiting for payday. I said that, didn't I? This is a short week. I just paid my rent. Look at me. I don't starve. I'm just not eating steak every night."

His eyes narrowed as he silently watched her.

"What? I do the best I can. I have my own place. I used to have a roommate when I first left my mom. That sucked. Try living with a stranger just to be able to afford the rent. She brought strange men home sometimes. I was always afraid one of them wouldn't be human. I'm doing way better now."

"Your furniture is old and doesn't match."

"So? You were just shedding hair on my floor."

"What does that have to do with anything?"

"Don't be a snob, Wen. That's what I'm saying. I don't look down on you for having a snout sometimes, so don't lift your nose over my home."

"I just hate that you struggle."

"Welcome to my world." She shoved her fork into the eggs and took a bite. "When does our adventure into getting me killed start?"

He scowled. "Today. I'm not going to let anything happen to you."

"Fantastic." She managed to not roll her eyes. "Where?"

"Washington state."

"That's a drive."

"We're flying. I brought a plane with me."

"You fly now? You got a pilot's license?"

"No. Micah has one and he's with me. It's his plane."

She glanced at the curtained window. "He's outside? You left him out there all night?"

"No. Of course not. We booked rooms at a hotel a few miles from here."

"What time do we leave?"

"As soon as we finish eating and showering. You'll need to pack light. We're supposed to be on the run with enforcers searching for us. Do you have a backpack?"

"Yes. So this Micah is our backup? That's good to know we're not going in alone."

"It's just going to be you and me. He's only flying us there. I want him clear of danger once we reach where it was reported the rogues hang out."

"Ah. He's family. Got it."

"What the hell does that mean?"

"You're taking *me* into this mess but keeping *his* ass safe."

"I'd never let anything happen to you."

"How many rogue Weres are there supposed to be protecting this ghoul maker jerk?"

"About a dozen. Horton keeps a few of his nest with him too. He became the master since his died. I was told he's leading less than four Vamps at most, at any given time."

"This ghoul maker is named Horton? No wonder he's an ass. I would be too with that kind of name. Is your intel good?"

"Yes."

"How can you be sure?"

"Micah and Graves trust their sources."

"Only a dozen rogue Lycans, plus a few Vamps." She chewed on a piece of toast. "Simple, right?" She hoped he heard her sarcasm.

"I can protect you."

"Who's going to protect *you*? You're one against bad odds. I know you've been trained to fight since you could walk, but give me a break."

"They'll want to gain information from me, and that means they'll need leverage."

She almost choked, and had to fight to swallow the food in her mouth. She glared at him. "Me. I knew I was bait."

"Leverage," he corrected. "They won't hurt you because they'd have nothing to use against me otherwise."

"You mean they won't *kill* me." She had a bad feeling. "I'm going to be a Vamp snack, aren't I? Damn it, Wen!"

He snarled and his eyes turned black. "I'll rip out their goddamn fangs if they even think about biting you." He slammed his fist down on the table. "You think I'd allow it?"

She dropped her gaze and winced. The cheap tabletop had split and dented inward. "Can you avoid breaking my stuff?"

He glanced down. "Sorry. They'll keep their fangs out of you and their hands off. I just meant that they'll know you're my vulnerable spot to get me to talk to them. They'll want intel on VampLycans since they obviously want to start a war. They'll keep it friendly, so I don't foresee you being in any real danger."

"You're going to feed this Horton bullshit."

"Yes. I'll wait for the first opportunity to kill him after I've figured out what he's done and who's involved with him."

"When the Vamps are sleeping?"

He nodded again. "It should be easy. I doubt most of those Lycans stick around all day to guard this asshole."

"Right. You said he was now a master. He'd already be dead if he was stupid. He managed to survive before when you said his nest was taken out. I think you're sorely underestimating this zombie maker, and it's a bad move."

"We'll learn the full scope of the situation once we get there."

"Right." She lost her appetite. "Oh boy. How exciting. We're going in blind and with low expectations. This is totally going to turn out great."

Wen arched an eyebrow and frowned.

"Damn VampLycans and their egos. Let me clue you in, honeybun. This isn't going to be a picnic without ants. These are freakin' Vampires and Weres who want to go to war with your kind. They aren't harmless or stupid. Rogues are crazy and logic doesn't fit into their daily lives. You underestimating them is going to get us both killed."

"Honeybun?" He appeared amused.

"That's the only thing I just said that you focused on? Come on, Wen. This isn't a game. If it turns to shit, you can take off but I can't run as fast as you do. I'd only slow you down, so my ass is going to be dinner or a chew toy. They'll catch me."

"You think I'd abandon you?"

She closed her eyes and lowered her chin. "You did before."

73

Wen slowly stood and unclenched his fists. "I couldn't stop your mother from leaving. We've been over this."

"I just think you're not giving this zombie maker creep enough credit. These guys are dangerous. You do have an ego problem. You think nobody can ever get the best of you but you need to see that this isn't some game."

He approached her and the urge to pull her into his arms almost overpowered him. He resisted. "I do know. I lost my brother. He was killed on the job."

She peered up at him. One of her eyebrows arched in question.

"I was attempting to underplay the risks so you'd feel safer."

"I know the truth, Wen." She reached out and placed her palm on his chest. "That's why you came to me. Rogues are nuts and don't live by any kind of rules. They are killers. It's why they need to be taken out. You're hoping for the best but we need to be prepared for the worst. You want me to feel better? Take this more seriously and stop trying to make it sound as if it's going to be a breeze."

"Okay." He admired her for her courage. He always had. "I honestly don't think you're going to be in that much danger or I wouldn't take you along. They'll want to use you against me. They'll see you as my weakness but we both know otherwise. You're the one they'll underestimate, Gerri. You're smart and resourceful. I taught you how to fight. You're not helpless. You said you killed a Vamp who came after you. How many humans can claim they've done that other than those who've stumbled across a Vamp while it was day sleeping? You took him out when he was awake and coming after you. There's a huge difference."

"I knew what he was and how to kill him."

"Exactly. You fought back. You always impressed me when I trained you. You use your smaller size as an advantage. They won't see you as a threat. *You're* my backup. It won't be me alone against them."

She nodded. "Okay."

"Go shower and pack light. Bring warmer clothes. The forecast is cloudy and some rain where we're going. I checked the weather."

"Aren't you going to shower with me?"

He glanced down her body. "If I do, I'll fuck you again. We need to get going. Micah is expecting to hear from me. I'll shower after you're done."

"Okay. I'll do that now and braid my hair."

"Leave it down."

"It's a pain in the ass if I don't braid it."

"I like it down."

She sighed. "It'll become a tangled mess."

"You had it down yesterday."

"Because I was running late."

"Leave it down, G.L."

"Whatever."

She left him and entered her bedroom. He waited until the water came on before he went in search of his cell phone. He pulled it out of his pants pocket.

"It's about time," Micah announced. "Where the hell have you been?"

"Get the plane ready. I'll meet you there in about half an hour. I'm with Gerri and she's agreed to help us." He hung up before Micah could ask more questions.

Was he going to get Gerri killed? He stared at the open bathroom door, listening to her splash around in the shower.

He clenched his jaw. He'd do anything to keep her safe. Part of him was tempted to just leave her there.

He glanced around her bedroom and anger rose. She lived with bars over her windows in a neighborhood that reeked of Vamps. He'd smelled them the night before when he'd entered the area. She wasn't safe if he left her, either. It would be better if he kept her by his side.

Wen had to admit he might have come to that conclusion for purely selfish reasons. He wanted to spend every second he could with her. It was the first time in years that he'd truly felt alive.

Chapter Four

"I have to handle these people." Wen jerked his chin in the direction of the airport employees.

Gerri translated that to mean Wen needing to mess with their minds so nobody asked too many questions. She winced but didn't protest. It wasn't right to mind control people but it was necessary. Wen would want his travel plans kept secret and under the radar.

"I'll just wait here while you do your mojo thing. How do you get around the cameras? All airports have them, even these small ones."

He reached up and tipped his sunglasses higher by half an inch so she could see his eyes. They began to glow. "The cameras are in the ceilings." His eyes dulled in color and he dropped the sunglasses back onto the bridge of his nose. "Go outside and give Micah your bag." He fixed his focus out the big window. "See the plane with the guy wearing the leather jacket? That's him. He's already got my bag. Give him yours so we can get in the air. We're already behind schedule."

She followed his line of sight and spotted a small plane. It was a six-seater, from her guess, and didn't look as bad as she'd feared. The pilot was crouched down inspecting the tires on the thing. He was a big man in that position but that wasn't a surprise, since she knew he was a Lycan. They weren't known for being tiny. "He knows I'm with you?"

Wen frowned. "Yeah. I told him I was bringing you along. Go on, Gerri. This will take a few minutes. Tell Micah I want wheels up in five."

She nodded and strode toward the exit door. She didn't worry about an employee being curious about her, knowing Wen would handle it. She pushed open the glass and stepped onto pavement. It was a small airport that didn't deal with big planes. She approached the guy, who was a good hundred yards out. He had straightened a little and opened a side compartment door, shuffling bags.

"Hi, Micah," she called out. "Wen said wheels up in five."

"Hey, legs. No problem." He avoided hitting his head on the plane and turned.

He kind of looked like Wen, with the blue eyes and dark hair. The family resemblance ended there, except he was also handsome. His mouth dropped open when he saw her. He abruptly shut it, and his nose wrinkled as he sniffed.

She paused about five feet away from him. The wind blew toward her, which meant he'd have a hard time picking up her scent. She didn't help him out by stepping closer. "Legs? Is that what you called me?"

"I thought you were Sherry." His eyes narrowed and he sniffed again.

"I'm Gerri. With a G. I take it you call this Sherry person legs?"

He opened his mouth again, then closed it. "Sorry. My mistake. I thought Wen said we were picking up someone by the name of Sherry." He recovered and took a few steps closer. "Hand me your bag."

She backed off a little. He wanted to get a whiff of her so he could tell what she was. *Legs.* He was also lying. He knew this Sherry person, and had a nickname for her. He thought she'd be someone else.

"Who's Sherry?"

"Nobody. Can I have your bag? You said Wen wanted to take off."

"I'm not a Lycan like you but I can smell bullshit."

Surprise registered for a split second but he masked it fast. "You're like Wen?"

"Nope. One hundred percent grade-A human, with no extras." She shrugged the strap of her backpack off her shoulder and offered it to him. "Who's Sherry?"

He spun away, loading her bag into the plane. "Nobody." His smile looked forced when he faced her again. "I take it you know about others?"

"I was raised with Wen's clan for a lot of years. My mother mated a VampLycan. They met when he was doing an art show. He was a tradesman."

He relaxed a little. "I didn't know they mated with humans."

"They normally don't. She was immune to mind control, and she kind of ended up in the middle of a fight with a small nest of Vampires who decided to crash his opening night at a gallery. He sold high-end stuff to rich people. The nest didn't like having a VampLycan in town and thought it would be a good idea to attack him. He ended up killing all five of them and had to wipe the minds of all the humans present." She paused.

"Except your mother," he guessed.

"Exactly. He didn't want to kill her though, and he spent a few days with her, trying to figure out what to do. Mom and Klentz fell in love. He took us home to Alaska with him. I was about a year old at the time."

"He accepted you. That's rare too."

"I was a cute baby. At least that's what Klentz always claimed. He was good to me." She felt a wave of sadness. He had been a loving dad, even though he hadn't been the one to get her mom pregnant. That had been some loser who'd abandoned her mom after finding out she was expecting. "He died in an avalanche when I was fifteen. He used to go out sometimes to drag home fallen trees to create his art. It was a freak accident. He probably would have survived, but it brought down some boulders along with a mountain of snow. He was crushed under them. My mom left the clan after that and took me with her." She paused. "Now you know my life story. Who is this Sherry?"

"She's someone who works with us from time to time."

"And you call her legs?"

He glanced away. "She's six-two."

"Ah."

He yanked open the door. "Climb into the back."

"Sure thing." She had to climb alright. He gave her a little help and she scooted into a seat. "Thanks."

"No problem. So…Wen wanted your help because you know what we're dealing with?"

"Yeah."

He sniffed at her again and his gaze traveled down her body, then back to her face. She could tell he was a little stunned.

"I'm the bait, and I can guess what you're picking up. Do I smell like Wen?"

"Yes. Strongly."

80

"That's the plan."

"He didn't tell me much."

"That's Wen for you." *Who the hell is Sherry to Wen?* She didn't think she'd like the answer. "He's real closemouthed about some things."

Micah sealed the door, then rounded the plane to take the pilot seat. The entire thing shook a little when he started the engines. He twisted in his seat, handing her a headset. She took it and put it on. He adjusted his, then spoke.

"Can you hear me okay?"

"Yes."

She turned her head, watching as Wen strolled out of the building as if he didn't have a care in the world. None of the employees even looked his way. He'd obviously manipulated their memories and they were fine with whatever story he'd implanted. He got inside the plane and put on a headset.

"Let's go, Micah. You're cleared for takeoff. They're holding all air traffic until we're gone." He turned his head. "You should probably take a nap, Gerri. We're going to be up all night."

Who the hell is Sherry?

She resisted asking for about ten seconds. "Who's Sherry?"

Wen's lips pressed into a tight line and he shot a glare at the pilot. Micah ignored him, maneuvering the small craft toward the runway.

"You didn't answer me," she persisted.

"Nobody." Wen put on his seat belt. "We're taking off. Buckle in."

"I'm not dropping this. Have you forgotten how stubborn I can be? Just answer the question."

He twisted his head to glare at her. "She's a lawyer who occasionally works for my clan."

"A VampLycan?"

"No."

"Lycan?"

A muscle jumped in his jaw and he really looked furious. "No. She's human. Trayis is always buying up land when he can to expand our territory, and she handles some of the deals when the owners are from the lower states. She's also helped us with some legal issues. She specializes in business law."

"Does she handle *you*?" Jealousy was an ugly emotion that wouldn't be denied. Though he'd said he'd slept with some humans.

He looked away. "We're taking off. Let Micah concentrate. It's windy today."

She refused to let it drop. "She knows what you are, doesn't she?"

He ignored her. That answered that. Sherry was one of his lovers. It hurt but it also pissed her off.

"Wen?"

He twisted in the seat. "What?"

"Does she know what you are?"

"Yes. She does." His eyes flashed a little, glowing blue. "She was saved by one of our clan about six years ago. She's immune to mind control, so we hired her. It was either that or kill her to keep her silent.

82

Now we're protected under client privilege because she's our attorney. Anything else you want to know?"

"Were you the one to save her?"

That muscle in his jaw twitched again. "Yes."

"Why am I here?"

That question seemed to be one he wasn't expecting. "I told you."

"You said you needed me because I'm human and know what you are. You already had Sherry. I take it you weren't willing to risk *her* ass?" That hurt.

His expression softened. "It's not like that."

"Fuck you, Wen." She leaned back against the seat and closed her eyes, fighting tears. He could have taken the other woman on his hunt but he'd chosen her instead. It was going to be dangerous. He wasn't willing to risk Sherry's life. Just hers.

"I told you the truth."

She flinched at hearing his snarled words. He was really loud over the droning engines as they sped down the runway. The plane lifted up into the air, swaying in the wind. She kept her eyes closed. Heights weren't her favorite thing, nor was looking at Wen at that moment.

"Damn it, don't ignore me," he demanded.

She lifted her hand and flipped him off. "Just shut up. I'm taking that nap." She hadn't put on her belt, so she just drew her legs up and curled sideways into the seat. It didn't matter if she was tossed around a bit at that moment. It was the least of her worries.

"It's not like that, Gerri. I wanted *you* with me on this mission. No one else."

She opened her eyes and glared at him. "Right. You fuck this Sherry, don't you?"

He said nothing.

"That's a big yes. You lied to me."

"I didn't."

"You implied that I was the only human who you could trust not to stab you in the back if they knew what you were. Guess what? Be glad I don't have a knife right now. And it wouldn't be your back I'd be aiming for. I'd take your balls."

"She doesn't matter, Gerri."

"Bullshit. You're keeping her far from this mess and I'm the one you're willing to sacrifice. Just shut up, Wen. I don't want to hear any more of your lies."

"I wanted to be with *you*!"

"Fuck!" Micah yelled. "Don't roar in my ear. I'm trying to fly."

"Stay out of this," Wen snarled. "You had no right to tell her about Sherry."

"I thought you said that's who we were picking up! Their names sound a lot alike. I called her legs and she started asking questions. I didn't say anything about you screwing Sherry."

"I'm the one getting screwed now," Gerri scoffed. "So he can keep *her* safe. She works for the clan, so she's more important."

"Goddamn it," Wen snarled.

84

He shocked her when he stood and climbed over the seats. It was a small, cramped area in the cabin. Micah started cursing and Gerri could relate. The plane tilted a bit. There wasn't a lot of space in the backseat and even less once Wen was almost on top of her. She slapped at him when he tried to force her to sit up. He was stronger, and she was afraid to really put up a fight in case Micah got hit, since he was flying the plane.

Wen ended up sitting next to her and dragging her onto his lap. He scooted over to the center of the seat. She fisted his shirt and grabbed a handful of his hair at the base of his neck. The urge to punch him was strong, but his eyes started to glow brighter.

"Don't pull that mind-wipe shit on me."

"I'm not."

She didn't look away. "I will never forgive you if you erase the last fifteen minutes of my life. I'll remember in time. You know my mother was immune. It doesn't last long on me. I'll dream the truth and eventually realize it's a real memory. My stepdad tested it on me and that's always what happened. I will hunt you down if you mess with my head, damn you. I know where you live."

"I just want to talk."

"Then remove the glow."

He closed his eyes and took a few deep breaths. His eyes were normal and beautiful when they opened again. "Sherry doesn't mean anything to me. Yes, I've fucked her in the past, but it was just sex. I wanted you with me for all the reasons I said last night." He glanced at Micah, then her. "I haven't lied to you. I just didn't tell you there was someone else I could have asked to go on this hunt with me. I wanted *you* at my side, G.L."

The silence stretched between them. She wanted to believe him but didn't dare. He was a VampLycan. They were known for their honesty but only to each other. One of them would lie to a human in a heartbeat to get what they wanted. Was he using her to keep Sherry safe? Did he love this lawyer? It hurt really bad to think so.

"Is her name Gerri or G.L.?" Micah sounded confused.

"Gerri, but I'm the only one who calls her G.L. It's an endearment." Wen kept staring at her. "Sherry doesn't matter," he rasped. "You do."

"I don't know if I believe you."

He frowned. "What will it take to prove it?"

"Kill Sherry?"

He scowled. "Is that a joke?"

Guilt struck. "I guess."

"I understand." He leaned in closer and nuzzled her head with his face, putting his lips next to her ear. "I want to rip apart all the humans you've let touch you. I'd love to see every one of them dead by my hands."

"It's not like there's many." She relaxed against him and eased her grasp on his hair.

"One is too many." He nuzzled her cheek again and whispered, "Trust me, golden locks. You're the only woman who matters to me."

She wanted to believe him so much it made her chest ache.

86

He adjusted his head a little and opened his mouth against her neck, nipping her. "I want to bite you. Nobody has ever made me feel the way you do."

She clutched his shoulders. "I knew it. You totally want to get me killed." His family would want her dead if he mated her.

He stiffened, as if reminded of what kind of outcome that would cause. He pulled her closer to his chest and sighed. "No. I'll do anything to keep you safe. Sleep. We're going hunting as soon as we land and the sun goes down."

She hadn't slept well the night before and was tired. "Thank you."

"For what?" He caressed her back.

"Not trying to wipe my memory."

"I would never do that to you."

She wanted to trust him. She just wasn't sure if she could.

* * * * *

Wen ignored his cousin and the way he kept glancing back at him with a curious expression. Gerri slept in his arms and he didn't plan to return to the front seat. He liked holding her. Not to mention, beating on Micah while he was piloting the plane would make them crash. He had removed her headphones so she'd sleep more comfortably.

"Sorry, man. I didn't mean to cause you any trouble," Micah said from the front. "I didn't realize you were serious about her. Who the hell is she, anyway?"

"None of your concern."

"Bullshit," Micah snorted. "We're family."

"I grew up with her. You know how I have Graves keep an eye on a human for me? This is her."

"He never shares anything you have him look into. I never ask. I take it she's important to you?"

"Very. Her mother took her away from the clan after her mate died. Carol was lost to her grief and just wanted a fresh start. She dragged her daughter with her."

"She told me that. Her mother was mated to a tradesman who died."

"I couldn't stop them from leaving. I begged her mother to stay with the clan but she wouldn't listen to me."

Micah twisted his head, studying Gerri. He grimaced. "Damn. I'm sorry. I see it written all over your face and in the way you hold her. Your parents would flip, wouldn't they?"

"You know how it is."

Micah paid attention to the instruments. "Graves and I have it easy. Our parents would love it if we brought *any* woman home, no matter the race, as long as we give them grandkids. Ten years ago, that wasn't the case. Mom was tossing every available bitch in our path who she felt would be strong breeders. Now it's just every woman with a pulse who she thinks might tempt us to take them to bed. Maybe that's the trick. Put off mating until they fear you'll never settle down."

"I like your parents."

"They've mellowed with age."

"That won't happen with mine."

"I know. I'm sorry, man. Gerbin dying really fucked up your life."

He felt a stab of pain in his chest at the mention of his brother's name. "He was their favorite. I miss him, and how things were before he died."

"Would they have accepted your G.L. if you were still the second son?"

"You call her Gerri." He thought about it. "Yes. They wouldn't have been thrilled but they would have accepted it."

"I don't envy your life."

"Me either."

The silence stretched and Gerri began to softly snore. Wen grinned, staring down at her parted lips. She was delightful. He'd worn her out with too much sex and not enough sleep the night before. No regret surfaced.

Micah cleared his throat. "You know Sherry isn't going to like this if she finds out. She's kind of possessive of you, and don't you have her working on this too, following all the police reports about these assholes you're going after, to see what they're into? It's possible she'll hear you were spotted with another woman."

"That's her problem, not mine. I was clear that I have no feelings for her."

"I know that, you know that, but women aren't rational. Hell, I saw how *that* one went off. She didn't like finding out that you bed hop."

He hated the pain Gerri had suffered over finding out about the lawyer he sometimes spent time with. Everything had changed. "You deal with Sherry from now on. I'll call you for updates and whatever else I may need you to ask her."

Micah twisted in his seat. "What?"

"You heard me. You're the in-between person for Sherry and I. You'll travel with her the next time she's sent somewhere for our clan."

"That's crazy. You're going to avoid Sherry just because it made your little G.L. upset?"

"I told you to call her Gerri. She has the right to be hurt." He stroked her hair. "I won't be able to look at Sherry or hear her voice without remembering today. I can't stand to see my G.L. in pain."

"Are you going to give up all women in the future?" Micah softly snorted. "Come on. You're being unreasonable. You just said you can't mate that little gal. We're not designed to go without sex for too long."

"G.L. thought Sherry was more important to me than she is. I don't ever want to give her that impression again. I'll promise her it's over between Sherry and I forever. And I always keep my word."

"You have it bad."

He knew it, and wouldn't even make denials.

"So what does G.L. stand for? I'm curious. Gerri is a strange name for a woman. I take it her last name starts with an L?"

"No. It's a nickname I gave her when we were kids. Golden locks."

Micah chuckled. "I see. Long blonde hair. It's cute. So is she. So, you're serious about G.L.?"

"I'm the only one allowed to call her that. Quit pushing. She hates her real name, Geraldine. She shorted it to Gerri. You can use that when you address her."

"Barbados," Micah finally muttered.

"What about it?"

"That should be far enough for you to go that your family won't find you when you sink your fangs into that little gal to make her yours. We both know it's only a matter of time with the way you're looking at her. A smart man would have left her behind when we took off, but you already can't let go. You might want to spend the rest of the flight wondering how you'll take to island life."

"I have too many responsibilities to my parents and the clan."

"Your priorities have changed. You just haven't realized it yet—but you will."

Chapter Five

Gerri woke when the engine noise died. She stared up at Wen. He smiled.

"Did you sleep well?"

"I take it we're not in Nevada anymore?"

"Washington," Micah answered from the front. He opened the door. "I'm going to secure my baby. It's getting windy."

Wen helped Gerri sit up and she stared out the windows. It seemed to be another private airport and they were parked near a few other small aircraft. "Looks like we're in the burbs."

"Burbs?"

"It's what I call the middle of nowhere."

"Micah picked this place for a reason. The security here is shit. That's good for us. We have to pick up the rental car I ordered and drive a few hours to reach where we need to be tonight."

"Fun."

He lifted her and climbed over the seat, opened the door, then helped her out. She didn't protest as he gripped her hips and gently deposited her on her feet. The wind whipped at her hair and she shivered, chilled by it after being so comfortable on Wen's lap.

"You'd think it would be warmer since it's summer."

"I blame the humans," Micah called out, hooking straps that were clipped to the ground to the wings of the plan. "Global warming from all their pollution. These freaky summer storms happen more and more."

Wen rolled his eyes and then winked at Gerri. "But he won't come live in Alaska. I've asked."

"No fucking way. You make me land my plane and take off on an old road when I fly up there. I like actual airports. I'm no bush pilot."

Gerri listened to them chat as she stretched her legs and watched another small plane land. It slowed as it came down the strip and then the pilot drove in their direction. "Company," she warned.

"It doesn't matter." Wen shrugged. "We weren't followed. Nobody knew I was coming."

"Do you want me to get the car while you handle business here? Make sure they refuel my baby?" Micah stared at Wen.

He nodded. "Take her with you."

Micah opened the side compartment and got their bags out. He tossed her backpack at Wen, then another one. The last thing in the storage compartment was a duffle bag with a strap that Micah shoved over his shoulder. He locked the panel down and then winked at Gerri. "Come on, G.L. Let's go pick up the rental."

"Her name is Gerri," Wen ground out.

"Sorry." Micah smiled though, not looking sincere at all.

Gerri paused. "What are you going to do?" She stared up at Wen.

"He's going to make use of his eyes with the airport employees so we're not technically here and I don't get charged for using their airport." Micah stepped closer and lowered his voice. "He wanted no trace of where we've traveled this time."

Wen scowled. "Shut it."

She thought about it. "You don't want anyone to know you were in Reno?"

He sighed. "No."

"I take it your clan doesn't know you asked me to help you out?"

Wen shook his head. "As far as they know, you dropped off their radar when your mother took you away. I'm keeping it that way."

"Would Trayis be mad?"

"I don't think so."

"Your parents," she guessed.

He lifted their backpacks and strode away. "I'll meet you soon."

Gerri watched him go and clenched her teeth.

"Hey."

She turned her head, looking at Micah.

"Don't bust his balls too hard. He's had it rough for the past thirteen years since Gerbin was killed. Did he tell you how it happened?"

"If you haven't noticed, he's not the most talkative person."

Micah snorted. "True. Come on. We've got a car to get, and I'll fill in the details since he won't."

He took off toward the large building and she hurried to keep up with him. "I'm listening."

"Did you ever meet Gerbin?"

"Of course, but he wasn't around much. He preferred hanging with the adults when he was home. It hurt Wen's feelings but he used to pretend it didn't."

"Gerbin was hard-core, you know? Serious. He visited our pack a lot since Trayis's mother and brother are pack."

"I didn't know that."

"Half-brothers, actually. Trayis and Arlis shared a Lycan mother. She was my mom's best friend. We're based in Colorado, with five other packs in the area. Three are friendly but two weren't. One of them wanted our territory and they attacked us."

"I'm sorry."

"Arlis became our alpha after that attack. He lost his parents and stepped up. Our pack managed to fight them off but we suffered heavy casualties. Trayis was furious that his mother was killed, and he wasn't about to lose his brother too. Gerbin became our guardian angel. Some Lycan packs make alliances with GarLycans, to gain a guardian to protect them from enemies, but they expect something in return."

"Like what?"

"Access to our women, if any of the GarLycans are seeking mates. Trayis didn't want that for us. A lot of our pack are related to his clan. The Lycans who founded our pack came from Alaska. He gave us Gerbin as a guardian without any strings."

"I know the history. The first-generation VampLycan grew up and the Lycans who raised them decided to leave."

"Having that many alpha types fuck up a pack structure, and there was a lot of fear after what happened with the Vampires."

"They thought there'd be a repeat? That the VampLycans might tear into Lycan minds and force them into breeding like the Vamps did?"

95

He shrugged, leading her to the front of the building and opening the door, waving her inside. "Maybe. The elders won't admit that though, if that was the case. It's my take on it. Anyway, after the attack on our pack, Gerbin was assigned to us almost full time while we recovered. He tracked the survivors of the pack that was responsible. Sometimes they fled into cities trying to hide."

"Into Vampire territory," she guessed.

"Yes. Gerbin didn't mind. Wen and his parents see him as a saint, but the truth is, he was kind of bloodthirsty. Don't say I said that. It would upset my cousin. Gerbin liked the killing and went after nests for the fun of it when he got bored. It ended up getting him killed. Wen tries to be as big a hero as he thinks his brother was. His parents expect it of him. I've watched the pressure he's under change him. So give him a break, because he sure as hell won't take it easy on himself. His life was taken away when his brother died. He stepped into Gerbin's shoes. It fucking sucks."

She let all that information sink in. "I love him."

"I realize. He loves you too. I know the stuff you learned about Sherry upset you, but he doesn't care about her the way he does you." He stopped by the customer service counter, lowering his voice. "I've flirted with Sherry many times. Wen didn't give a shit. He snarls at me for even using your nickname. He'd beat me nearly to death if I even joked about kissing you."

A man walked out of the back room and Micah smiled. "Hey. My girlfriend and I had a rental dropped off here for pickup." He withdrew his wallet. "I'm Fred Tobis. I got an SUV. Have they delivered it yet?"

"I need to use the restroom, Fred." She wondered why he was using a fake name but she went along with it.

"Hurry back, sweets." Micah winked. "I'll miss you." He turned to the guy. "We're going to visit her family so I can ask her dad for her hand in marriage."

She smiled and blew him a kiss. "I'll hurry."

She fled to the ladies' room and used the toilet. Everything Micah said kept circling in her mind as she washed her hands afterward and finger combed some of the worst tangles out of her hair. But it was what he *hadn't* said that bothered her.

Wen would never go against his parents' wishes. He'd never mate her. His entire life had become about being a replacement for Gerbin.

She left the bathroom to find Micah waiting outside the door. "That was fast."

He smiled and turned. She followed him outside. The man who'd been behind the counter pulled up in a blue SUV. Micah signed the papers, took the keys, and opened the passenger door for her. He tossed his duffle in the back before taking the driver's seat. They pulled away.

"What about Wen?"

"We'll pick him up soon. We didn't want anyone seeing the three of us traveling together from the airport."

"Oh."

"He usually doesn't hide his travels, but now I know why this time is different." He pulled over to the side of the road a block away from the airport. "Have any ID? Give it to me and I'll hold it while you're with him. I want your cell too. You don't want any of the bastards you're going up against to learn your real identity."

She hesitated but then slipped her driver's license and ATM card out of her pocket. It was tougher to give up her phone. "Please don't lose them."

"I won't. I'll be staying in a hotel not far from where you're going as backup. My brother is meeting me there. Wen said he had this, but we'd rather be safe than sorry."

"Graves?"

He arched his eyebrows. "You've met my brother?"

"No but Wen has had him keeping tabs on me. He admitted as much."

He nodded. "Graves does a few jobs for Wen that I don't ask about, just like he doesn't usually ask me where I fly our cousin."

"Thanks for sticking around in case we need help."

"Family should always have your back. How good are you at remember numbers?"

"Why?"

"I want you to memorize my cell phone number. You get into trouble, call. We'll come."

"Tell it to me."

He repeated it about six times before she nodded.

Movement caught her attention and she turned in her seat. Wen yanked open the back passenger door and tossed in their backpacks. He got in and shut the door. "Let's go."

* * * * *

Wen glared in the rearview mirror at his cousin, who avoided meeting his gaze. He didn't like the way Micah kept talking to Gerri and smiling. He wasn't being as flirtatious as normal but it pissed him off all the same. Every time Gerri laughed at something his cousin said, he clenched his fists tighter.

"Are we almost there?" He tried to keep his tone light.

"Soon." Micah finally looked at him and grinned. "So, Gerri, what is your favorite color?"

"Blue," Wen stated.

"Red," she blurted at the same time. She turned in her seat. "I'm not fifteen anymore, Wen. Blue used to be my favorite color." She faced forward. "I took a painting class a few years ago for fun and my teacher said there are two hundred and eighty-five shades of red. Isn't that cool? I like the darker hues."

"I'll remember that."

Wen growled. "So will I."

Micah met his gaze in the rearview mirror and Wen gave him a killing look. His cousin cleared his throat and became silent. Time passed without anyone speaking until they reached a crowded part of Seattle.

"I'll drop you off here," Micah announced, pulling over to a curb. "There's a diner down the street and you're only a few miles from your target."

Wen shoved open the door, hooked both backpacks, and got out. Gerri did too. She waved at his cousin. He caught her hand and tugged. "Come on."

"What crawled up your ass?"

He stared down at her. "Excuse me?"

"You're in a really bad mood. I'm the bait, so if anyone has the right to act that way, it should be me."

"Why will he remember what your favorite color is?"

She frowned. "Are you jealous?"

"No." He hesitated. "Did he hit on you while you were getting the rental?"

"Of course not. He's your cousin. Give me a break."

"He's a player. I can't keep track of his girlfriends. He never stays with one woman for long."

She arched her eyebrows.

"I just don't want you to get hurt later."

Her lips pressed together.

"What?"

"You're not going to be around, so what do you care? You've made it clear you're only going to be part of my life for a short time. You'll be back in Alaska, or with Sherry—if I even survive this."

He tightened his hold on her and jerked her closer. "It's over with her. I will never touch her again. I swear on the life of my parents. She means nothing."

She lowered her gaze to his chest. "Put your sunglasses on. Your eyes just went all evil version of Lycan."

He let her go, uttered a curse, and pulled them out of his pocket to cover them. "Better?"

She lifted her chin, regarding him with a sad expression. "I'm not going to fight with you. We've done that enough. I'm getting tired of it, aren't you? There's no reason for you to be mad. Your cousin was just being nice to me, nothing more, and I swear I'll never sleep with him, okay? I'm so not interested. Spare me the promise about Sherry too. You can't ever mate me and you're not going to be a monk. She's in the same boat I am."

"What does that mean?"

"We're just filler in your life until you have to settle down with a VampLycan. Now...I'm starving. We missed lunch and it's dinnertime. Plus, the Vamps will come out soon. We'll be hunting them or they'll come after us. Either way, I don't want to deal with that confrontation on an empty stomach."

"Don't ever say that you mean so little to me again."

"Fine."

"You're in a shit mood."

"So are you."

She was right. "I'm sorry." He tried to calm. "I'm just worried."

"Me too. I don't like being bait."

"You're not bait. You're leverage."

"So you keep saying. What's the difference again?" She headed toward the diner.

He followed. "They'll see you as valuable because Horton needs me. That means they won't risk hurting you."

"You're assuming he's somewhat sane and rational."

They entered the diner and took a quiet seat in a corner, far from the windows. He put his back to the wall so he could watch the other customers and see the door. The bags were shoved to the floor by their feet. Gerri sat across from him. The waitress brought them drinks, took their orders, and all the while, Wen mused over the choices he'd made.

"Why are you being so quiet?"

He pulled himself from his thoughts. "Just going over possible scenarios," he lied.

"Like what?"

"I'm gearing up for what's to come."

"Fine. You do that. I'll just sit here."

He knew she was irritated but he ignored her, letting his gaze dart around the room, watching for threats. It was a dangerous mission. He never should have brought Gerri in on it, and part of him blamed Lavos. He really liked the lead enforcer of Lorn's clan, but the guy had mated a human. Wen had felt envy. All he thought about was Gerri, how much he missed her, and that ache had become so strong he'd just wanted to see her again. That's why he'd volunteered to go after Horton. He knew it would send him out into the human world and he'd seen a chance to spend time with her.

102

It was selfish. Seeing the hurt she'd felt over his sex life had made him realize just how difficult saying goodbye to her would be for them both. Regret came next. She'd admitted that it had taken her a lot of time to get over him. He should have left her alone. He hadn't been thinking about what was best for her.

He shot furtive glances at her as she played with the wrapper from her straw. The phone in his pocket had him itching to call Micah to come pick her up. She'd be safer with his cousin. He could come up with another plan that didn't involve her. She looked up and caught him watching her.

"What?"

"Nothing."

"Bullshit. You should see the expression on your face right now. If you grind your teeth any tighter, I think your might break something. What's wrong?" She tensed and lowered her voice to a whisper. "Did someone come in who's a threat?"

He scanned the room again and inhaled. "No. Only humans are eating with us."

The waitress brought their burgers and fries. Gerri waited until she'd left before speaking again.

"Let me guess. Are you rethinking taking me on this mission with you?"

"How did you know?"

She smiled. "We grew up together. You got that same look when you came up with that plan to build us a tree house and then realized what would happen if I ever fell out of it. It scared you, watching me climb up and down to our hideaway, and you always kept close so you could grab me." She licked her lips. "Yeah. Same expression now as then."

"Maybe it's best if I have Micah come back for you."

"I lost my job." Her eyes narrowed. "I flew in a plane to get here." She picked up her burger, glanced at it, then stared at him. "As stupid as it is for me to say this, there's no going back."

"That's not true."

She leaned in closer, lowering her voice. "I smell like you. It's put a target on my back, and you promised to stay with me until I don't. Suck it up, buttercup. Believe me, if I wasn't all in on your crazy plan, I'd have ditched you as soon as that plane landed."

"Why?"

"You know why." She bit into her burger, dropping her gaze.

Sherry. She wasn't going to let that go. *Damn.* He had a lot of regrets already, and now he could add to them. He wished he'd never slept with the lawyer. He knew how deeply that jealousy could burn—he'd felt it every time Graves had told him G.L. was dating some man. She hadn't lived with any of them, so he'd been able to tell himself she couldn't be in a serious relationship. Sometimes he even liked to pretend she hadn't allowed any of them to take her to bed. He knew better now though, after sleeping with her. She hadn't been a virgin.

"Stop thinking what you are, Wen."

"You don't know what is on my mind."

104

She snorted and took a sip of her drink. "I'm in this. I've had time to think more since you told me your crazy plan. You've got to get close to this zombie maker, and showing up with me is about the only thing that's going to convince him you're not there to wipe him off the Earth. Let's face it, it's so insane that it just might work. I mean, your backup is a human. They're never going to suspect the VampLycans put you up to this."

"I know. I'm still worried about you though."

"I don't want you tortured and killed, Wen. You go in alone without me and that's probably what will happen. I'm leverage for them to use against you, remember? It's a good plan. We're doing this together. I have your back."

He stared at her, knowing if he got her killed, he'd never forgive himself.

Chapter Six

Gerri softly grumbled, shoving her hands inside her pockets. "This is miserable weather. It hasn't rained but it feels damp all the same. I'm actually cold."

"It's supposed to be sixty-two degrees. That's mild. We're also near the ocean. I can smell the salt in the air." Wen wrapped an arm around her waist in an attempt to warm her. "You've lost some of your tolerance for the chilly temperatures."

"I never liked the cold. I froze my ass off but I had warmer coats and owned thick gloves in Alaska. You say sixty-two like it's normal for summer or something. Brrrr! I'll take eighty degrees any day over this."

He smiled but it looked forced. "It won't be too long."

Her guts twisted. That was code that they were being followed or he'd picked up a scent. She wanted to ask which, but didn't dare voice it because sound carried. It would alert whoever he must have sensed or smelled that they were aware of them. "Really?"

"Yes." He glanced to his left, then right. "We'll take shelter soon."

In other words, they'd probably be attacked and he'd have to fight while she tried to stay out of the way. She gripped the small container of mace that she'd packed. It was laced with battery acid, something she'd added after being attacked by that rogue Vamp. It wouldn't kill a Vamp or a Lycan but it would sure blind them for longer than a few minutes, and hurt like hell while they healed. That might give them the time for Wen to share the story he'd made up. If they were really lucky, someone would believe it.

"Awesome," she muttered. "I can't wait to get you alone, stud."

He squeezed her waist as if to assure her…or maybe give her a heads up that they were about to have company.

All doubt left when he quickly let her go and snarled, moving in front of her in a protective crouch as two men dropped from a nearby roof to land in the empty alleyway in front of them.

She withdrew her mace but kept it fisted in her hand to hide it. Forewarning was asking for trouble. Surprise was all she had since she was no match for their strength and speed, whatever they were.

It took seconds for her to identify each man's species. It was weird seeing a Lycan and a Vampire working together. They usually gave each other a wide berth.

"What do you want?"

She couldn't see Wen's face with his back to her but there was no missing his snarled tone, or the fact that his hands on the pavement now sported some wicked-looking claws.

She forced her attention off him and glanced behind her, spotting two really pale faces near a Dumpster. *Vampires.* They wore all black and had that floating-head appearance going on that she found creepy as they remained in the deep shadows of the night. She turned all the way around to face them head on, keeping her back to Wen.

"Two more," she whispered. "White heads." He'd get the term, since he'd taught it to her as a kid.

"I'm aware."

Wen really sounded scary when he partially shifted, and she was glad he was on her side. VampLycans could fight. A Lycan and three Vamps wouldn't stand a chance against him. She hoped they knew that too.

"You drop on her and I'll dust your ass," Wen warned.

She jerked her chin up. The Vampire on the balcony above her froze. The damn thing looked ready to pounce, and she hadn't even spotted him. She swallowed hard and inched back closer to Wen.

"He's really protective of me and means every word." She reached down, dug her fingers inside her pocket and wiggled out the metal compact she kept in there. She tossed it up at him. "Catch. That's what's left of the last Vamp who tried to bite me."

The white head caught the container and opened it. She watched his expression and heard the low hiss of rage. He closed it and glared at her with malevolence in his eyes.

"Yeah. Those are Vamp ashes," she taunted. "They belong to the last moron who thought I looked like dinner. My mate has zero tolerance for someone else trying to take my blood. I wouldn't piss him off."

"Gerri," Wen hissed. "I've got this."

She winced. She probably should have told him about the souvenir she'd kept, but it made an effective point. That Vampire who'd attacked her in her old apartment had deserved what she'd done to him, but it had been hell cleaning up the mess he'd left behind. There had been a lot of vacuuming involved. UV lamps weren't easy to come by either. She'd kept some of his ashes, wanted a reminder in case she ever grew lax with her security again. She'd been that pissed.

The Vamp pocketed her compact. She hadn't really expected to get it back.

"What are you doing here, half-breed?" The animalistic tone of the stranger assured her it was the Lycan speaking. "You're far from home and not welcome."

"I don't give a shit if you like my presence or not," Wen snarled back, louder, winning the scary-voice pissing contest. "Move out of my way."

The silence grew eerie. Gerri was tempted to look back to see how dog face reacted to being told to move, but she didn't dare take her attention off the three white heads. They could move fast and take her to the ground in the blink of an eye if she glanced away.

"Why are you here?" The creepy voice with a slight hiss to it had to be the Vampire. "Who are you looking for?"

Wen's tone changed slightly, a little less threatening. "I'm here because I want to be. We don't want any trouble but I'll kill you if you attack us. We're just passing through, if you're pissed we're in your territory."

"Why are you traveling with a *human*?" Dog face spat the words.

"She's mine," Wen growled. "You got a problem with that?"

"Stop," the Vampire ordered. "Let me handle this. What do you mean, you're just passing through?"

"Do you want me to speak slower for you?" Wen snarled. "We've been traveling for a while. Let us pass and leave us alone."

"Are you mated to the human or are you addicted to human blood?"

"She's *mine*," Wen repeated. "Every part of her. I chose her over my clan since they refused to accept her."

"She's human," the Lycan said, continuing to state the obvious. "Why would you choose her?"

"Instincts won't be denied." Wen bumped against Gerri's backpack as he straightened to his full height to let her know he was right there.

"He's mostly Werewolf." The Lycan sounded disgusted. "It's one of our flaws. We fall for someone we're screwing and have to claim her. He must have been really desperate to fuck something, if she was his choice. Any decent Werewolf wouldn't touch a weak, spineless bitch."

"Don't call her that," Wen threatened.

"I'm not a bitch," Gerri muttered. "But I can act like one if you insult me again."

"You told her about us," the Vampire hissed. "You know the rules. You broke them."

"She worked for my clan. Decker forbid me from touching her but I was her guard. He sent a few bastards to kill her so we left—after I dumped their bodies on his porch."

"Why would he allow a human there at all?" The Vampire sounded suspicious.

"It's none of your business. Get out of our way," Wen snarled.

"You want passage through my city." The Vamp paused. "I demand answers."

"You're in no position to ask me shit. I'll kill you all if you try to stop us."

"Baby," Gerri crooned, purposely trying to sound needy. "I'm cold and hungry. Just answer them so we can find a cheap motel or something."

"Fine," Wen huffed. "Decker has used a few of them with mind control to spy on the towns around our territory. They give us a heads up if there's any hint that the other humans are catching on to what we are. Now will you leave us the hell alone?"

Gerri kept silent but was impressed with how easily Wen could lie. It sounded plausible. A VampLycan like Decker would never trust a human to work for him, but they might guess that. That clan leader had been the most feared and loathed of the four clans. Even Gerri had heard horror stories about him. Some of the meaner kids had threatened to send letters asking Decker to kill her in her sleep. Humans had Santa to send their wishes to. VampLycan bullies had Decker. He had become the boogie man of her childhood. She shivered just thinking about him.

Wen reached back and gripped her hip. It wasn't easy to do since their backpacks kept them apart by a few feet. She took a deep breath and forced her mind away from the past. The future looked grim enough, as she made sure the Vamps hadn't advanced while she'd been distracted. They remained in their same positions, almost resembling horrific statues.

"We could give you shelter and food for your human." The Vampire paused. "For a price, of course."

"Forget it." Wen pressed against her again. "You'd sell our location to my clan. No thanks. Let us pass or I'll fight you to the death."

"We're not associated with your clans."

"You'd be motivated by the price on our heads." Wen deepened his voice. "Move or die. We're out of here."

"They are hunting you?"

"As if you don't know that. Were you looking for us?" Wen snarled. "Did you already alert them? Are they on their way to kill us?"

"How long have you been on the run?"

"A while." Wen paused. "We're still alive despite their best efforts. Take my advice and forget the bounty. You aren't the first group of morons who've tried to collect. I'd tell you to ask them how that worked out, but I had to kill every last one of them. Decker won't pay it anyway. He'll send an assassin rather than money. He's a lowlife bastard who looks down on anyone not VampLycan. Move out of our way and allow us to pass."

The Vampire lifted his hands. "We have no alliances with the VampLycan clans. They are hunting me as well."

"Sorry, but I'm not buying it. You'd have to do something seriously shitty to get on their radar, and you're just a few Vampires hanging out with a Lycan. I admit that's weird, but nothing to bring them down from Alaska. Unless you knocked up a bitch to breed one of my kind?"

"I created a soldier and left it in a town near them." The Vamp smiled. "That got their attention."

"Soldier?" Wen didn't sound convinced. "What the hell does that mean?"

"It's our version of strong Vampires with expiration dates. They're mean, tough, but completely unstable unless they're fed blood by us."

The Vampire paused. "Notice how I'm here and not there? They go rabid. It's a beautiful thing to behold. A soldier will kill anything that moves or has a heartbeat they can hear."

Gerri hated the Vampire already. He sounded really proud of leaving a hyped-out zombie to murder innocent people. But it didn't surprise her. Humans were cattle to most Vamps. There were supposedly some who were different, but she'd never come across one. She'd done her best to avoid anything nonhuman though.

"Then that means we *really* want to get the hell away from you, if you're being hunted too." Wen shook his head. "I've kept us alive by being smart. I doubt you can outwit any of the enforcers they'll send after you for long. You'll lead them right to us. No thanks."

"Nest, back away and go," the Vampire ordered.

The Vamp on the balcony turned and jumped, disappearing onto the roof. The two by the Dumpster slipped away into the darkness. Gerri wasn't certain if that was a bad or good thing. Had they really left or were they going to hide out of sight and launch a sneak attack?

"VampLycan, we offer you shelter for tonight," the master continued. "At least accept that. We could help each other."

"I don't see how."

"You're a long way from home and we're in the same situation. VampLycans will send enforcers after me. We could join forces."

Gerri masked her features. They were falling for it, or at least seemed to be. But she wasn't trusting him at all. It could be a trap. She just hoped Wen's low opinion of their intelligence wouldn't get them killed.

"No." Wen lowered his voice. "I have no reason to trust you."

"We have common enemies."

"You could be my enemy as well." Wen hesitated. "Get out of the way or I'll kill you."

"Don't be so hasty. I'm a hundred and eighty-two years old. I have age and experience. This is my world, more so than yours. You VampLycans tend to stick to your own territory. Think about it. Your chances to avoid capture are better if you have help. We could work together."

"Capture, hell. They'll kill her, make me watch, and then I'll die next. I suppose you want me to believe you're offering to help out of the goodness of your heart?" Wen snorted. "Give me a break. That bounty on us must be huge. I didn't think Decker would care that much about the other guards I had to kill. They weren't important to him; no one is. But I must have been wrong."

"I have more money than I could ever spend. I'm not interested in a bounty. Call me Horton. What's your name?"

Wen didn't give it. "What do you want then, Vamp?"

Horton sighed. "So stubborn. Fine. I need information. I have to know the number of VampLycans in each clan. I want a detailed account of how they work and any weaknesses they may have. Who do they fear? Why? How can I get their enemies on my side so we can work together?" His voice rose. "I want to take those bastards out. Those sons of bitches killed my master and my nest. I'm going to make certain they pay for that."

Gerri fought to mask her features. Wen seemed to be right about the master wanting to wage a war with VampLycans. He held a major grudge.

114

"I don't believe you," Wen said. "You're lying. If what you've said is true, there's no way you would have escaped them if they'd killed your master and wiped out your nest."

"I wasn't there. I'd been sent to go get more feeders. I returned the next night to find them all ashed."

Feeders? Gerri shivered. He meant victims. The bastard was admitting that he'd kidnapped humans to feed to his nest.

"Why were you in Alaska?" Wen sounded angry. "You must have been if you left one those soldier things near their territory. Are you working for the VampLycans? Are you some kind of bounty hunter for them? I knew it! You're tracking us, aren't you?"

"No!" Horton hissed. "We were there for another reason."

"I still don't believe you." Wen's voice deepened into a snarl.

"They slaughtered our nest for no damn reason other than we were in Alaska. Fuck the VampLycans! They believe they have the right to kill anyone they want. I'm going to make them pay."

Wen was silent for long seconds. "They forbid me from claiming my mate. That's against our nature. Someone needs to take them down."

She knew those words must have been tough for Wen to get out. Memories flashed through her mind of the years she'd watched him train to fight, and the pride that showed in his eyes when he spoke of what it stood for, being a VampLycan. They were the defenders of the weak. They righted wrongs. Mostly it was Lycans they defended, but still, it was honorable.

115

He'd shared all the stories with her that he'd been told by his older brother. He'd adored and worshipped Gerbin. He'd been Wen's superhero for going out into the world and killing evil bastards who needed to be wiped off the face of the Earth. Now Wen was the one doing it.

She really hoped they wouldn't die too.

Wen seethed, but he hid it. The bastard Vampire was so close but he could pick up the heavy scent of Lycans. They were lurking between the buildings on both sides of them, probably ready to attack on command. He breathed through his nose, picking out the scents. The intel had been off. There was more than a dozen of them, closer to two.

It had been a mistake bringing Gerri with him. At this point, he just wanted to kill Horton. The rogue Lycans would probably scatter without the Vamp keeping them together. He might have been able to dust the ghoul maker and escape before the Lycans could attack, but not with her. She'd slow him down too much, even if he grabbed her and carried her over his shoulder. It would also be stupid. He wasn't there only to kill Horton. He needed to figure out who else was working with him, whether or not the council was ordering nests to target VampLycans, and if any Lycan packs were buying his bullshit.

He pushed his rage down. A depraved asshole like Horton had killed Gerbin and changed Wen's life forever. He regulated his breathing, cleared his mind, and thought things through.

"Fine. I'll give you information in exchange for you telling me some locations where only humans exist. That way I don't have to worry about anything coming after my mate or selling our location to your council, any packs, or to the VampLycans." He paused. "I need money too. I had to leave all mine behind when we ran. I'm sick of stopping random humans and making them hand over the cash in their wallets. None of them seem to carry much of that anymore. I can't risk making them go into banks with all the fucking cameras they have."

The master grinned, his expression smug. "I can give you that."

"You try anything, one of your people even looks at my mate, and I'll rip off your fucking head," Wen warned. "Am I clear? She may only be human, but she's *mine*." He snarled. "Got it, Horton?"

"You really should learn to trust, VampLycan."

"The name is Wen. And I'd never be that stupid. I like breathing."

"We now have an alliance. Follow us."

Wen snagged Gerri's hand and began to walk, keeping a good fifteen feet between them and the Vampire and his Lycan pal. She didn't try to grip him back. She was smart. He could release her in an instant and attack if the need arose. She even trailed him by a foot so he was in front, able to defend her if necessary.

It reminded him of a memory from the past. Trayis had gone to the clan child caretaker at the start of one summer with Gerri in tow. Everyone had seen the human child from afar but her parents had kept her close to home, away from the other kids until that day. Their clan leader had explained she had fragile bones, couldn't heal as fast as they could, and would never grow claws or fangs. He'd warned all the other kids to be gentle with her in their play, and that there was no honor in harming someone so much weaker. Trayis had also made it clear she was part of the clan and harsh punishment would come down on anyone who hurt her.

It hadn't stopped some from saying mean words to her. They pointed out she was smaller than she should be, compared to other kids her age. Some enjoyed making her gasp and smell of fear by unleashing their claws and jumping at her in mock attacks. Wen had felt sorry for her. Her hair had also fascinated him. She had so much of it. It was blonde, almost white, and ran in ringlets down her back. Her mother would always tie it in a ponytail but after a while it would come loose, spilling around her face.

Gerri had spent all her time indoors, reading books, rather than playing outside with the others. He had never understood her reasons until he'd finally asked her why. Some moments in life stuck in one's mind, and that was one of them. She'd peered up at him with her big blue eyes and tears had formed inside them.

"My dad says I'm easy prey, and I should stay inside where I'm safe. He doesn't want anything to happen to me. Trayis said I needed to be around other kids but they won't chase away anything that comes after me. I almost walked into baby moose last week. I couldn't hear or smell it. It was a good thing it was alone or I might have been attacked. I'm going to have to become a craftsman like my dad or stay inside all the time like my mom does when I grow up. I tried to lift my dad's chainsaw so he could teach me to make sculptures, but it was too heavy. One day, when I'm bigger, I'm going to do that every day until I'm so good I have a future."

Wen had pitied her. He'd started taking her outdoors and even taught her how to fight. She'd been really smart, had a sense of humor, and he'd enjoyed spending time with her. Their bond had grown until he couldn't imagine life without his G.L.

His grip on her hand tightened as he followed the insane Vampire into one of the buildings down the block. He wasn't going to allow anything to happen to her.

The Lycans followed. They were quiet but he could still pick up the sounds they made. It was going to be bad if they were being led into a trap.

Vampires were greedy and selfish. He had something Horton wanted though, and Gerri was the only leverage he could use against Wen. He'd thought it out well and tried to relax. He'd had to risk his life often in the past on these kinds of missions but this one was different. G.L.'s life was on the line too.

The interior of the building was nicer than the exterior. Someone had spent money having it repainted. Horton turned after they entered and smiled. "Welcome to our current home. It's guarded twenty-four-seven by Joel's pack."

The Lycan curled his lip, glaring at Wen. He got the message loud and clear. The alpha of the rogue pack wasn't happy about having them as guests and made no bones about it. Wen returned his attention to Horton.

"I need food and a bed for my mate."

"Of course." Horton turned, walking up the stairs. "This way."

119

Wen yanked Gerri around to his other side and put his body between her and Joel as they passed by the alpha and climbed the stairs. It was a five-story building, from what he'd counted from the outside. They stopped on the fourth floor and the Vampire threw open a door near the top of the stairs.

"Here you are. I'll have one of Joel's pack bring something for dinner. Expect food in twenty or so minutes. I want you downstairs while she eats. We have information to exchange."

"You think I'm going to leave her alone?" Wen shook his head. "It's never going to happen."

"I don't trust humans. The pack will keep an eye on her."

"I don't trust anyone here," Wen countered. "She remains at my side." He took off his backpack and tossed it on the floor.

Gerri did the same.

"We have common goals." Horton frowned. "We both want to hurt the VampLycans enough to keep them from ever coming after us. It would be stupid to harm her. You wouldn't tell me what I want to know if I did."

"It would be stupid to leave her alone in a building like this one." Wen sharply inhaled. "I've picked up the scents of at least four Vampires and over two dozen Lycans since we've met. Do you know what I *haven't* smelled? Any women from any race except for Gerri. I'm not leaving her alone to fall victim to some asshole who thinks she's an easy meal or something to fuck. You're a master. I shouldn't have to tell you the temptation she poses in this scenario. Why the hell don't you have any women here?"

Horton's mouth firmed into a tight, white-lipped line. Wen figured he wasn't going to answer, but then the Vamp surprised him by closing the door at his back, giving them privacy.

"They didn't last a week. Fucking animals," Horton whispered. "It wasn't mine who killed them. Joel's men were too rough with the two whores I bought them. I turned them, thinking they'd be able to survive this rabid bunch, but I didn't foresee how violent they'd be during sex."

Wen cringed inside, imagining the horror those poor women must have faced before their deaths. First, they'd been turned into Vamps, then thrown at a Lycan pack. He doubted they signed up for what they'd endured. "It's a learning curve, dealing with rogues."

"I wouldn't say that too loud," Horton whispered. "Joel takes offense. He's too irrational at times to completely control but I am stuck with them for now. They want my money, and I need them to guard us during the day."

Wen believed that. There was no other reason why rogues would hang with Vampires unless they got something out of the deal. It had to be either for money or they needed someone to do a little mind tuning on humans. "My mate stays at my side."

"Fine. We'll get you fed, and then both of you will come downstairs. I turned two apartments into an office. Try not to insult Joel." Horton rolled his eyes. "Fucking Werewolves. They can turn on you." He spun, quickly opened the door, and left.

Wen closed the door and locked it. It wasn't a solid door but the locks would at least give them a split-second warning in case of attack if someone tried to break it down. Gerri opened her mouth but he shook his head, easing around her to check out the apartment. It smelled of a human and was a bit dusty, as if it hadn't been lived in for weeks.

It turned out to be a one-bedroom apartment with a bathroom, kitchen, and small living area. There was no fire escape, so the windows were attack proof. Someone would have to climb to reach them, and the building wouldn't permit that without balconies. He checked for any obvious recording devices next but found none. Gerri stayed close to him as he searched, shadowing him from room to room.

Chapter Seven

Wen finally faced her. "Stay in character," he mouthed.

Gerri wondered if he heard someone in an apartment next to theirs or if he'd seen a bug she couldn't. "I'm worried, baby." She winked. "Are you sure they aren't going to turn us over to the VampLycans?"

"I don't think so." He raised his voice a little. "I know the clans would attack any Lycans or Vampires that were hanging out together. They'd be paranoid about that. I think we're good. Relax, mate."

"I'm just so tired of always running." She batted her eyelashes at him. "Thank goodness you're so big and strong."

He smiled, amused. "There, there, baby. Don't cry. You know I can't stand it when you do. You're being so brave for a human."

She lifted her hand and flipped him off, then spun away. There was no way she was going to pretend to sob if someone were listening to them. It sank in that they were four floors up in a building with Vamps and Lycans. She'd caught it when Wen had stated he smelled at least two dozen rogues. That was more than they'd expected. At any second, they could attack. Wen would be greatly outnumbered.

He grabbed her around her waist, turning her in his arms, and pressed her against the wall. It stunned her enough to gasp as he lifted her right off her feet.

His lips came down over hers and his tongue swept into her mouth. He also pressed his body against her and wiggled his hips until she spread her thighs, wrapping them around his waist. She moaned as he rubbed the length of his stiff cock along her pussy.

She clutched at him, turned on. He smelled so good and felt so right. It was insane to fool around while they were in a nest of crazy Vamps and rogue Lycans, but she didn't shove him away. He finally ended the kiss and stared into her eyes. His were glowing. She didn't fear him messing with her mind. He was just turned on too.

"Better?" He whispered the words. "You were scenting of fear."

"So you decided to make me hot and wet?"

He grinned. "Yes." His nostrils flared. "Mmmm."

"Doggy sex treat," she muttered.

"*My* doggy sex treat though. You being aroused will mask some of your emotions for a little while and maybe put these assholes off their game, if they're watching you more so than me."

"We just established they have no women here. Are you sure this is the best thing to do? Tag, I don't want to be it."

"Horton wants info too much," he murmured, letting her down. "He's motivated to keep them in line." He released her and checked out the apartment again.

She watched him, staying against the wall. Her legs felt a little shaky. It would have annoyed her, except she'd seen the front of his pants. She wasn't the only one his little make-out session had affected. He sported a huge bulge. She tore her gaze from him, looking for anything that could be used as weapons if they were ever attacked in the apartment. There wasn't much. Whoever had lived there before hadn't owned many things.

124

Wen came back to her, looking grim. She arched an eyebrow. He snagged her hand and led her to the corner, where a couch sat, and pointed. She spotted a dark stain. It looked like dried blood. She looked at him.

"Human," he mouthed.

It meant the nest and rogues had probably taken the building by force instead of buying it. Horton had admitted to using feeders. She had a bad feeling that the last resident had become food. Her gaze went around the room once more; she was pretty certain a man had lived there. The apartment didn't have a homey feel to it, instead feeling a little cold. That was probably a good thing, since Vampy women hadn't fared well with the rogues.

"Shit," she mouthed back.

Wen grimly nodded.

A knock sounded on the door and Wen let her go, pointing to the kitchen. She moved fast, putting the small island between her and the living room. Her gaze landed on a pan left on the stove. It looked clean but heavy. It would work if she needed to hit someone. Wen motioned for her to stay back before he opened the door.

A Lycan stood there holding a large bag. Even Gerri could pick up the scent of food from across the room. Wen took the bag. The Lycan turned, not saying a word, and stomped off. He hadn't looked happy, tasked with getting them something to eat. Wen closed and locked the door before approaching her.

"Think it's safe?"

He shrugged, placing the bag on the counter. "Horton wants us alive."

"But drugged would be better, I'm sure. It would make us more manageable."

The bag sat there untouched. Gerri was glad they'd eaten at the diner. Wen snatched it up again, strode to the fridge and stuffed the bag inside. They'd have to eventually find a way to eat that didn't involve the enemy bringing them possibly drugged or poisoned food. Wen stared at her, his expression clear to read.

"Get that look off your face."

"What look?"

"It's the tree house, all over again. I'm in this, Wen."

"I worry," he admitted.

"Me too."

"It won't be long. Just stay next to me, be prepared for anything."

She nodded, then closed the distance between them. He looked surprised when she snuggled into his chest, wrapping her arms around him. A second later he held her tight.

"It's going to be okay." She had to have faith.

He lowered his chin to rest on the top of her head. "Two days," he whispered. "At most. Then we'll be out of here."

She filled in what he didn't say aloud. He must think that would give him enough time to learn everything the clan wanted to know. She just hoped he was right. The Lycan alpha made her nervous. He outright hated her, had made that obvious, and he had a crazy look in his eyes. It meant his entire pack would be as unstable. Otherwise they wouldn't follow him.

Time crawled by until Wen loosened his hold on her. "We need to go downstairs."

She nodded, releasing him. Wen met her gaze. "You stay close to me, got it?"

"Like a flea on a dog."

A quick grin flashed across his face and he shook his head. "Brat." He sobered and walked around her.

She followed close, waited for him to open the door, and then shadowed him. No one was waiting for them and they didn't run into any of the Lycans until they reached the bottom floor. Joel and two of his pack stood by the front door, blocking it as if they planned to escape. The alpha pointed to a door.

"In there."

Wen reached back, gripped Gerri's arm, and tugged her to his side as they passed them. She knew he did it to keep her protected, putting his body between her and the rogues. He knocked, the Vampire yelled at them to enter, and Wen shoved open the door. He pushed Gerri in first.

The apartment had been mostly gutted of furniture and the living room had been turned into an office. Horton sat behind a desk. He yanked a cell phone from his ear and placed it down in front of him. His gaze locked on Wen. "Have a seat."

Gerri glanced around but there weren't any chairs.

Wen growled low. "I don't think I belong on the floor. Nor does my mate."

Motion had Gerri spinning, watching as a Vampire carried in two dining room chairs from the hallway. Wen adjusted her, forcing her to step closer to the front of his body. The Vamp put the chairs down near the desk then fled.

Horton waved them to sit as the door closed behind them. Wen released her and jerked his head. She took the seat farthest from the desk. He moved the other chair closer to her, then sat. He scowled at Horton.

"I see you as an equal, VampLycan. Put your fangs away. We're friends."

"I wouldn't go that far. What do you want to know in exchange for telling me human-only areas? I'm far from territory I'm familiar with. We traveled through Canada but my mate had a hard time living in the wilderness. The cities were filled with Lycans and Vamps. Then we crossed into the United States yesterday."

"We'll get to that. What clan did you belong to?"

"Decker's. I already told you that."

"Yes, Decker. You didn't like him?"

"I hate the bastard. He'll kill us all if given the chance."

"Why were you a part of his clan then?"

Wen hesitated.

"Just tell him the truth, baby," Gerri urged. "We aren't given a choice."

Horton fixed his gaze on her. "You aren't, perhaps, but he's a VampLycan."

"Be quiet, mate." Wen reached over and put his hand on her leg. "I was born into Decker's clan. That's how it's decided. Decker kills anyone who tries to leave his clan. Not to mention the other clans don't like Decker, so they would be uneasy accepting one of his members. They don't trust us because of him. He really would send an assassin after you instead of payment if you contact him about the bounty on our heads. He's greedy and dishonest. He uses anyone he can to get his way, and then murders them when their use is up."

Gerri remained silent. Most of what Wen had said was the truth, except where he'd been born.

"What about her? I can't see Decker trusting a human."

"She had a family he threatened to kill if she defied him. He murdered them long ago, but she didn't know that. Once she realized, he fucked with her head to keep her spying for him."

"How did she become your mate?"

"I was one of her guards. He never sent her into human towns without one of us keeping an eye on her. We also made sure she stayed in the cabin he'd put her in. He figured she'd try to escape. He fucked with her head so much, she was becoming an empty shell from the mind control. It was just a matter of time before he killed her and found a replacement. But I fell in love with her, so when the order came down, I fled with my mate. We've been on the run ever since. Now tell me where Vamps and Lycans prefer not to live so I can take her there."

Horton remained silent. "How many VampLycans are there in Decker's clan?"

"Six hundred and thirty-two," Wen answered.

Gerri remembered her lessons from Wen as a child and focused on her heart rate, keeping it steady. He was lying and she didn't want to give him away. He had added to the number.

"The other clans?"

"Around the same amount. They don't exactly give us information easily about their clans. Decker wants to rule all the clans, not just ours."

"Who do VampLycans fear?"

Wen studied the Vamp, also aware of Gerri at his side. He kept his hand on her thigh in case she gave him away when he lied. He figured he could do something sexual, like inch his hand up to her pussy, to account for her spiked heart rate if the need arose, but she didn't let him down.

"Who do VampLycans fear?" Horton glared at him. "Tell me."

This jerk had probably met Decker, since he'd sent his nest to Alaska. It wouldn't hurt to tell the truth. "The GarLycan clan."

"Why?"

"The bastards can fly, shell their bodies to near rock, and are ice cold with their emotions."

"But we've been told VampLycans have a tight alliance with them."

"Used to. Past tense. We don't have any women they're interested in anymore. They don't trust anything Vampire blood. None of them want to breed with a VampLycan."

Horton expressed his displeasure with that information by hissing. "Why do they hate Vampires?"

"No fucking clue. They just do. Once the pure-blooded Lycans all left our territories, things grew tense. Decker was always trying to become friendly with Lord Aveoth but he wasn't having any of it."

"So GarLycans won't come to the defense of VampLycans?"

"I wouldn't say that."

"Why?"

"Our territories are close to each other. They don't want Vamps anywhere near them."

"You must know why they hate us. Tell me the truth."

"I don't know." Wen sighed, getting irritated. "Ever met a GarLycan?"

"Of course not."

"Lucky you. They're cold bastards. You think you Vamps corner the market on being heartless?" Wen snorted. "They make your kind seem downright cuddly and chatty. They keep to themselves and don't share information with us. At least not with Decker. I don't know how they interact with the other clans."

"So the clans aren't close at all?" Glee showed in Horton's eyes. "That's good news."

Wen forced a smile. That used to be true, but not anymore, not since Lorn had taken over Decker's clan. Now they worked together. "I don't see how that's helpful to you. You said they took out your nest. Which clan attacked you?"

"Decker's. That bastard lied to us."

Wen flew from his chair fast, pretending to be outraged. "You know him? This *was* a trap. I knew it!"

"Sit. He sent us to Alaska with false information. He said he still controlled his clan but they came after my nest anyway."

Wen growled, his fangs and claws growing. "Talk, Vamp. What in the hell are you saying? You have an alliance with Decker?"

"We believed we did. He went to our council, promising to help them take out their enemies. He even promised my master a VampLycan to use however he wanted. He swore no one would retaliate when he sent us to Alaska. That was a lie." Horton motioned for Wen to sit.

Wen hesitated, then righted the chair, planting his ass on it hard. "Decker always lies."

"I contacted the council about the loss of my master." Anger had Horton hissing. "They didn't care. Decker is in their good graces right now, and they are protecting him in Chicago. He wiped out a few nests that refused to take their orders. It's blasphemy for those conceited assholes to choose the VampLycan over their own kind. My master was loyal to the council."

That was one piece of the puzzle. Now he knew why the council would work with Decker. "So Decker is with your council?"

"Yes."

"Why?"

"Don't you know?" Horton stared at him with narrowed eyes.

"I fled with my mate a few months ago. I haven't been in contact with anyone from my clan. I knew I couldn't trust them."

"I wasn't given all the details. I'd hoped *you* could tell *me*." Horton calmed, seeming to think as he tapped his fingers on the top of the desk. "I was just on the phone with another master who hates the council. He's heard a rumor that Decker's clan had sent him packing, and that's why he's turned to the council."

"The clan turned against Decker?" Wen tried to appear stunned. "Wow. I had no idea."

"They are still hunting for you, VampLycan. My source confirmed it. You still need me. Word has spread to be on the lookout for you and the human spy. The bounty is huge, and your clan has contacted every pack and nest with your photos."

The Vamp could lie well enough to impress Wen. He couldn't detect any change of scent or heart rate coming from him. There was no bounty out on them. "I'm sure they want us dead. I killed other VampLycans to save my mate."

Horton leaned back in his chair, folding his hands together over his chest. "I need to think. Perhaps I've gone about this all wrong."

"You're considering collecting the bounty?"

"No. Not that. I blamed all the VampLycans for the death of my master. Perhaps it's just Decker I need to focus on." He suddenly leaned forward, staring intently at Wen. "You know him well, don't you?"

"Yes. I grew up in his clan. That's why I'm telling you to never trust him. He'll fuck you over every time."

Anger flashed in the Vamp's eyes. "And the council is protecting him."

133

Wen watched the Vamp close, taking in every twitch of his facial expressions. He could guess what Horton was thinking. He'd claimed he wanted to start a war with VampLycans, but he really just wanted revenge on Decker. He was more than happy to help him come to that conclusion.

"Decker will use your council and kill them when he's gotten whatever he wants. That's how he works. Then he'll find someone else to use to gain what he wants next."

"Good," Horton hissed, his rage building as his eyes glowed, his fangs elongating. "Those bastards deserve it. King Charles was better than all of them combined. A swift death is too damn good for the council members, and Decker isn't allowed to get away with what he's done. He set my master up to be slaughtered."

"Sounds like Decker. He probably laughed his ass off. The jerk is fucking insane."

Horton rose, and in a blink, attacked the wall nearest his desk, punching holes into it. Gerri's heart rate spiked but Wen gave her thigh a gentle squeeze, not taking his attention from the Vamp. If he turned his rage on them, he wanted to be ready to protect her.

Horton finally stopped. He smiled when he faced them, as if his bloody hands and the damage to the wall amused him. "You're going to tell me everything about Decker."

"Fine. I still want to know where I can take my mate that will be safe, and I need money."

"You don't care that I plan to kill your clan leader?"

"He stopped being my leader the moment he ordered the death of my mate. I have no loyalty to that bastard. I never liked him."

"I must plot." Horton paced. "Go upstairs. We'll speak tomorrow night. I want you to tell me how best to get his enforcers to turn on him. Think hard and long, VampLycan." His gaze drifted to Gerri, then back to Wen. "You want to keep your mate safe. I want revenge."

"Understood." Wen rose to his feet, holding out his hand. Gerri took it and he led her out of the room.

Chapter Eight

Wen shoved a piece of furniture in front of the door, lifted their backpacks, and carried them into the bedroom once they'd locked themselves inside the apartment. Gerri followed him around. He ditched the backpacks, then did another search of the apartment. He shook his head, implying nothing had changed since they'd left. She relaxed but he still lifted a finger to his lips, hinting for her to keep her voice low if she spoke.

"We're safe here, sweetheart." He said that loud, in case the pack was listening from another apartment or the hallway.

"I know. I trust you. Should we get some sleep? I'm tired."

"Sure." He took her back into the bedroom.

She began to strip but Wen shook his head, just removing his shoes. Gerri hated sleeping in her clothes, but she knew Wen didn't want them naked in case of an attack. She just removed her shoes as well, then climbed on the bed.

He pushed her to the side nearest the wall, and took the outside of the bed as they settled down. Then he pulled her close, pressing his mouth against her ear as they cuddled up together. "That Vamp is fucking nuts," he whispered.

"I agree. So can we leave yet?" He'd know she was really asking if he could just kill Horton already. He wasn't playing with a full deck of cards, so it was best if he was taken out quickly. Anyone who'd spent any time with him would have seen that too. Whatever he'd said or done in his bid to start a war probably wasn't taken too seriously by anyone with a brain.

Wen hesitated. "Not yet. He's just looking for a target for his rage. Now he's focused on Decker."

"I get what you're saying." It would be nice if Horton killed Decker. "He can't touch him though. His own council is keeping that jerk safe." She couldn't see a reason to let Horton live since there was no way he'd be able to get to the ex-clan leader.

"Let's give it time," Wen whispered. "At least he might change his tune if we allow him to contact his friends."

In other words, Wen hoped the false rumors Horton had circulated about VampLycans would be put to rest if he ranted about Decker and the council instead. "Then I hope he has a big mouth," she whispered.

Wen chuckled. "It will make him seem more unstable. We'll give it some time, let him do his thing, then mission over."

"Got a plan about how to do that?"

"It's going to be tougher than I thought but we'll see what happens during the day."

She guessed he was hoping the Lycans would grow bored hanging around the building and thin out some while the Vampires slept. It would be easy for Wen to kill them while they slept. "Still a lot of company around us, huh?"

He pulled her closer. "Yes."

"They aren't going to let us out of here without a fight, are they?"

He shook his head.

"Is it safe to sleep?"

"We'll take turns. Are you tired?"

"No. That nap I took helped. You sleep first. I'll wake you if I hear anything." She might not have his keener senses, but someone would have to come through the door or a wall to get at them. That would be plenty noisy enough for her human hearing to pick up.

Wen's hold on her eased after a while and she knew he had fallen asleep. She shifted her head a little, listening for any sounds. The floor overhead creaked, as if someone walked above them, but the rest of the building was silent. It left her with time to think.

Once Wen felt it was time to kill Horton, they would have to fight their way out. It would also mean her time with Wen would almost be over. She curled into his big warm body a little closer, inhaling his scent. Tears filled her eyes but she fought them back. It would be hell giving him up a second time. She'd loved him when she'd been a young girl and those feelings hadn't changed. They might not be as close as they once had been but her heart didn't care. It wanted to keep Wen forever.

Her mind found another option. Maybe Wen could use her on future missions; they would get to spend more time together. He was young for a VampLycan, though. She'd age but he wouldn't. One day, she'd either become too old to be sexually appealing to him, or he'd find a mate he could take home to his family.

It would come with another steep price if she made that her future. She'd have to give up the thought of ever getting married or having her own family. The loneliness would also be unbearable each time he was back in Alaska, until he could return to her.

The unfairness of it broke her heart. Anger surfaced too, all directed at Wen's parents. They'd never liked her but they should want their son to be happy. Instead, they'd forced him to step into Gerbin's shadow, and to shoulder all the responsibilities of first son that went with it. Wen had honor. He'd do anything to please the couple that had given him life.

She wondered if they realized how miserable they made their son, or if they even cared.

A noise outside near the street drew her attention, and she carefully rolled away from Wen, climbed out of bed, and peeked out the curtain. Dawn approached, the sky a glow in the distance, the night not so dark. Street lights were still on, so she had no problem spotting Horton and Joel below in the backyard of the building.

They seemed to be arguing. Horton pushed the bigger alpha, making him stumble. Joel responded by flashing fangs and rising up, puffing out his chest. It was a defiant act, even a threat. Horton backed out of sight but he remained outside, judging by the way Joel glared where Gerri assumed a door must be.

Joel finally nodded, spun, and motioned with his hand. Two men stepped out of the shadows along the back wall. She hadn't spotted them with her human eyes before that. They met him in the middle of the small yard. A short discussion ensued, then the Lycans broke apart. Joel returned to the building but his two men returned to their positions in the shadows.

She let the curtain go and returned to the bed to curl up with Wen.

"What is it?"

She should have known he'd wake the moment she moved. "Tension between our new friends," she whispered. "Alphas don't like to take orders."

"No, they don't. I might not have to take out the Vampires after all."

She smiled, snuggling into him tighter. "No shit, but that leaves us with an unhappy pack."

"It wouldn't be a problem if they weren't rogues."

"Because they wouldn't be working with a crazy Vamp?"

"No, because I'd challenge for alpha and kill theirs."

"You don't want a pack."

"No, but I wouldn't have to fight all of them at once. I'd disband them."

"You could do that?"

He shrugged. "It doesn't matter, since they don't follow the rules."

"Go back to sleep."

She stayed awake long after Wen dozed. It was more important that he got plenty of rest instead of her. He was the one who'd be doing the fighting if shit hit the fan. She did smile when Wen muttered unintelligible words in his sleep, obviously dreaming.

* * * * *

Wen jerked awake. G.L. peacefully slept next to him. He carefully got out of bed so he didn't disturb her and checked his cell phone. It was afternoon but there were no texts. He stalked out of the bedroom and into the living room, rubbing the back of his neck. It hadn't been a nightmare that woke him, but more of his past replaying in his head. The day the clan had learned of Gerbin's death always haunted his dreams, but the fact that he was effectively in enemy territory had probably been the cause this time.

He wanted to punch something, the anger still gripping him. It had been devastating to learn of his older brother's death, but worse, he'd gotten into a physical fight with his father. It would be the first of many over the years since that day.

"What's wrong?"

G.L.'s soft voice made him turn. He hadn't heard her at all, too distracted by his memories. She was adorable with her mussed hair and sleepy gaze. He crossed the room and pulled her into his arms, just needing to hold her. It didn't matter if they had a day or a week. Their time would be too short.

She wrapped her arms around his waist, clinging to him. "What happened? I'm sorry I fell asleep."

He kissed the top of her head. "Everything here is fine. It's all quiet." He listened to the building around him, double checking. "I probably should do recon."

He tried to release her but Gerri tightened her grip and lifted her chin. He looked down, staring into her beautiful eyes.

"What's wrong? Are we in deep shit? Just tell me. I'm in this with you a hundred percent."

He stroked her hair away from her face. The curly ringlets wanted to wrap around his thumb and he smiled. "We're fine. This is a 'me' issue. I had a dream and woke agitated."

"What kind of dream?"

"It more like a bunch of memories merging together and replaying as I slept."

"Talk to me," she whispered. "Your eyes are really dark. Do you need to shift?"

He got control of his Lycan side and forced his body to relax. "Better?"

"Yes. They're a pretty blue again."

"Are you trying to tell me they aren't attractive when I'm shifted?" He liked to tease her.

She smiled. "You're always attractive when you're in skin. I don't care what color your eyes are." Her good mood faded and she grew serious. "Talk to me, Wen. When I walked out here, you looked ready to attack someone."

"I relived the day word came to us of Gerbin's death."

She pulled him over to the couch and tugged on him until he sat next to her. "Tell me about it."

"I should see how many Lycans are guarding the building."

"It won't matter if you do that now or in a few minutes. Talk to me. Please?"

He could deny her almost nothing when she stared at him with that vulnerable look on her face, making him guess his refusal might hurt her feelings. "Hang on a minute."

He left her on the couch and turned on water in the kitchen sink, then turned on the shower in the bathroom. He flipped on the television in the living room, then sat next to her again. All those noises would help hide their voices if anyone was listening from other apartments. He leaned in, speaking softly.

"I heard my mother's shrieks and rushed to their home."

"You didn't live with them still?"

He shook his head. "I'd built a cabin nearly a mile from them. I'd hit maturity age a few months before. I'd been outside, chopping wood when I heard her. I dropped the ax and ran. A group of the clan, including Trayis, was gathered in front of their cabin. My mother was on her knees, my father beside her with his arms around her. Trayis turned, and I just knew Gerbin must be dead." He paused, emotion almost choking him. "My father lifted my mother and carried her inside. Trayis told me he'd been contacted by the pack Gerbin played guardian to. A nest of Vampires had killed my brother. Everyone in that area was aware of who he protected, and they taunted the pack by sending his bloodied clothing to the alpha."

"I'm sorry, Wen." She took one of his hands in hers, holding it tight.

"The healer came and sedated my mother. She wouldn't stop wailing and carrying on. Gerbin was her heart."

"You are too," Gerri whispered.

He forced a smile. "There is a bond with a mother and her firstborn that I've always been aware of. I know they love me, but Gerbin..." He shook his head. It hurt knowing it would have been easier on his parents if he'd been the one to die instead. "My father came outside and ordered me to go after the nest responsible. He couldn't leave my mother alone in her grief to seek vengeance. It was up to me."

Gerri frowned but said nothing.

"Trayis said I wouldn't be going alone. Gerbin was his friend and one of his enforcers. He put together a team to assist me."

"Good. I take it you were able to kill them all?"

He nodded. "Yes. We'd hoped to retrieve Gerbin's body to bring home for burial on clan lands, but the ones we tortured before death said their master had burned his body."

"I'm so sorry." She pressed against his side.

He debated on telling her the rest.

"What else?" She peered up at him with narrowed eyes.

G.L. had always known him too well. "I returned home to discover a naked VampLycan waiting for me in my bed. My father wanted me to take a mate, and he began sending them to my house to test matings. He tried to order me to fuck and bite them, even if I didn't have the urge."

Her mouth parted and he saw jealousy glint in her eyes. He more than understood. "I was furious. He informed me that with Gerbin gone, he and my mother expected a grandchild immediately. They feared something would happen to me too. I had to put locks on my cabin to keep him out, so he couldn't let more women in. Trayis eventually gave me land farther from theirs after a few years of that bullshit happening every few months, so I built another cabin. One tougher to break into, so my father couldn't allow women inside to wait for my return."

She lowered her gaze to his chest. "Did you test matings with those women?"

"No. I threw them out."

"I'm glad Trayis helped you."

144

He snorted. "It wasn't just for my sanity; it was pissing off other clans my father had reached out to, looking for unmated women to come meet me. They were insulted when I threw their clothes at them, ordered them to get dressed, and shoved them out of my home. Trayis ordered my father to stop."

"Did he?"

He shrugged. "In a way. He stopped breaking into my home before the women arrived to give them the impression they'd be welcomed when I returned. He'll probably have one staying with family when I return from this mission to push at me. I'll get invited to dinner and a woman will be there. My parents do that shit every time I go on a mission."

"That must be rough."

He studied her and smiled. "I've never fucked them, G.L. Not once. I knew it would be pointless because I'm not even attracted to them." His humor fled. "I also don't trust anyone who my father sets me up with. They want that grandchild too damn much and I'm sure those women are smart enough to know they're being used, and they're allowing it. Hell, they're willing to birth a child with me knowing I don't want it."

"But it's not like you could get a VampLycan pregnant unless you mate to one."

"That's not true."

She looked surprised.

"We're part Lycan. I deal with a lot of them since I go on missions often for the clan. In some cases, they can bypass the mating requirement if their numbers are so low they're facing extinction as a pack."

"I don't understand."

"Mind-over-matter kind of thing. A Lycan can force her ovaries to work, force herself to ovulate to get pregnant if she's motivated enough, even if she's not mated. We're all aware of what happened to poor Bran."

"Who?"

"Bran. He used to be a member of our clan until one of Decker's women set her mind to fool him into getting pregnant. She masked the scent of her ovulation and had sex with him. He didn't even know he had a son until after Veso was born. He left our clan to care for his son, since she didn't want to raise him, but she refused to allow Bran to bring Veso to our clan."

"I never heard anything about that."

"We don't like to discuss it, but since it happened to Bran, every male is given that talk now once they hit adolescence, to avoid a repeat."

"Was there a talk about humans?"

He grinned. "You bet there was. My father lectured me often about how you couldn't control your body, so I wasn't allowed to touch you. He didn't like the way I spent so much time with you. As soon as I started getting boners, he pulled me aside."

"I bet he did. Why did that woman do that to this Bran?"

"Because she was with Decker's clan. Some of them have no honor. Decker wanted stronger bloodlines and sent her after Bran. Veso is strong. He refused to become an enforcer for Decker but he's agreed to be one of Lorn's, now that he's taken over."

"I've missed a lot while I've been gone. I can't believe Decker no longer leads his clan."

"It's been great all around. Now if only Lord Aveoth could find the bastard so he can't give us more trouble. He's hiding with the Vampire Council."

"Why do you think the council is even bothering to offer him sanctuary?"

"Are you kidding? To have a VampLycan and a group of his enforcers in their debt?"

"Got it. Power. Greed." She paused. "But they already rule all the nests."

"Word is that not all Vampire nests like the council."

"You mean rogues."

"No. Some nests are decent ones, but they don't want to be under the thumb of the council anymore. The council keeps the peace, from what we know about it, but it's also are run by a bunch of outdated thinkers. They forbid Vamps from being too friendly with humans or other races."

"Isn't that a good thing?"

He hesitated. "One of the clans has become friendly with a master. I'm not allowed to share too much information but Trayis requested permission to talk to this guy, since we're dealing with the fallout of Decker going to the Vampire Council. He wanted as much intel about them as possible. This master said the council are a bunch of elitists who think they're too good for all other races. Mich—" He cleared his throat.

"This master is more of a modern thinker. He wants peace between everyone. The council wouldn't be thrilled if they knew he allowed Lycan packs to roam in his territory, or that he doesn't treat humans as if they're cows. He has a rule that none of his are allowed to feed off them. They only use bagged blood in his nest and pay humans to donate it. The council would frown on that."

"Because humans are cattle to Vamps."

"The council seems to believe that. There are nests who want them disbanded so they don't have to fear censure if their modern practices ever comes to light."

"Would this master be punished if the council found out he lets Werewolves into his territory and pays for human blood so no one is bitten?"

Wen nodded. "They'd think he was unfit to lead his nest. They'd sanction his death."

"Yeah. I can see why the council might need to be disbanded."

"That's for another day. One nest at a time." He straightened up. "I need to see how many are guarding us during the day. I won't go far. Lock the door when I leave and scream if anyone comes at you. I'll stay within hearing distance."

She clung to him when he tried to rise.

He hesitated, peering into her eyes. "What is it?"

"You changed the subject, I noticed. Why were you so upset when I woke up?"

He couldn't help but smile. G.L. did know him too well. "I'm fine. I told you. It was just dreams."

"But?"

"I don't want to let you go...and I realized what's going to happen when it's time for us to part."

"Some VampLycan is going to try to bed you."

"*That* won't happen. It's just that when I'm with you, I try hard to forget about reality. That dream made me realize nothing will be able to change."

"As in, your parents will never let me stay with you."

"Yes." He sighed. "I must recon, G.L."

She let him go that time, releasing his hand. "I know. Mission first. Go. I'll stay on alert."

He stood and walked to the door. Gerri was on his heels. He unlocked the door and sniffed, picking up the strong scent of Lycan. He eased out into the hallway without looking back. The door gently closed and he heard the locks slip back into place.

Chapter Nine

Gerri glanced around the chain restaurant. "I'm shocked they let us leave."

"We have eyes on us," he muttered, glancing around. "Two Lycans just entered. They followed us all the way here."

"I figured."

The waiter dropped off their food and Gerri dug in, starving. She swallowed her mouthful and then caught Wen's eye. "Can they hear us?" She mouthed the words.

He smiled. "You look lovely tonight, sweetheart."

She'd take that for a yes. "Thank you for the meal."

"It's my honor to care for my mate."

She really wished that title actually belonged to her.

Hunger kept her focused on the food in front of her, so their lack of conversation for the next twenty minutes wasn't a problem. They didn't dare eat anything in the apartment or whatever the pack brought them. She knew the only reason they'd been allowed to leave was because Wen had argued with Joel. He'd been blunt. He wouldn't risk them being drugged. He'd demanded they be allowed to leave to get their own food.

Wen paid the bill and they left. Two men along the counter rose to their feet. She glanced at them. They were muscular, rough-looking thugs, and she didn't need a special sense of smell to tell her those were the two Lycans.

Wen kept hold of her hand as they returned to the building. The sun had gone down while they ate. It wasn't a surprise when they entered the front door to find Horton and one of his Vamps waiting.

"In my office, now," Horton snapped.

She allowed Wen to maneuver her to keep his body between her and the others. He seated her and took the chair next to her.

Horton dropped into his chair behind the desk, glaring at Wen. "You have a problem with my hospitality?"

"I was raised with Decker. I don't trust anyone. It's safer that way."

Horton frowned. "Why do you say that?"

"Decker would give bad food to his so-called guests to sicken and weaken them. I'd be easier to handle if you did the same. I can survive almost anything you feed me but my mate can't. That's why I insisted we be allowed to go out before dusk. Lycans can't control the minds of humans in the eating establishment we just visited."

Horton visibly relaxed. "You're a paranoid bastard."

"It's why we're still alive."

"I can respect that. You aren't stupid, are you?"

Wen growled. "No. I'm not."

"Fine. I told Joel to allow you to eat wherever you want. You'll have guards. To keep you safe, of course."

Wen arched his eyebrows. "If you say so."

"I don't control all the Werewolves in this city. We're now friends. I want to keep you and your mate safe."

Gerri watched the two men, keeping her mouth shut. Horton was a manipulative creep. He hadn't ordered Joel to let them go. He'd been sleeping when they'd left, but she noticed how he'd worded that to make it sound as if he'd had a say in the matter. Those Lycans weren't following them for their safety either. They were being watched.

She wondered what Horton's next move would be. It didn't take long to find out.

"Did you think about what I asked? I need to know how to get Decker's enforcers to turn against him. Tell me how to do that."

"Tell me where I can live with my mate without fear of Lycans or Vamps attacking her," Wen countered.

Horton scowled. "I'm making you a list of areas in the United States where there are no nests or reported packs. It takes time. You have the answers I need now. Tell me what I want to know."

"Give me money then. Something in exchange." Wen let his fingernails grow into claws. "So far, all you've given us is a place to stay. I could have provided that for my mate without you."

Horton hissed and Gerri tensed in her chair, half expecting the crazy Vamp to lunge over his desk at Wen. Instead, the Vamp seemed to calm down after a few seconds. She relaxed too.

"Fine." Horton bent down and opened a desk drawer. He tossed a package to Wen.

Wen caught it, opened the flap, and peered inside. He frowned, glaring at the nest master. "This can't be more than a few thousand dollars."

"Call it a down payment. There's plenty more where that came from."

Wen passed it over to Gerri to hold but he kept his attention on the Vamp. "Decker is paranoid and doesn't trust anyone, even his own enforcers. Is there any way you can get Vamps who are near his enforcers to do things for you?"

Horton nodded. "Yes."

"Have them talk to Decker's enforcers about something stupid and innocent, like the weather, but have them do it where Decker can see them together yet not hear what's being said. He'll ask his enforcers what they were talking about. He won't believe their answer, instead he'll assume Vamps are trying to sway his enforcers away from him."

Gerri caught on faster than Horton, and added, "Decker will think his enforcers are lying to him. Why would Vamps approach his men just to say it's a beautiful night? He's too paranoid and won't believe it's that innocent."

Wen flashed her a smile. "He'll think they're becoming disloyal and try to kill them." He stared at Horton. "It's what he does."

"That sounds too simple." Horton didn't look convinced.

"That's the beauty of it," Wen murmured. "What would happen if you saw your Lycan pack talking to another master a few times and they told you the discussion was about the weather?"

Anger glinted in Horton's eyes. "They are betraying bastards. That wouldn't be the case."

"See? Decker thinks that way about everyone, including his own. It's the only reason he survived being clan leader for as long as he did."

"It's a good plan *because* it's so simple," Gerri stated.

Horton narrowed his gaze at her. "I didn't ask *you*."

She sealed her lips. He didn't like humans. Message received.

"Don't speak to my mate with that tone." Wen stood and snarled at Horton. "We're going upstairs." He held out his hand.

Gerri took it and they left the office. The Lycans and Vamps waiting outside allowed them passage to the stairs. They didn't speak until they were back inside the apartment and Wen had checked out the space to make sure no one had been inside while they'd been gone. She stashed the money in her backpack, not wanting to leave it laying around for someone to steal. Wen returned to her.

He pulled her into a tight hug. "Soon," he whispered.

"You want to see if he can actually do damage to Decker. I get it. It would be nice if they all turned on each other." She smiled and rubbed her cheek against his.

"I'm also curious about where he'll finally say we should go. As if there's such a place that anyone could ever be safe from VampLycans." He gripped her arms and pulled her away from him, a smile on his lips. "The North Pole?"

"I like Santa, and I bet elves are cute. I'd so live there with you. We could get jobs making toys."

He suddenly lifted her off her feet, striding forward until her back bumped against the wall, and took possession of her mouth. She gasped

154

and his tongue delved between her lips. His kiss left her breathless and instantly turned her on. He had that effect on her. She wrapped her arms around his neck and hugged his waist with her spread thighs.

He shifted his hips, rubbing his stiff cock trapped inside his pants against the center seam of her jeans. She moaned against his tongue as he tormented her clit. She resented their clothing, wishing they were naked and he was inside her.

He suddenly broke the kiss, his eyes glowing when she stared into them.

"I want you," she admitted.

"It's such a bad idea. We need to stop." Frustration showed on his handsome face and his eye color darkened to black.

"Easy, honeybun." She knew that endearment had amused him before and she needed him to calm a bit. It really could hurt him to go that far over into his Lycan side without shifting. "Why can't we do this? We can be quiet."

"Because there are two dozen Lycans in this fucking place and you smell incredible when you're turned on. They'd pick up the scent no matter how quiet we are. It would make some of them hornier than shit and they'd break in here to try to get at you. I'd fucking kill them, and we don't want a bloodbath yet."

"Shower." She jerked her head toward the bathroom. "We can shove our clothes against the bottom of the door. There's a fan in there. We can lock our scent in that one room. And I saw chemicals under the sink."

His eyes glowed again. "You're so smart." He kept hold of her and carried her into the bathroom, using his foot to kick it closed. Then he put her down. "Strip."

She didn't need to be told twice. She bent, tore off her shoes, and worked on her pants next. He disrobed faster than she did and shoved his clothes against the bottom of the door. He bent over, yanking open the cupboard under the sink, and brought out a spray bottle of shower cleaner, resting it on the counter.

Gerri loved the sight of his beefy bare ass. He had the best body. All muscles and sexy skin. He stepped around her, turning on the water as she finished undressing. She thought they'd go into the shower but Wen had other ideas as he gripped her hips. She got ahold of his biceps and then he lifted her off her feet. Her back hit the bathroom door, his mouth on hers a second later.

She wrapped around him, clinging to him as he kissed her. It had been hell to sleep next to him without being able to do more than cuddle. Their time was short and she wanted him. The sex was incredible, and the memories would have to last her a lifetime.

He entered her in one fast thrust. She gasped, tearing her mouth from his. He was big, she'd been ready, but it still came as a surprise.

"Sorry," he groaned, burying his face against her throat to leave wet, hungry kisses along her skin. "Fuck, G.L. Did I hurt you? You're so damn tight and small."

"No. Next time go a little slower on the entry."

He chuckled. "You are very wet."

"No shit. You make me that way. Move. I'm ready."

He rolled his hips, pinning her tighter against the door. She ran her hands up his arms to get a firm grip on his shoulder with one hand, wrapping her other arm around his neck. He withdrew a little, then thrust up. Gerri moaned his name.

"Shush," he growled. "We don't want them to hear you."

Right. She forgot everything when Wen was inside her. She lowered her face and pressed it against the top of his shoulder. He fucked her hard. The door creaked a little but she managed to smother the sounds she was making. He moved faster, angled his hips to drive up into her a little deeper, and she was lost. The climax built until it tore through her and she wanted to scream. She bit him instead, sinking her teeth into his skin along the top of his shoulder.

"Fuck," he snarled, tearing his mouth away from her. His body grew rigid and he groaned, coming hard enough that he shook against her.

They clung to each other as they caught their breath and Gerri released his skin, lifted her head a little and smiled at where she'd bitten him. No blood showed but he would probably have a bruise for an hour or so. Her teeth had dug into his skin enough to leave marks.

Her amusement quickly died when Wen lifted his head and stared at her. His pupils and irises were the same black color.

"You need to shift."

He closed his eyes, taking deep breaths, and gently pulled his cock out of her. Gerri hated it when he lowered her to the floor and forced her to release him. He spun away, entering the running shower.

She leaned against the door and knew she'd fucked up.

Wen fought for control as the hot water ran over his head, down his body. He could shift but he didn't want to give that part of himself control right now. The urge to bite Gerri, to mate her, to taste her fucking blood and make her take his, was so strong it left him quaking on his legs.

He heard her approach, probably to join him in the tight space. "Don't."

She didn't touch him. "I'm sorry. I'll go in the other room."

"Don't you dare. Just give me a minute."

"Right. Scent."

"We have to wash first, then spray the room before we open that door. I won't have those bastards coming after you." He clenched his fists, blinding rage hitting him so strongly his heart pounded. The thought of any other man even wanting to touch her made him want to kill.

"I'm so sorry, Wen. I didn't think about it when I bit you. I just wanted to muffle the sounds."

"I know." He sucked in air, held it in lungs, and blew it out. He repeated that for a good minute or so. "This isn't your fault. I'm the one who can't bite."

"Is the urge just as strong?"

He debated on telling her the truth.

"I'll take that for a yes. I'm sorry. I won't bite you again."

He hated his life in that moment. His parents. Hell, even Gerbin. How in the hell had he allowed himself to be killed by the nest he was tracking? His brother should have been more careful. Then Wen would be free to

158

mate G.L. He'd have gone after her when she'd turned eighteen. He tortured himself by mentally going there. They'd have kids by now, since he couldn't keep his hands off her. Just the image he created in his mind of her belly swollen with his child had him longing for that possibility. He wanted it so bad.

"Shift," she urged. "Do it. You're too far over the line."

Maybe it was for the best. He wouldn't try to fuck her in fur. He bowed his body and, while the space was tight, the hot water distracted him as his bones popped, the fur coming out, and he dropped to all fours.

He finally raised his head when it was over, looking at her. She stood naked next to the shower, watching him with tears in her eyes. He was causing her pain somehow. He regretted involving her in this because of it. It had been selfish to pull her into his life just because he hadn't been able to stay away. His weakness to see her, his inability to stay away, had brought them to this point.

She entered the shower stall and closed the door. "It's okay, baby." She reached for the shampoo. "I'll wash you."

He pressed his body against the side of the tile.

She frowned. "Okay. I won't. No touching? That's going to be hard. Damn, city showers are cramped, aren't they?"

She used the white liquid she'd dumped into her hand to rub against her skin, even down to her sex, to wash away what they'd just done. He maneuvered to give her a little space. She ducked her head under the water. He couldn't keep his gaze off her. She was his. He knew it, felt it, and it went against everything inside him to resist the urge to shift back, fuck her again, and exchange blood to bond her to him.

159

He had to close his eyes finally when she started washing her long hair. It was torture, since he wanted to be the one doing it. It helped that he was in fur though. He managed to turn in the shower so his tail was the only thing brushing up against her body. A gob of something hit his tail and he flicked it. She gasped.

"Watch where that goes."

He turned his head and opened his eyes, amused finally. She gave him what she probably thought was a dirty look but it was cute as hell. He flicked his tail again, slapping against her thighs.

She spun, presenting him with her ass. "Don't even think about it."

He was tempted to slap her ass but kept his tail still. She finished with her hair and got out of the shower, then faced him as she dried off. "You ready to shift back yet or do you need more time."

He hunched over, closing his eyes. When he was done, he straightened on two legs. "Spray the room while I wash my hair."

"You're going to hate it."

"Better than having to fight Lycans with hard-ons if they catch the scent of sex."

"True enough." She closed the shower door and the false scent of pine filled the room. He grimaced, breathing through his mouth. "How the fuck can humans stand that shit?"

She laughed. "Most city people have never been in a forest to know the difference and we don't have super-sensitive noses. Snob."

He growled low and finished his shower. Gerri was dressed, minus her shoes, when he opened the door to grab a towel. He noticed the way her gaze slid down his body.

She gave him her back. "I'll wait in the other room."

"Don't go far and leave the door open."

"Trust me. I'm not going to make it easy for someone to attack me while you're getting dressed."

She was smart. His G.L. always had been. She went out of his sight but did as he'd asked, leaving the door wide open. He caught glimpses of her as he put on his clothes. She seemed to be distracting herself by cleaning up. Regret surfaced once more. She'd be home safe if it wasn't for him. He faced the steamy mirror and used his palm to wipe it, noticing right away the redness of his skin along the top of his shoulder. He leaned in, hating for once how quickly he healed. The mark she'd put on him had almost completely faded.

It caused his chest to ache. He wanted her to scar him, wanted her teeth to break his skin. "Fuck."

"You okay?" She came to the doorway, peering up at him.

He forced a smile. "I'm hungry." It just wasn't for food. He wanted his mate.

"I guess we'll be going out again."

"No. We're in for the night. I don't want to distract Horton."

She nodded. "Okay."

He watched her walk away, and then left the bathroom, flipping off the light. God damn his parents and their old-fashioned ways.

161

Chapter Ten

Wen was being so quiet it worried Gerri. Something had happened when they'd had sex. He wouldn't talk to her about it and acted as if nothing was wrong. She'd bitten him. That had to be it. It had been thoughtless, since she knew he had the urge to bite her.

Then again, thinking wasn't something she did well when Wen was naked and making love to her.

They'd gotten a few hours of sleep but a loud commotion had them both out of bed at three in the morning. Wen went to the window, pulling back the curtain. "Fight."

Gerri was beside him in seconds. Two large men were battling in skin but their claws were out. There was enough light in the backyard that she could see the tears opening up in their clothing as they hit each other, and the bloodshed it caused. Her gaze lifted to the other buildings, noting lights coming on around them.

"What morons," Wen muttered.

"I know. Someone will call the cops."

Horton appeared, along with Joel. The alpha moved fast, shoving the two Lycans apart and snarling loud enough to be heard by the neighborhood.

"Is this what you call keeping them under control?" Horton sounded pissed, since he shouted it.

They all moved inside but Wen cocked his head as he released the curtain. "Shit."

She couldn't hear what he did. "What?"

"They're still fighting downstairs but I hear sirens."

It wasn't long before she picked up the faint sound of a patrol car or two coming. "It's not a biggy. Horton will mind wipe them and make them go away."

"True. Maybe I should assist."

She latched onto his arm. "Or not. It looks as if Joel's pack has some infighting. I don't want them attacking you if they're comparing their dicks."

He scowled. "What?"

"That's a roundabout way to say resettling the pecking order. You know how Lycans get."

"I do, but how the hell do *you* know?"

"I told you my mom is with a pack. They fought whenever one of them thought he was hot shit and wanted to advance his placement in the pack. It's a rogue thing mostly, as far as I can figure. I hope not all packs are like that. Otherwise, how in the hell do they survive each other?"

"It will look good if I assist. We're trying to fit in."

"Fine."

"Stay at my back."

"You know it." She followed him out of the bedroom, took a moment to grab a few steak knives, and they left the apartment.

The fighting had calmed a bit on the first floor but there was some snarling and pushing going on when they arrived. Horton appeared furious, glaring at Joel.

163

"Stop them now!"

Joel struck one of the fighting Weres in the face, taking him down. The other one he grabbed by his throat and choked until he passed out. He tossed the limp body next to his one-time opponent. He glowered at Horton. "Deal with the cops. They just stopped outside."

"I hear," Horton hissed. "Drag them out of sight."

The sirens stopped. Joel and another Lycan grabbed the downed men and carried them toward a door at the end of the hallway.

Horton frowned at Wen. "I hate fucking dogs. Useless and trouble."

Gerri saw Wen tense but he didn't respond. She guessed Horton had forgotten the man he'd just said that to was half Lycan. She rubbed Wen's back, hoping it soothed his temper. She might sometimes call Lycans hybrid dogs but Wen knew she liked to joke around. Horton, on the other hand, had meant it as an insult.

The police pounded on the door and Horton walked over to it, flinging it open. "Thank goodness you're here. Come in. Two men got into a fight. We've subdued them."

Two cops walked in, looking leery and nervous as they glanced at Wen then Horton, and finally at Gerri. She forced a smile.

The taller of the two addressed her. "Are you hurt, miss?"

"No. I'm fine. I was upstairs with my boyfriend when the fight broke out. We came down to see what was going on."

Horton closed the door and the cops turned, each putting a hand on their weapons. Horton's eyes glowed and Gerri lowered her gaze fast, not wanting to test how well he could fuck with someone's mind.

"Take your hands off your weapons." Horton lowered his voice to a soothing tone. "Keep looking at me."

She saw both cops react, dropping their hands at their sides. She shifted behind Wen to block her view of Horton, just in case. He was a master and she didn't even like to hear his voice. It had a quality to it that made her want to do what he said; she'd gotten the urge to look at him when he'd ordered the cops to do so.

Wen reached back and took her hand. That helped. He grounded her.

"Nothing happened here," Horton stated.

"That's not going to work." Wen squeezed her hand and released it. "The humans from other buildings must have seen them fighting and called it in. I saw what went down from above. May I handle them?"

"Fine." Horton snapped.

Wen approached Horton then glanced back at her. Their gazes met. "Turn around, honey."

She did as he said. He didn't want to risk her staring into his eyes. In seconds, his husky voice told her he must have unleashed his glowing mojo. "Two teenage wannabe actors were practicing for a video they want to make. The blood was fake. You talked to them, warned them that you'd arrest them for disturbing the peace if they ever do that again. Understand?"

"Yes," the two cops stated in unison.

More seconds ticked by until Wen's voice sounded again. "There are people out in the street. Tell them it was just some teens pulling a prank with costumes and props for a video. Assure them that everything is fine. You may go now."

The door opened and Gerri spun around, watching the cops walk outside. Wen closed the door and leaned against it. He stared at Horton. "Humans aren't *totally* stupid, and telling them nothing happened wouldn't have worked. You should know better."

"I don't give a shit what humans think as long as they leave me alone."

Wen pushed off the door and drew closer to the master. "Do you care about VampLycans? I don't want them showing up here, damn it. They might be using police reports trying to find us. A call going out about a fight, injuries, and no arrests would raise red flags."

"Fine." Horton looked annoyed. "I let you handle them. I don't think anyone could mistake those two assholes for teenagers though."

"The police report will list them as teenagers. If adults had pulled that shit, the cops might have arrested them. This way it looks believable."

"Whatever." Horton turned and threw open the door to his office. "Get in here."

Wen waved to Gerri to follow him. The Lycans hadn't come back out of the room they'd gone into. Both of them entered the office to find Horton pacing behind his desk.

"Close the door."

Gerri shut it and walked up to stand slightly next to but a little behind Wen. They both watched Horton. He looked agitated and furious.

166

"This is the third time shit like this has happened. Fucking dogs!"

Gerri glanced up at Wen, saw a muscle in his jaw clench, but he hid his anger fast. His features masked his emotions and didn't show when he spoke. "What did you expect from a rogue pack? They aren't stable. It's amazing they haven't turned on you yet."

"I'll fucking kill them all!" Horton shouted.

The door behind them banged open. Wen reacted by snagging Gerri around her waist, lifting her, and carrying her to a corner. He dropped her on her feet and put his body in front of hers. She peered around him, watching Joel storm inside.

"You got a problem with me and my pack?"

"Yes," Horton hissed at him, flashing fangs. "You can't keep them in line."

Two Vamps entered, then three more Lycans. Hostility hung in the air as they glared at each other. Gerri tensed, wondering if a fight would break out. Wen must have been worried too, because when she glanced down at his hands, his claws were out. She reached for the two knives she'd hidden under her clothes, withdrawing them.

"Control those fucking beasts," Horton ranted. "Every time the cops are called, it's drawing attention to us that we don't need. What's so hard to understand about that, Joel? If you can't keep them from fighting, fucking kill them all."

Gerri saw hair sprout over Joel's skin and his bones popped as his features changed, his snout pushing out. He threw back his head and howled.

Gerri tightened her grip on the handles of the knives. She heard people running over her head, coming down the hallway.

The alpha had just called his pack.

The Vamps attacked the Lycans closest to them and Horton leapt over the desk to slam into Joel. "Help me, Wen!"

Wen didn't budge, staying in front of Gerri. Furry bodies ran into the room. It wasn't a big enough space to accommodate them all. Glass broke across the room and a fourth Vampire landed in the melee after crashing through a side window. Gerri could even pick up the iron stench of blood filling the room with her human nose, it was so thick.

Wen snarled, a scary sound. "Don't even think about it."

Two Werewolves were coming at them, their four-legged bodies low, prepared to launch an attack. Gerri pressed tighter into the corner but kept the blades pointed at the wall in case they slammed into Wen, knocking him into her. She didn't want to accidently stab him. He backed up farther, blocking her view of everything but his broad back.

"VampLycan!" Horton yelled.

"You're on your own." Wen lowered his voice, "Get ready to move, Gerri."

"Right with you," she promised.

Then the fighting suddenly stopped and the room grew quiet.

Gerri couldn't see anything and she had no idea what the silence meant. Wen shifted his body a little, and then she saw Horton across the room, holding a limp Joel against his chest. The alpha was bloody. So was Horton. Crimson covered his mouth and jaw, even his throat.

"I'll fucking kill him if you don't stop right now," Horton hissed. "I drink any more of his blood and he won't survive."

The wolves lowered to their bellies, their gazes locked on Horton. One of the Vampires lie on the floor, covered in blood and torn up from multiple bites. Gerri realized one of his hands had been bitten off. She looked away, her gaze taking in more. One wolf was dead. His eyes were open, blood soaking his fur. She was glad to be pressed up against the corner, since her knees weakened. The room was covered in red stains and puddles.

"Get the fuck out of here and I'll return your alpha to you breathing," Horton ordered.

The wolves backed out of the room, some of them badly injured.

Two of the Vampires checked the one still on the floor. A darker-haired one lifted his head. "He's lost a lot of blood, Master."

"Then fucking feed him," Horton snapped. He shoved Joel's limp body to the floor. "And take this one out of my fucking office. Don't bleed him more. His heart is barely pumping. We still need him."

Wen stepped away from Gerri but stayed close. "Is this what you call keeping control of your territory?"

"Fuck you, VampLycan!" Horton lifted his hand and pointed at him. "I told you to help me."

"This wasn't my fight." Wen shrugged. "You already had backup from your nest. Besides, you're a master. If a fucked-up pack can take you out, you deserve to die. I was protecting my mate."

169

Gerri inwardly winced. There was that VampLycan arrogance she'd always hated. They weren't the most sympathetic race when it came to Vamps, and they could be too blunt. She bet Horton wasn't too fond of what Wen had just said, either. One glance at his reaction assured her she was right. He looked furious.

She opened her mouth to try to defuse the situation but then pressed her lips together. There was nothing she could think to say that could twist Wen's words into something nicer. It would probably only worsen things, since she was human.

Horton took a step toward them but stopped. He suddenly laughed. "True." He spun away, walked into the tiny kitchen area, and bent over the sink. He turned on water, washing his face.

Horton kept his back to them. He took his time washing his face, dried it, and then removed his shirt. He disappeared out of sight, probably into the apartment bedroom. He returned wearing a clean shirt. He looked around and curled his upper lip.

"Clean up this fucking mess," he told one of his nest, who walked back into the room from the hallway. "At least I'm not hungry anymore." He smiled at Wen. "It wasn't a boring evening."

"There's that." Wen kept his tone neutral.

"Go upstairs with your mate. We'll handle this mess." Horton took a seat at his desk.

Gerri hid her knives. Wen turned and stunned her by gripping her hips. She gasped when he just tossed her over his shoulder, hooked an arm behind her legs, and strode toward the door. He took the stairs two at a time, until they were back in the apartment. He slammed their door, locked it, and headed into the bedroom.

"Want to tell me why you're carrying me like a sack of grain?"

He bent and dumped her on the bed. "I didn't want you walking through blood."

"Thanks?" She frowned. "Now what's the real reason?"

"They were doing triage in the damn hallways. I didn't want you to see that."

"Don't give me that bullshit." She removed the knives and put them on the nightstand.

"Fine. I just wanted to get you up here before the pack can regroup. I have no idea how hurt Joel is, and if his pack will lose their damn minds if he dies." He crouched in front of her. "It could turn bad again."

"Do you want to leave now?"

"Soon."

She stared into his eyes and lowered her voice. "After dawn?"

He nodded. "I'm going to kill that fucker," he mouthed.

"What about giving him time?" She knew he'd understand. He'd planned to give Horton time to cause Decker problems.

"Things changed just a few minutes ago."

"Because of how unstable the situation is?"

"You could have been hurt."

"We already knew that. What really changed, Wen? Be honest with me, damn it. We're in this together."

171

Wen hesitated.

Gerri leaned forward and snagged his shirt with both hands, fisting it. She yanked him closer until their lips were inches apart, holding his gaze. "What is it?" She kept her voice at a whisper.

"I heard the Vamp talking, the one who carried out the Vampire who got hurt."

"What did he say?"

"He ordered one of the Lycans to go find a blood donor to feed to his friend."

That didn't sound bad. "And?"

"The Lycan said 'just grab that asshole's mate. She's human'."

"Not surprising. I knew they'd see me that way."

His eyes darkened. "The Vamp said 'not yet. My master has plans for her. He's going to make her strong enough to survive you assholes for longer than a few days'."

Understanding dawned, and she knew why Wen seemed so freaked out. "You shouldn't be surprised that he plans to fuck you over. *Us*, I should say. He's a bad guy."

"He said the Vampire women he turned didn't last with this group. He's planning on turning you into a soldier. I'm not willing to risk him getting you alone somehow." He reached up and cupped her face in his hands. "I can't save you if he does. There's no coming back from that. You'd slowly go mad and become a killer. I'd have to take you out."

She replayed in her mind everything he'd told her about those amped-up zombie versions of a Vampire. She also didn't want to amuse a pack in the worst way imaginable. "I'd want you to."

"We leave in the morning. I'll take you to safety, then come back to handle this mess."

"We're a team."

"I want you the fuck out of here, G.L. We're done."

Pain twisted her heart. He wasn't just talking about this mission. He'd have to return to Alaska once his scent faded from her, and she'd go home. She released his shirt. "I'm your partner in this until the end. We do what you need to do and walk out of here the way we came in. Together."

"It's too dangerous."

"I'm your fucking backup, Wen."

He licked his lips and eased his hold on her. "No, baby. You just became a liability. I'll be too worried about you instead of focused on what needs to be done. I'll take you out of here for food in the morning and get you somewhere safe. Then I'll come back alone." He rose up. "Discussion over. Get some sleep." He stalked out of the bedroom.

Tears filled her eyes but she wiped them away. She knew he'd break her heart.

Wen was furious as he poured a glass of water from the tap and drank it down. He knew there would be some risk involved for Gerri but he'd never thought Horton would want to turn her into a soldier and hand

173

her over to be a sexual plaything for the rogues. It made him sick to his stomach and enraged at the same time.

The Vamp and Lycan speaking in the damn hallway should have known he could hear them. It was just luck that they were stupid or underestimated his senses. Horton had been running water to clean off the blood on his face, or he'd probably have heard the same conversation, alerted him that Wen was on to him.

It took all of his control to not grab Gerri, smash a window, and jump out of it with her in his arms. He wanted her out of the building now. There was no telling when Horton planned to grab her, or how.

He stormed into the bedroom, wanting to stay close to her. She had removed her shoes, lying on the bed with her back to him, curled into a ball. He knew she wasn't sleeping though.

He couldn't stretch out next to her. He was too stressed and worried about her safety. He stayed in the doorway, on alert. He had an advantage at that moment. He could protect her for a few hours. Some of the Lycans were hurt from their fight with the Vamps. They probably wouldn't go on a rampage or listen to Horton until their alpha was either dead or recovered enough to give them orders.

It was best to wait until dawn, when the Vamps were tucked away. Maybe Joel would wake and order his pack to flee the building. That would be perfect, but Wen wasn't counting on rationality from the pack. They probably still needed whatever the hell they were getting out of the deal with Horton too badly to walk away.

He reached up and rubbed the back of his neck. He'd get Gerri to someplace very public and secure, then come back to kill Horton. Once that was done, he'd meet Micah at the airport. They'd be out of the area by noon. He could take Gerri home and stay with her until his scent faded.

It would also mean keeping his damn hands off her for a few weeks. That would be hell, but he wouldn't leave her vulnerable to attacks. Her life meant more to him than his selfish needs. That lesson had been learned. She was in danger because of him.

She's accused him of being willing to sacrifice her life. He wouldn't. No matter what it cost him.

He went over what he'd learned. He knew the Vamps slept in the basement. He'd seen them coming out of there. It made sense. They probably had some kind of escape route. He would if he were a Vamp. A city probably meant sewer tunnels. He'd have to hit hard and fast.

Horton would be able to move during the day. He wasn't sure about the other three in his nest. They'd fought well but the one who'd gone down didn't seem that old. He probably wouldn't be able to fend for himself once the sun was up. That left him dealing with three, plus the Lycans. The Vamps would die first, so Horton didn't have time to escape.

It wasn't going to be easy to get back inside the house without Gerri. The Lycans would be suspicious. He'd faced harder missions though. The most important thing was her safety.

Chapter Eleven

The house was silent when Gerri and Wen descended the stairs. Both of their backpacks remained inside the apartment. They didn't want to alert anyone that Gerri wasn't coming back. One Lycan sat in a chair in the hallway. He rose to his feet, looking a little leery.

"I'm taking my mate to eat. Do you want us to wait until a few of your pack can tag along?" Wen kept his tone calm.

"Go."

Wen kept hold of her hand and led her out the front door. No Lycans were in sight. They didn't talk until they'd made it down the block. "That was weird," she muttered.

"No lookout at the front. Only one guard downstairs and he didn't give us any shit. I wonder if Joel died?"

"You haven't slept at all. You didn't hear anything?"

"I heard movement, doors, but no one was talking loud enough for me to overhear anything. I watched the back window but nobody left that way. There's no view of the front from the apartment they put us in."

"I guess that's good for you if there's only one guard."

"It makes me wonder where the hell the rest of the pack is." He kept glancing around. "But yeah, I need to hit Horton and his nest first. I don't want him escaping."

"He'll be trapped in the basement."

"Doubtful. Most Vamps have escape routes if they're smart."

"He's old enough not to be helpless when the sun is up, right?"

"Definitely. I'd bet at least one of his Vamps has been feeding off him too. He'd want backup if he's ever attacked by the Lycans. The more he lets them drink his blood, the stronger they become."

"Maybe all three of them have been getting master blood."

"Not the one who got so hurt last night that they had to carry him out of the room. He went down too easy. That could have changed though, once we went upstairs. Horton would have seen how weak that nest member was and probably will have wanted to fix that. I would have."

They reached a little cafe and Wen opened the door. "After you."

She ducked under his arm and walked up to the counter. Wen withdrew cash from his wallet. She ordered them two coffees and some breakfast burritos. "Eat first."

He paid the cashier. "I need to make a call. I'm going to duck into the bathroom. Watch the door and take a seat near the glass so you can be easily seen. I wouldn't be surprised if we were tailed."

"Got it." She forced a smile and took a seat at table near the front door. Her gaze traveled along the street. People were out and about but none of them looked as if they could be Lycans. She'd had years of practice watching people, being on alert.

Wen returned to the table within a few minutes. She looked up when he took a seat across from her. "Micah will fly us out right after I'm done. I want you to meet him at the airport. Do you remember the name of it?"

"Yes. That's a long drive if I have to pay a taxi."

He slipped her a wad of bills under the table. "That will cover it."

177

"Okay." She tucked the money in her pocket. "So you're going to go back to the building, then meet us?"

"That's the plan." He held her gaze. "I scouted the back. There's an alarm on the door but I grabbed an employee. I had him to turn it off. I'm going to eat, then go out the front. As soon as I do, you hit the back door. Don't draw attention to yourself by running. Hail a cab as soon as you can. Don't stop for anything, G.L."

She was worried about him. "Got it. Simple."

He studied her. "You won't do some dumbass thing and try to follow me, will you?"

She grinned. "No."

"You thought about it though."

"Guilty. Then I realized I'd only distract you. I'd be shit backup if I needed saving. I promise I'll take off out the back and head toward the airport. You promise me you won't die."

He reached across the table to take her hand. "Not a chance."

One of the employees brought their coffees, and breakfast burritos stuffed with scrambled eggs, bacon, and hash browns. Gerri didn't have much of an appetite but she managed to eat one.

Wen downed all four she'd ordered for him. "I need to go."

"Please be careful. I'm not saying goodbye to you yet. You promised to stay with me until your scent is gone."

"I always keep my word. You be careful."

"I got the easy part. I wish I had my phone. I'm going to be worried about you."

178

"I'll be about an hour or less behind you. Micah will be waiting at the airport." He stood. "Ready?"

She got up and rounded the small table, grabbing hold of the front of his shirt. He stared down at her.

"Don't die," she whispered. "A kiss for luck?"

His mouth twisted upward. "I'm not going to need it but I won't turn down a kiss from you."

She went up on tiptoes as he lowered toward her. His lips brushed hers gently. She wanted to deepen the kiss but he pulled away.

"It's time, G.L. Be careful. Now move that lush ass of yours and no looking back."

"Same to you." She let him go with regret. The words "I love you" caught in her throat but she swallowed them down.

He turned away, pushed open the door, and strode back in the direction they'd come.

She spun, walking toward the back of the cafe. The exit sign was near the bathroom. She pushed the door open and ended up in an alley. She turned in the opposite direction Wen had gone and strolled away. A few bums were sleeping but no one stopped her. She hit the street and saw a kid sitting at a bus stop texting on his phone. She went right up to him and pulled a twenty dollar bill out of her pocket.

"Hey."

He lifted his head, glancing at her, then the money.

"I need to make a call. I'll be real fast and it's local. I lost my cell phone. Can I borrow yours for one minute?"

He hesitated then handed it over. She slipped him the money and dialed Micah.

He answered on the first ring. "Who is this?"

"Gerri. Wen is going in alone. He needs backup. Do you have the address of where we were?"

"Give it to me."

She rattled it off. "Help him. I'm on my way to the airport."

"Will do. He's not going to be happy about this."

"I don't care. He wouldn't let me go with him and I hate the idea of him being alone. Is your brother still around?"

"He is. Both of us will go."

"Be careful. Two dozen furs and four others. Got it?"

Micah chuckled. "Someone can hear you?"

"I borrowed the phone. Got to go. I see a taxi. Be careful and don't let anything happen to him."

"We'll do our best."

She ended the call and passed the cell back to the kid. "Thanks."

"That was the easiest twenty bucks I ever made."

She walked over to the street and waved to the taxi oncoming. It pulled over and she slipped into the back. "I hope you've got some time, because I need a ride to the airport." She gave him the name, so he wouldn't assume she was going somewhere local.

The guy gaped at her. "You know that's a private airport, right? It's not a regular one."

"I know."

The driver faced forward. "Okay. I want a hundred up front."

She pulled out the money, hiding the large stash from him, and offered up two hundred. "I'm not going to screw you over by running up a tab I can't pay. Just get me to the airport."

He glanced at the bills, then her. "Okay."

She turned in the seat, glancing back at traffic. It was possible someone might try to follow if the Lycans had been watching them. It was her job to make sure that didn't happen. Her mind went to Wen.

Please be okay. Please come back to me.

* * * * *

Wen entered the house, his face a mask of fury. The Lycan leapt up from his chair in the hallway. "Where's the woman?"

"We got into a goddamn fight. Do you have a mate? They can be infuriating! The fact that she's human makes it ten times worse. Your little fight last night upset her and now she doesn't feel safe here. I protected her, didn't I? Yes, I did!"

The Lycan gawked at his rant, then recovered. "You need to find her. She knows about us."

"She's having one of those girly iced coffees and donuts down the street, told me to give her space. I'm picking her up in ten minutes. Space? What the fuck is that about?" He paced, as if agitated. "She's my mate. There's no such thing as *space*."

"You need to get her *now*."

181

Wen spun, walking closer. "I know. Mates can drive you crazy."

He threw a sucker punch, surprising the Lycan.

His fist made contact with the guy's nose, snapping his head back. Wen moved fast, caught him, and snapped his neck. Then he carried the body to Horton's office and dropped it there. He closed the door, then moved quickly while the coast was still clear to the basement door.

It was locked. He withdrew his hunting knife from his ankle holster, wedged the blade between the door and frame, and popped the cheap lock. He eased the door open. The scent of Vamp filled his nose. They were definitely sleeping down there. Fresh blood hit his nose too. He grimaced, silently entered the stairwell, and eased the door closed behind him. He made sure it remained locked, his eyes adjusting to the dimness.

He inched down the stairwell into the finished basement.

The sight of eight bodies shocked him. They'd been callously dumped on the floor. He only picked up a few heartbeats, and they were faint. He silently mouthed a curse. He hadn't expected victims. He walked closer and crouched beside the one nearest him.

There was blood around the man's mouth. Wen leaned in and sniffed.

Dread hit hard as he glanced at the others. He could see some of their faces. They had blood around their lips too. Vamp blood.

Fucking Horton had turned them.

Another heartbeat suddenly joined the others. They were turning from dead to undead.

Wen sheathed his knife to free his hand. He touched the one next to him, using his finger and thumb to open the eyelid. Rage hit next as he stared into the bloodshot eyeball of the unconscious victim. Not a Vamp. It was going to wake up a soldier. He was certain of it. The proof was in the eyes, and the fact that he had died before turning.

Just to be sure though, he released the eyelid and leaned in closer to study the man's complexion. He saw the beginnings of very faint, darkening veins under the skin, but the victim still smelled human. That fight last night must have made Horton worry about the Lycans outnumbering his nest.

It was a fucked-up situation, but Wen knew what he had to do. He rose up, ignoring the still bodies. They wouldn't be dangerous until the sun went down and they were done turning. He had more pressing matters to deal with first.

He walked down a small hallway, paused near a closed door and frowned. It was a security door with at least four locks. He moved to the next room and eased that standard door open. It was a storage space with some furniture inside, no scent of Vamp there. Next, he went to the room across from it. It contained cleaning supplies, some paint, and other things that were probably used to maintain the building.

He returned to the furniture storage and glanced around, found metal bed frame rails, and lifted two of them. He tested their strength by trying to bend them. They held. He kept very quiet, entered the hallway, and studied the enforced safety door. He set the rails on the floor and returned the maintenance storage room. There was no rope but he found cables. They'd work. He returned to the hallway and tied them tight around the railing, then pushed the railing against the walls across the door, pressing his body up against them to keep them from falling. He attached the cords to the doors that opened inward.

The Vamps might try to open the door from the inside but they'd have difficulty. He backed away, eyeing his handiwork. The rails would work as a reverse brace. The door wouldn't open more than about four inches before the rails slammed against it. He grinned, then entered the room with furniture that was right next to the Vamps'.

He eyed the drywall, glad it wasn't brick. He took some deep breaths, rolled his shoulders, and then bent, retrieving his hunting knife. He withdrew another one from his boot, rose up, and surged forward.

He hit the wall hard, using his shoulder and tucking his head, going straight through the cheaply constructed barrier.

All four Vamps were there. They had set up two bunk beds. Horton woke and rolled out of a top bunk. He hissed as he landed on his feet, looking confused as Wen shook off debris from the wall and insulation.

"What the hell are you doing?"

Two of the Vamps stirred but they were more sluggish. The fourth didn't move at all. It was a mistake that Horton hadn't made him stronger after he'd survived the Lycan fight. Then again, Wen wasn't surprised. He didn't think much of the bastard.

"What do you think? You want to turn my mate into a soldier. Fuck you!"

Wen lunged, going for the closest Vamp, who'd managed to get to his feet. Wen took his head off with his blades and dust filled the room.

184

He went after Horton next.

The master hissed and leapt, jumping back onto his bunk. Wen knew he'd try to dive over him to get to the wall he'd broken through, or attempt to reach the grate he saw on the floor under one of the beds. That was probably the escape route out of the building. He couldn't let it happen.

He shoved one of his knives into the heart of the second Vamp to free his hand, grabbed the guy by the throat, and threw him at Horton.

Using his superior speed and strength to reach them quickly, Wen tossed the Vamp aside and grabbed Horton. He punched out with his second knife, the blade sinking into Horton's neck.

The master screamed, the sound coming out more of a gurgling noise.

The injured Vamp leapt on Wen's back but he ignored it, keeping hold of Horton as he gripped the handle of the blade and violently twisted.

He felt fangs sink into his shoulder, the bastard on his back trying to weaken him. But he refused to let go of the master.

Horton stared at him with horrified eyes for a precious second—and then it was over. His head came off and he burst into ash.

Wen stabbed the Vamp behind him in the head, reached back to fist him by his hair, and ripped him off him. He threw the bastard on the floor, trying to use his boot to stomp him in the ribs, but his foot slipped in all the blood coating the guy's upper body from the stab he'd taken to the chest earlier.

The room spun but Wen ignored the dizzy moment, fell on the Vamp, and yanked his knife free. He hacked at his neck, removing his head. The body under him disappeared into ash.

Wen sat there on his knees, slowing his breaths before reaching up, feeling the rip in his shirt. It was soaked.

He turned his head, angling it enough to see how much damage had been done. The bastard had torn him open with his fangs. It would heal, but he'd bled a lot. He stayed down for a few more moments, taking deep breaths. He finally rose, reached the sleeping Vamp, and ended him with the flash of his blade.

He picked up his other blade, wiggled through the hole in the wall, and left the furniture storage room. The master and his Vamps had been taken care of. Now he just had to deal with the soldiers.

More heartbeats sounded now. The dead were coming back to life. They couldn't be saved, it was too late for them, and they wouldn't turn to ash if he removed their heads. He'd have to kill them and destroy the bodies with fire.

Guilt hit but he pushed it back. Their fates had been sealed the moment Horton had forced his blood into them, then killed them. He couldn't allow a bunch of bloodthirsty savages to be let loose on a city.

Noise sounded above his head and he tensed. It was a miracle the Lycans hadn't already come downstairs. They had to have heard the fight that had taken place in the other room. He sheathed his knives, no longer needing silence.

He unleashed his claws and waited. It didn't take long. The door above burst open with the sound of wood cracking. Footsteps thundered down the stairs. Joel was the first one to arrive.

"It's over," Wen told him. "Horton is dead. Just walk way."

More Lycans filled the room behind Joel. The alpha held up his hand, glaring at Wen. "What did you do?"

"Look at the bodies on the floor. Do you know what they are?"

"Dying humans." Joel glanced at them, curling his lip. "The Vamps feed off them."

"Wrong. Your little fight with Horton last night must have made him uneasy. These *were* humans, but by sundown they'll become soldiers. Think super-tough Vamps with bloodlust unlike anything you've ever seen. They'll recover faster than a normal Vamp and grow more insane every time they're injured. He brought them into this building to use against you. And they would have turned your pack into food. Understand? I did you a favor."

"Horton was going to make us rich."

"You're an idiot if you believed anything that Vampire told you, Joel. He was using you until you weren't needed anymore. Then he would have slaughtered your pack with these things on the floor. Did you hear him last night, ordering me to fight your pack? Notice how I didn't? My beef isn't with you."

More Lycans eased into the room. Wen kept track. There were nineteen of them. He was greatly outnumbered and damn sorry he hadn't brought his guns to the fight. He would have, but he'd had to get Gerri to safety, and the risk of humans on the street noticing he wore weapons

187

would have drawn attention. And he hadn't had the opportunity to return upstairs to grab his backpack.

Joel snarled, hair growing along his body. "Fine. We'll ransom you for the reward money."

"I hate to break it to you, but I cut my own deal with the VampLycans who were hunting me. I called my old clan after that fight last night. They wanted Horton dead. He pissed them off even more than I did. The bounty is gone. You won't get a fucking cent for me." Wen wasn't about to admit there hadn't been a real bounty. "It's over."

"You cost us a lot of fucking money, VampLycan," Joel snarled. "You're going to die for that!"

They attacked in pack formation. Wen tensed, knowing he'd have to fight his way to the stairs they currently blocked. It would help if he could bottleneck them there, take on fewer at a time. He'd have to reach the stairwell first though.

At least the dead humans weren't a threat until the sun went down and they awoke soldiers.

Six Lycans hit him at once, pain shooting up his arms from their claws, and Joel tried to go for his throat. Wen slashed out, his knife making the alpha scream in agony.

The Lycans began shifting, growing fur, and pushing against each other to get to him. He staggered back, throwing them off and dropping his weapon in order to free his claws. Then he tripped on a damn soldier body and went down.

Fangs tore into various body parts and he roared, twisting to protect his belly, then shoved up from the floor. He got to his feet and fought hard. It was tempting to shift but he was just as lethal half-shifted. It also made it harder for them to do as much damage with his clothes on.

He fought on, killing any Lycan that got close enough. At one point a wolf leapt at him. Too late, he tried to duck—but the Were sailed over his head, clearly on purpose, slamming into another Lycan that had been sneaking up from behind.

Wen identified the markings on the fur and laughed. Graves had come.

He spotted another familiar furry body by the stairwell, tearing out a Lycan's throat. Micah was there too.

He was going to survive after all.

Wen felt dizzy and almost dropped to his knees as another set of fangs sank into his arm. He threw the bastard, smashing him against a wall. His claws plunged through the Lycan's throat as he held it there. The enemy died fast.

He let the body fall, snarling as two more of the pack attacked.

Chapter Twelve

Gerri was worried as she sat on a bench outside the private airport. A guard inside had started circling her, so she'd left the interior to wait where she could see the parking lot. Once in a while she'd go inside to use the bathroom and glance at a clock on the wall. Wen and Micah should have shown up over three hours ago.

Something is really wrong. The thought kept repeating in her mind.

She'd called Micah's number a dozen times from the payphone but it had gone straight to voicemail. He couldn't exactly call her back since he had her cell. She regretted handing it over to him, along with her license. What if they never showed? She only had about a hundred and sixty dollars left out of the wad of money Wen had given her. She'd be stranded in Washington with no one to call for help.

A black classic muscle car pulled into the lot and parked. Gerri watched as a big man climbed out and she was on her feet in a heartbeat. It was Micah. She rushed toward him, her gaze darting from him to the passenger side. Wen didn't get out. Micah walked to the front of the car and waited for her. She realized he was alone as she got closer to the car.

"Where is he? Is he okay?"

Micah gripped her arms, his expression grim. "Wen got hurt but he's healing."

"Oh God." She'd known it in her gut. "How bad?"

"The pack tore him up quite a bit before we got there but I swear he'll be fine."

"Where's your SUV? Is he driving it?" She stepped to the right, staring at the entrance to the parking lot.

Micah pulled her back and leaned down a little, holding her gaze. "He's healing. Graves is tending to him while he's down for the next few days."

She closed her eyes, fighting the urge to be sick. VampLycans were fast healers, so his injuries had to have almost killed him if Micah's brother had to take care of Wen. It meant he was in really bad shape.

"Gerri? Look at me."

She opened her eyes.

"Wen is going to be fine. I wouldn't lie to you."

"Take me to him."

His hold on her tightened. "He ordered me to fly you home and stay with you until he's able to join us. I'm going to protect you while you're carrying his scent."

"No. Take me to Wen."

"It got messy, Gerri. Do you understand? Wen wants you where you'll be safe. That's home and far from here. The police might be looking for you at some point if they interview any of the neighbors around the nest building. You and Wen were seen in that neighborhood."

"What happened?"

"Wen took out Horton and his little nest but the bastard had made soldiers. They were still turning but hadn't changed completely yet. The rogue pack was pretty pissed and decided to try to tear apart my cousin. It was a bloodbath. Do you know what it means when you kill newly made soldiers?"

She shook her head.

"Freshly made ones leave bodies behind. Plus we killed the pack, and they don't ash either. There was no way to remove all of the dead in a populated area without someone noticing, not to mention the blood would have remained. It meant taking down the building to destroy the evidence."

She stared up at him, stunned.

"We had to set the building on fire, then make it explode," he explained. "That drew human attention. I'm sure by now the cops are interviewing people to try to figure out what the hell happened. You could have been seen, understand? The cops might want to talk to you."

"Shit." He was right.

"There was no choice. My brother is an expert at that kind of thing. Nothing will remain that the humans will be able to make sense of, if they even bother to dig out that basement. He made sure it was hot enough to obliterate anything down there. Our kind don't burn the same as humans do. It's something to do with our blood. We're pretty sure it's the same with the soldiers. They all had heartbeats by the time Graves had rigged everything."

"Heartbeats?"

"Don't ask." Micah looked around. "I need to go inside, file a flight plan, and get us the hell out of Washington. Right now, the police will hopefully believe the explosion was caused by a gas leak. Graves made a 9-1-1 call from inside the building right before it blew, saying he smelled gas. The farther you are from here, the better, in case they think it was arson."

"Do you think I'll get blamed?"

"No. You were here before that building went. You've been inside, right? These places have cameras."

"Yes, until one of the guards kept staring at me. Other people were here to meet pilots or owned planes. I just sat inside, worrying about when you and Wen would get here. I think I was making him nervous so I came outside."

"Then you have an alibi. Now let's make sure it's a good one. I'm sorry I'm late. I'll say I got a flat tire if anyone asks." He released her. "Your bag is in the trunk. Let me grab it and mine. Travelers have luggage."

She followed him to the back of the car, where he retrieved her backpack and his duffle. "Rental?"

"My brother's. He kept the SUV. The backseat is soaked in Wen's blood. I'll report it stolen in the morning. It will be found sometime tomorrow, a burned-out shell. That will give Graves time to torch it tonight."

Her stomach was tied up in knots. "How bad is Wen? Be honest."

"We got there and heard the fighting in the basement. The pack was all going at him. Lots of bites, but he's got all his fingers and toes."

That didn't make her feel any better.

Micah led her inside the building. "I'm your boyfriend."

"Are you still Fred Tobis?"

"Yes. Just don't talk unless you have to. Draw as little attention as possible. We don't have Wen with us this time to flash his bright blues to erase memories."

"Got it."

Micah pointed to a set of chairs. "Take a seat. I have to go deal with the paperwork. Use the bathroom while I'm gone too. I'm hoping I get us in the air within half an hour."

"Can I call Wen?"

He frowned. "He's probably sleeping, Gerri. It's the best thing for him while he's healing."

"I'll feel better if I can hear his voice. Please?"

He hesitated, then fished out his phone from his back pocket. "Only use this phone, never your own. Speaking of, I put yours in your backpack. Don't copy his number down for later. We're using VampLycan-owned cells, and they scramble the numbers in case one is ever taken by an enemy. They show up as caller unknown with no info. You call him from your phone, and everyone who has access to your records will have his number. Not to mention, *your* number will show up on *his* phone, probably your name too, and his clan will be able to track your cell. That would be very bad, considering I know damn well Wen doesn't want his parents to find out he's been with you."

"I get it."

He looked down at his phone, using his thumb to touch the face. "Keep it short. He needs to heal." He handed it over. "Hit connect when you're ready. I'll give you privacy. I should be back soon."

194

She took the phone, her heart pounding, and watched Micah walk up to a counter, talking to the woman behind it. Gerri took a seat and pressed her thumb down. She lifted the phone, putting it to her ear. Seconds passed and then it rang. She closed her eyes as it rang again, then again.

"Please pick up and be okay," she whispered.

Five rings later and it clicked. "Hello?" It was a woman's voice.

Her eyes flew open. "I'm sorry. I must have the wrong number."

"You don't. This is Stellia, correct?"

Gerri was taken aback. That was the clan healer's name.

"Trayis said you might call," the woman rushed on. "I apologize for answering Wen's phone but he's in the shower. I heard his phone ringing in his pants so I answered it. He's feeling a lot better since he drank some of my blood."

Gerri finally managed to speak again. "Who is this?"

"Trayis didn't tell you my name? Well, he did say you were out hunting and he'd have to send someone to get you when I spoke to him earlier. You probably didn't get many details. I'm Sherry. I work for your clan, and I'm the one Wen bit so he could heal faster. Tell Trayis he was right. My blood worked. I ordered Wen and I room service. I admit I'm a little lightheaded, but Graves pulled him off me before he took too much blood. I figured we both could use some food."

"I want to speak to Wen." Sherry was with him? He'd *bitten* her? What the hell was going on? Anger and pure jealousy hit hard.

"Sure. Hey, babe..."

"What?" Wen's voice could be heard faintly in the background.

"Your doctor is on the phone and she wants to speak to you."

"Tell Stellia I'll call her back."

Gerri lowered the phone and disconnected it. Her chest hurt. Sherry had called him "babe" and he'd answered to it, as if it were normal. It was blatantly obvious they were sharing a room if she could talk to him while he showered. Hot tears burned her eyes but she blinked them back.

Time passed slowly, and finally Micah came back from where he'd disappeared with the airport worker.

"We're all set. Ready to go home?"

She managed to stand. "Yes."

Micah stopped in front of her, studying her face. "Are you okay? You look really pale."

Wen had finished his mission and he didn't need her anymore. He was with Sherry. "I think I'm going to be sick."

She spun, darting toward the ladies' room, barely making it to a stall before she threw up the breakfast burrito she'd had with Wen earlier that morning.

* * * * *

Wen felt better. Blood wasn't stuck to his skin or matting his hair anymore. He walked out of the bathroom and flinched when he caught sight of Sherry. She sat on the edge of the bed, gripping his cell with both hands, looking ready to faint.

"I told you to stay flat." He crossed the room, taking the phone from her with one hand, gently pushing her onto her back with his other. Guilt came next. He'd done that to her. His gaze went to her bandaged arm, glad it was covered. He couldn't remember biting her. Everything had been a blur, from the time the fight ended to waking up in the SUV with Graves and Sherry.

"Good idea." She chuckled. "I hope the food comes soon. I usually get a cookie and some orange juice when I donate blood at the annual hospital drive, but this is worse. I think I need a cake and an entire orange tree."

"It's not funny. I could have killed you. What in the fuck was Graves thinking? Why the hell are you even here?"

She cracked her eyes open, her smile fading. "You sound mad."

"I am. I don't even remember taking blood from you."

"You wouldn't because you were unconscious. Your fangs were out though. You looked like you were dying. Jesus, Wen. I was so terrified I called Trayis, and he said you needed blood. Graves was going to give you his but I volunteered. It made sense. Blood loss was the last thing he needed, since he'd just told me about all the bodies he had to burn. I sure as hell couldn't do that job for him while he recovered. He scratched my arm and I put it in front of your mouth. You latched right onto me."

Wen crouched next to the bed, careful to grip the towel around his waist so he didn't lose it. "That doesn't answer why you're here."

"Trayis asked me to come. We didn't know until I got here yesterday that your cousins were around in case you needed help."

"Why would he send *you*?"

"In case you got arrested or something, I guess. I don't ask Trayis why. He says go, I go. I might handle business law, but I know how to bail someone out. You know that. Imagine my surprise, though, when I ran into Micah at the bar last night. What are the chances of us staying at the same place?"

"You always pick a five-star hotels when you travel. So does my cousin. This is the closest one to where I was undercover."

"True." She smiled again. "Why don't you lie down with me? That would make me feel better." She patted the bed. "You could distract me with amazing sex until room service comes with our order."

Wen rose up and backed away. "I could have killed you, Sherry. Did Trayis mention that? You *never* bleed for an injured one of my kind. I'm half Vampire and have no control of how much I drink in that condition."

"Graves pulled you off my arm when he said you'd taken enough. You were fucking bleeding from like thirty places. What was I supposed to do? Let you die? What's wrong with you?" She tried to sit up but then lay back down. "Shit. The room is spinning."

"Of course it is. I took too much blood. Goddamn it." He reached up and shoved his wet hair back from his face. "I should take you to a hospital. You probably need blood now."

"You could give me some of yours."

He backed up until he hit the wall. "No!"

She flinched. "Why are you snarling at me?"

"We can't ever exchange blood. *Never,* Sherry."

198

"Oh, that's right. It's how you VampLycans mate, isn't it? Would that really be so bad?"

"I don't feel that way about you."

"We're good together, Wen. Don't we have a lot of fun? I wouldn't mind spending all my time with you. I can't say I'm a big fan of Alaska; it sounds like a godforsaken kind of barbaric hell, between the winters and all those animals I've heard about. But I'd deal with it to be with you. That's saying a lot."

"It was just sex. You know that."

"It could be a lot more."

He shook his head. "It's over, Sherry. I'm sorry."

"What in the hell do you mean by that?"

The door beeped and then opened, admitting Graves. He stepped inside and smiled at Wen. "You look a lot better."

"Thanks for your help, but why are you even here?"

"You mean because you didn't ask for my help? You should have. Micah asked me to come."

Wen frowned.

"It was getting boring in Colorado." Graves crossed the room. "How you doing, legs? Feeling better?"

"Wen is being an asshole. I saved his life but he's acting as though I cunt-punched his mother."

Graves arched his eyebrows, glancing between them.

Wen sighed. "You shouldn't have let me feed off her."

199

"You had more blood *outside* your body than left inside by the time the fighting was done. I had to carry you out to the SUV—which was a bitch, by the way. Broad daylight. I wrapped you in a blanket and stuffed your body into one of those plastic garbage cans with wheels, then rolled you out of the building. You don't fit well inside one, either."

"Then what happened?" Wen asked, curious.

"I got you to the SUV we'd parked in the alley next to the building. Micah stayed behind to guard the building. Sherry flipped when she unwrapped you to see how bad you were, then called your clan leader. He said to give you blood. I would have done it, but we had a basement full of corpses to deal with. I shoved her arm against your fangs, you did your Vampy auto-drinking thing, and when she almost passed out, I yanked her away. At that point, you woke up enough to growl at us. I bandaged her up, and she babysat you while I went back into the building."

"Where's Micah?"

"You told me to tell him to leave. You were demanding he fly G.L. to Nevada immediately, so he took off to do that. Who the hell is G.L.?"

Wen softly cursed. "Fuck. You'd know her as Gerri or Geraldine. Micah didn't tell you she was with me?"

"No." Graves frowned. "He didn't tell me much at all."

In all the confusion after Wen had woken, he'd figured she was still waiting at the airport. He needed to speak to Micah. He was stunned at the amount of time that had passed when he saw the hour displayed on the phone screen. The call went to voicemail.

"Call me." He hung up.

"Who's woman you two are talking about?" Sherry sat up.

He ignored her, focusing on Graves. "How did I get into the hotel? I can't remember."

"Sherry stayed with you in the SUV. Micah had taken off to pick up my car, to do what you'd told him. I set fire to the house your Vamp had been playing in, so the humans wouldn't find a body dump. I made it go boom." Graves chuckled. "Big boom."

"The hotel," Wen prodded.

"We dumped a shitload of water on you after stripping you out of your clothes, since you'd stopped bleeding. I had grabbed your bag Micah had found inside the building before he left and took it to the SUV. We dressed you, shoved a baseball cap I found on your head to cover that mess, and you stumbled next to me. You don't remember that?"

"No."

"People thought you were drunk. Graves helped you walk." Sherry was watching him with narrowed eyes. "No one gave either of you any shit. You're both muscled as hell, so they probably thought you'd get into a brawl."

"I laid you on the floor in the bathroom so we wouldn't have to explain bloodstains to the maid later, and then I went to buy you some more clothes." He wrinkled his nose. "All yours were dirty in that bag. The new stuff is in the room next door. I wasn't sure if you were up or not yet, so I dumped the bags in there."

Wen reached up and rubbed the back of his neck. He glanced at his phone. "How long ago did Micah leave?"

"Hours ago."

It meant he'd had time to get to Gerri at the airport and board his plane. They were probably in the air. "Fuck."

"Who is G.L.?" Sherry sounded more agitated.

Wen dropped his hand from his neck and glanced at Graves. "Can you get me those clothes, please?"

"Sure. I'll be back in minute."

"Make it five. Sherry and I need to have a talk."

"Okay." Graves left.

Wen waited for the door to close before he held her gaze. "Remember how I told you one day I'd find a woman and realize she was my mate?"

Sherry tensed. "Don't say it."

"You asked. I answered. That's why it's over between us."

She licked her lips, then frowned. "Why did you send her to Nevada?"

"Because I was out of my head. I don't even remember doing that."

"She's a Lycan? Isn't Trayis going to have a problem when you bring some rogue home with you that you met during this mission?"

"She's not a rogue."

"Bullshit, if she was hanging out with those assholes who almost killed you."

"She's not one of them. I can't mate her because she's human. My parents would kill her."

202

Sherry looked relieved.

That pissed him off. "It's over between you and I, Sherry. She found out about you and it hurt her. I swore to her that I'd never touch you like that again."

"And you always keep your fucking word, don't you, babe?"

"Yes."

"Just like that, huh? We've been seeing each other for years. You go home but you always come back to me."

"You'll travel with Graves or Micah for clan business from now on. I'll send another VampLycan if one is needed. It just won't be me."

"Over a woman you say you can't even be with?"

He hesitated. She would probably rant to Trayis, repeat what he'd said, but he and the clan leader were friends. Trayis wouldn't tell his parents about Gerri, especially after he talked to him. And he planned to do that today. "I can't mate her. I didn't say I won't see her and spend time with her every chance I get."

"In other words, I've been replaced. Is she younger than me?"

"You and I weren't committed, Sherry. It was no secret I had other lovers. So have you."

"Fine. See both of us. I've shared you with other women before. We'll just keep doing that."

"No. There's only one woman I want. I might not be able to make her my mate, but she owns my heart. I don't want anyone else."

"You son of a bitch! She *is* younger, isn't she?"

"No." He regretted hurting her. "I have to call Trayis and Stellia now. I'm sorry."

"You've been through a lot and aren't thinking clearly. It was a tough mission. You'll change your mind and want to see me again."

"It's not going to happen."

Chapter Thirteen

Gerri had climbed into the back of the plane during the flight, lying about needing a nap. She just hadn't wanted to talk. Micah would either flat-out lie to her or try to give her some clan bullshit on why Sherry was with Wen if she asked. The attorney did work for the clan, after all. That excuse didn't explain the intimate setting she'd pieced together from that phone call.

At least Wen hadn't totally screwed her over by sending her home unprotected. As long as she stuck close to Micah, he could fight off anything nonhuman who got a whiff of her. Of course, they'd be in trouble if an entire pack or nest came after her. He was just one Lycan.

Micah secured the plane and got their bags out. "I have to fill out paperwork and then we'll head to your place. I hope you have a comfortable couch, since I'll be staying with you until Wen gets here."

She nodded.

"Are you okay? I swear Wen will be fine. I've seen him recover from far worse. Hell, six years ago he took four slugs to the chest."

That didn't help. She might be hurt and angry, but the thought of someone shooting Wen didn't sit well with her. He might deserve a punch to the balls though. "I just want to get to my place and eat something."

"I know I'm not the man you want here, but Wen will come as soon as he can." He locked the storage compartment and pocketed the key, then pulled out his phone to glance at the screen. "Wen called."

Her heart hammered. "Call him back once we're out of here."

He frowned but shoved his phone back into his pocket. "I thought you wanted to talk to him."

"I do. I just want food first."

"I forgot." He assessed her.

"That I'm human?"

He nodded.

She usually would have been insulted but this time she used it to her advantage. All nonhumans were arrogant. "I'm not as sturdy as you are. Guilty. I'm still exhausted. I feel like ten miles of bad road. I'll be back to my normal self after I eat and get more sleep."

He led her inside the small airport through a door and jerked his head toward the public waiting area. "Use the bathroom. This won't take long." He passed her backpack over.

"I'll be waiting. Just do what you've got to do so we can leave."

He turned and strode toward one of the employees. It left her alone with her thoughts. Would Wen actually come see her or did he plan on making Micah be her protector until his scent faded? Only time would tell. He'd either show or he wouldn't.

She had no idea what to say to him. Maybe yell because she was hurt over what she'd learned with that phone call...or should she just let it go? He couldn't mate her. That was one fact she did know for sure. He'd have to return to Alaska without her either way.

At least he couldn't mate Sherry either. She was human. It was petty, she admitted that, but it eased some of the pain of Wen being with the

206

other woman at the moment. He was also injured, so she doubted he was in any condition to have sex.

Loud voices drew her attention and she turned her head, watching four large men walk into the airport together. They were having an animated conversation, one of them laughing, as they each pulled black wheeled suitcases behind them.

She dismissed them and dropped her head, debating on if she should just get it over with when Micah came back by asking him to call Wen. He obviously wasn't in the shower anymore. The flight had taken hours. Whatever he had to say about allowing Sherry to stay with him while he'd sent her away, he owed her an explanation. She wanted to hear it.

"What do we have here?"

Gerri startled and lifted her head, staring up at the four men. They had changed direction and approached her without her noticing. She glanced at each face. They weren't bad-looking guys, ranging from their mid-twenties to maybe late thirties. One of them released the handle of his suitcase and dropped into the seat next to hers. He leaned in, putting his arm around her. Her body went rigid as she turned her head, holding his gaze. They were brown with amber highlights. She was pretty sure he wasn't fully human.

His nostrils flared. "Hello, sweetheart. Don't make a scene." His hand on her side dug in and she felt four sharp tips. *Claws.* He could rip her open if he wanted to. The silent threat was there.

She glanced around, searching for cameras, but the bulky bodies standing in front her blocked most of her view.

"No one can see," the man pressed up against her said. "What's your name?"

Options filled her head on how to get out of the mess she was in. The sun was still in the sky, so they had to be Lycans. Fur bats wouldn't need an airport. They'd just wait until dark and fly anywhere they wanted to go. They'd smelled Wen and come after her. She studied their clothes. They dressed nice, with expensive shoes, and those suitcases weren't cheap. All those clues hinted that they weren't rogues. They more than likely belonged to an established pack, probably a local one.

"I asked you your name." He allowed his sharp-tipped fingers to rub her shirt. It didn't hurt but she was aware of each claw. He sniffed at her again, then scowled.

She could stall them until Micah came out and saw the dilemma she was in. It was a public place though. Witnesses would see them fight. That was a big no-no. *It's a public place.* She licked her lips and held his gaze.

"I bet there are security cameras in here. Everyone has cell phones now and they love to take videos to upload to the internet when they see drama." She paused. "I don't want to cause a scene, but it will be an epic one if you don't let me go."

He growled low, not happy.

"Screaming, tears, shrieking. All of the above. Count on it. I've got a set of lungs on me, despite my size. Understand? Get out of my face."

He straightened, his arm sliding along her back. His claws lightly raked her but he didn't cut her shirt. He leaned back a little, eyes narrowing, as he stopped invading her personal space.

"Thank you." He seemed in charge. That meant he was the highest-ranking one out of the four. "Now go wherever you were heading before you came over here. I don't want trouble. Neither do you. Let's pretend we never crossed paths. That's easy, right?"

"Who the fuck are you?"

One of the other men sniffed loudly. "I want to know what the fuck that is."

She glanced at the one who spoke, then back at the man next to her. It sank in that they couldn't identify the scent that had drawn them to her. At least the one standing couldn't. "I'm someone you don't want to mess with. I'm having a bad day. I am so not in the mood to find out what you want with me. Just walk away."

The leader's nose flared. "You're very brave for someone alone."

"Who says it will stay that way?"

He glanced around, and so did the three men with him. She took the opportunity to do the same. Micah was still out of sight. That was probably for the best. He might not keep his cool. She was trying to.

The Lycan beside her held her gaze again. "I think you ran away from someone. We won't hurt you, but you *will* tell me who you belong to."

"*What* you belong to," the blond man standing muttered.

She kept staring at the one sitting next to her. "I belong to no one, I didn't run away, and none of this is your business. I can appreciate what you're trying to do but it's not necessary. I'm no danger to you or yours. I just want you to leave me alone."

"Ballsy," the blond snorted.

She glanced up at the man. He seemed to be the outspoken one in the group. "You have no idea. Do yourselves a favor. Walk away." She returned her gaze to the one in charge. "Four men surrounding one woman looks creepy as shit to my kind, if you need an FYI. Humans will think you're sexual predators or something. I won't have to cause a scene if you stay much longer. Your presence will do that."

"I want you to stand up and follow me out to my car. We're going to have a private conversation."

"That's so not going to happen. I'm in no mood to be kidnapped. Thanks but pass. I wasn't kidding about the epic screaming fit I'll throw."

"You're bluffing."

"I'm not. You try to force me out of here and you'll be starring in a trending video on the internet." She hesitated, assessing him. "Neither one of us wants that. I've known about other races my entire life and have kept them secret. Do you understand? This bullshit isn't necessary."

His mouth pressed into a tight line. "Known what?"

He was going to play dumb now? She wanted to roll her eyes but refrained. Lycans could be prissy. "Do you even know what you're smelling on me?"

He frowned but she saw uncertainty in his eyes.

"Maybe you haven't smelled one before. I'll help you out. VampLycan," she whispered. "He's an enforcer. You so don't want to fuck with me, because he would make you wish for death—and he'd grant it. I'm not a runaway, up for grabs, or a fugitive. I grew up with him and we're lovers. He had to do something for his clan but he's going to be back with me soon. That's why I'm alone. He trusts me. You should too. Is everything clear now?"

The guy had paled as she'd talked. He swallowed hard and rose to his feet. "Yes."

"Fantastic. Are we good?"

He gripped his suitcase handle. "Yes."

She glanced at the three Lycans with him. They looked fearful too. Sometimes the truth was the best way to deal with a situation. "Have a great day." She waved.

They took off, striding fast away from her. A few minutes later, she spotted Micah. He walked directly to her. "We need to leave right now."

"You ran into the friendly foursome?" She grabbed her backpack and stood.

He gaped at her.

"It's okay. They stopped to have a chat with me. I dealt with it."

"Are you okay?" He lowered his gaze down her body.

"I'm fine. They seemed to think I was a stray they needed to wrangle."

"How did you deal with them?"

"We had a heart-to-heart chat. I pretty much explained that Wen—minus using his name—would rip off their heads and shove them where the sun doesn't shine if they screwed with me."

Micah's eyes widened more. "Are you fucking insane?"

"I was a little more polite than that. I was giving you the condensed version."

He grabbed her arm and hauled her toward the exit doors. "That was Mace Manson."

"Nice name. Who is he?"

"The son of the local alpha, traveling with his security team." He hustled her outside and led her to long-term parking, unlocking a gray sedan. He threw himself into the driver's seat, twisted, and tossed his duffle bag into the back.

She noticed the rental sticker on the bumper as she hurried to the passenger side. It was unlocked so she climbed in, shoving her backpack over the seat to the back too. "Where's the fire? I told you, it's handled. They left me alone."

"Close the fucking door and put your belt on. You threatened the son of an alpha, damn it." He started the engine, craning his neck around, peering everywhere.

She shut the door and put on her belt. "He said we were good."

Micah snarled, throwing the car in reverse. "I was only gone fifteen minutes."

"You're being paranoid. Sometimes honesty is best. Didn't your mother ever teach you that? They aren't going to mess with us."

"I'm not risking it. We're going to your place, packing you some clothes, and then I'm taking you to my pack. Ever been to Colorado? Because you're about to."

"You're overreacting, Micah. They are afraid of VampLycans and I made it clear I'm with one."

"I'd rather be paranoid than stick around to be attacked by a once-friendly pack. We have alliances with some. The Manson pack is one of them. Mace saw me. He knows my scent, and now yours. They might try to track us down since we're near their territory. Wen would have my ass if anything happened to you, Gerri."

She sighed, not in the mood to fight with him. "I've never been to Colorado. Well, at least I can't lose my job since Wen already got me fired."

* * * * *

Wen was furious as he paced the room. "Don't order me to come home right now, Trayis. I told you. I need to protect Gerri until my scent fades from her."

"Are you still in love with her? Are you planning on bringing her home if I allow you time to go get her? Is that your plan? Grab her and return?"

"You know that's not possible."

"Do you still love her, Wen? You obviously must, since you had her with you."

"That's irrelevant. I can't ever mate Gerri. You know why."

"Isn't it time you stood up to your parents?"

"It's not that damn simple, Trayis. You know it. They'd never accept her."

Trayis's voice calmed. "You're not Gerbin. It's not natural for them to treat you as if you are. You've allowed them to dictate your life. It's

213

always been a personal family matter that I haven't stepped into because it hasn't affected your duty to the clan." He paused. "Until now."

"What does that mean?"

"You volunteered for this mission with Gerri in mind, didn't you? It's why you were vague about the details of how you'd convince Horton you were rogue. You planned to talk her into going on this mission with you so you could spend time with her."

Busted. He didn't try to deny it. "I got the job done. Horton is dead, and that rogue pack won't be a problem anymore either."

"You put Gerri at risk and dragged her into VampLycan affairs. Do you have any idea how much bullshit whining I had to deal with when I agreed to allow Carol to leave with her daughter? The elders felt they posed a threat because they knew about us. I couldn't force Carol to stay, and I sure as fuck wasn't going to kill her. Your father suggested that, by the way. He argued they were both threats to our clan and offered to kill them himself."

Wen snarled. He wasn't surprised. His father had never been happy about his feelings for Gerri.

Trayis went on as if hadn't interrupted him with his angry outburst. "I had faith that Carol and Gerri were trustworthy. Not once in the past fifteen years has there been a problem—until now."

"Gerri is no threat to the clan. She'd never betray us to humans."

"I know that," Trayis snapped. "Hell, out of all the clan females I've had to deal with as a leader, she was the best. Little Gerri never played mind games with the boys or caused fights. I worried about her constantly though because she was so fragile and sweet, something other

214

VampLycan children aren't. You fucking walked her into a nest and a rogue pack? What the hell were you thinking? I demand an answer right now."

Wen tried to calm.

"Answer me," Trayis snapped.

"I wanted to spend time with her," Wen admitted.

"You couldn't do that without putting her in danger? You were obviously keeping tabs on her. Couldn't you have just visited her to say hello? Why in the hell would you take her on one of the most dangerous missions I've sent you on? Do I have to spell it out for you what they could have done to her if you'd been killed? Fucking rogues, Wen. They have no honor."

"She wasn't hurt."

"She could have been!"

Wen flinched and jerked the phone farther from his ear when his clan leader yelled. "I wouldn't have allowed that to happen. Why are you yelling at me?"

"Gerri was raised in this damn clan under my protection. I promised Klentz when he brought her here as a baby that I'd do my best to always keep her safe from other VampLycans. I just never imagined I'd have to protect her from *you*. I'm giving you a direct order to come home now, Wen." Trayis paused. "Your ass better be on the next commercial flight out of Washington and on its way to Alaska. Don't make me personally come after you. I will. You are not to call Micah or Gerri. I will contact my brother, ask him to assign Micah as her guard, and make certain she's safe until she can seamlessly blend in with humans again. You don't have her best interests as a priority. I do. Now get your ass home."

Trayis disconnected the call. "Fuck!" Wen was so mad, he crushed the phone in his hand.

Across the room, Graves looked up from his laptop. "He made some good points. You did put a human in danger."

Wen knew his cousin had probably overheard most of the conversation with his Lycan hearing. "I didn't ask for your opinion."

Graves shrugged. "This has not been your best week. You've pissed off your clan leader and the hot lawyer. All over Geraldine. Want to talk about it? I never asked when you had me scoping out her life. I don't like to pry."

"Keep it that way."

Graves went back to typing on his keyboard. "Want me to book you a flight to Anchorage and hire a bush pilot from there to drop you near home?"

"No. I'll do it."

"You just destroyed your phone."

"I'll buy a burner or use the hotel one."

Graves sighed. "I wouldn't fuck with Trayis. You've already filled your quota on stupid lately. He was really pissed. You know my brother will keep this woman safe."

"I told her I'd be the one to stay with her. Not Micah. Stay out of this."

"Not a chance. Trayis just gave you a direct order. You don't want to fuck with him, especially since Arlis is his half-brother. They're tight. You'll get us in some shit with our alpha if you make this a bigger mess. I don't need my ass handed to me by Arlis because you're in a mood. It would fucking suck worse if I'm ordered to tie your ass up and transport you home by force. Don't do that to family."

"What the fuck were you even doing here? I didn't call you."

"I told you, Micah did."

"What did he tell you?"

"To get my ass to Washington because he might need some backup. I didn't need to hear more. I love road trips." Graves turned in his chair to look at him. "So...Geraldine?"

Wen took a seat on the bed. "Gerri. She hates to be called that. Her mom only used that name when she got into trouble."

"She really your mate?"

Wen nodded.

"Why the hell haven't you claimed her?"

"My parents."

"I love my parents, but I wouldn't give a fuck if they didn't approve of whoever I was drawn to. They could deal with it or stew. I'd still have my mate sharing my bed every night, cousin. It's not right to deny that shit. A mate is your priority if you find her."

"Your parents are a lot mellower than mine."

Graves snorted. "Not really, but the difference is that they know what boundaries to never push with us. You let the lines get blurred,

217

Wen. Never get between a man and his mate. You know that family is everything to me. They're my motivation to keep doing what I do for my pack." His eyes bled black, then back to bluish-gray. "I'm dead inside about everything else. It's the price I paid with this position. I have no regrets, but you can bet your ass that if I felt something for a woman that ran deeper than temporary lust, I'd pity anyone who tried to take her away from me. It wouldn't matter who."

A chill ran down Wen's spine. He knew what Graves did for his alpha, and what he was capable of. "Even Micah?"

Graves suddenly smiled. "He'd never be that stupid. And it's not as if I have a chance in hell of ever finding a mate anyway."

"You don't know that for sure."

"I do. You have to have a heart to find love. I lost mine the day our pack was attacked."

Wen stared at his cousin, horrified. "You loved someone who was killed," he guessed.

Graves turned back to his computer. "Go home, Wen. I'll help my brother keep the woman you're too dumb to claim safe."

"It's not like that."

"Right."

Wen snarled. "I'd have to kill my parents if I mated her. What kind of fucking choice is that?"

Graves glanced over. "One *they* forced you to make. It's not your doing, man. Think about that."

"My father is an elder. Trayis couldn't allow that to go down."

218

Graves kept typing. "Our pack could always use you."

"You know I can't leave my clan."

"*Can't* comes out of your mouth a lot, cousin. It's fucking sad."

Wen stormed over, looking at the screen of the laptop. "You're playing fucking bingo and chatting with the other players while giving me life advice?"

Graves shrugged. "At least I'm doing something I have a chance of winning and making friends at the same time. You? Not so much."

Wen snarled.

Chapter Fourteen

Gerri was nervous as they entered the cabin. She stared opened mouthed at the logs along the walls and the huge wooden beams. Micah closed the door with his foot, holding onto her suitcase, his duffle bag, and her backpack slung over his shoulder.

"We're here!"

She shot him a dirty look.

He grinned. "Sorry. You have human hearing. Was that too loud even for you?"

A door jerked open to the right and a tall, bulky man stepped out. He had black hair, dark brown eyes, and she instantly guessed he was probably Micah's father. Their facial features were a lot alike. He wore a red flannel shirt that was rolled up to his elbows, faded jeans, and was barefoot. He studied Gerri with a curious look, then stared at Micah.

"Mandy went to the store and should be back soon." He slid his gaze back to Gerri. "I'm Angelo, Micah's older brother."

"Oh." She wasn't sure about Lycan customs; the pack her mother had hooked up with hadn't been normal. He didn't offer his hand, so she stayed back and just nodded. "I'm Gerri. It's nice to meet you."

"Knock it off, Dad. There's no reason to lie to her. She knows we're Lycans. And take out your nose plugs. You were gluing your model ships again, weren't you? I know that shit stinks. Take a whiff of her."

Angelo stared at her again. He turned his back to them, reached up, and removed the plugs from his nose. He shoved them into his front pocket then turned back, and his nostrils flared as he inhaled.

Gerri smiled. "You could certainly pass for his brother though. It's not necessary to pretend. I know Micah didn't fill you in on any details when he called to tell you he was bringing me home with him. He made the call in the car with me sitting right next to him. I was actually raised in Trayis's clan. I assume you know who that is?"

"Of course." Angelo walked closer. "You're a half-breed? I'm picking up human but also Wen's scent."

"Full human. My mom was mated to a VampLycan. I was almost a year old when they met. He adopted me. As for Wen, that's a longer story."

Angelo shot his son a confused look. "What's going on?"

"We'll go into it more later. We're starving and I'm exhausted. We've been driving since yesterday to get here."

"He wouldn't let me drive," Gerri muttered. "And we didn't make any stops except for gas, food, and potty breaks."

"I have better reflexes than you do." Micah dropped their bags and approached his father, grabbing hold of him.

Gerri felt a little envious as the two men bear-hugged. It was obvious they were a close-knit family. Angelo reached up and fisted some of Micah's hair, smiling as they pulled apart. "Your mom thinks you're bringing home a woman to surprise us."

"Shit. I *told* her I was guarding a woman and wanted to stay with you guys since I'm single. It wouldn't be appropriate to expect Gerri to stay at my place. It's a one-room cabin. I don't even have a wall up to enclose the bathroom. Why in the hell would she assume that?"

Angelo hesitated before he spoke. "You know your mother. She hears what she wants to. You were bringing someone home, and you're right, it wouldn't be appropriate for you to take her to your place unless you had already mated her. We assumed she'd be an important human girlfriend you were planning to bond with, and wanted our approval."

"Is she really at the store?"

Angelo snorted. "Kind of. She went shopping to buy more human-friendly clothes to impress your 'girlfriend'. I told her that she dresses fine but you know how she is. The fact that you finally wanted us to meet a woman was enough for her to start planning your mating ceremony. You called after the shops closed last night and she wanted to be there first thing this morning when they opened. We didn't expect you to arrive for another hour or so."

"Fuck." Micah growled next.

"She'll be disappointed, but at least you know she'd welcome a human."

"Thanks, Dad." Micah scowled.

"She really wants grandbabies."

"I know. Trust me, I've heard it before." Micah rolled his eyes. "Why can't *you* give her another baby?"

Angelo threw up his hands, backing away. "Don't even go there. I'm lucky to still have my balls after *your* labor. She was threatening to rip them off with her claws." He looked at Gerri as his hands dropped to his sides. "Micah put her through sixteen hours of hard labor. It set a record for longest Lycan birth in our pack. He was always stubborn."

"It's not my fault."

"You asked. I'm reminding you. Find a mate and get her pregnant. And trust me, pick a human. They've got to be less terrifying in labor than your mother was. I have scars. She tore into me during the worst of her pain." He eyed Gerri again, cocking his head. "You're carrying Wen's scent, but it's not strong enough for him to have mated you. Are you attracted to my son?"

"Don't even think about it, Dad." Micah shook his head.

"What? She obviously liked Wen well enough and he didn't scare her away. You're smaller than he is and less intimidating. Not by much, but it counts to women." Angelo stepped around his son to get closer to Gerri. "Did the condom break? It happens. How long ago was it? We should be able to tell if you got pregnant within three days. If you're not carrying a VampLycan, how would you like to have little Lycan babies? Micah would make an excellent mate."

"Fuck!" Micah got between them. "Stop. You're embarrassing me. Gerri doesn't want me. Her and Wen—"

"He won't mate her unless he knocked her up. We all know that." Angelo shoved him out of the way, holding Gerri's gaze again. "My son, on the other hand, will. Don't let what he said about his cabin run you off. He's still building it. We can get a crew out there and make the place

223

really nice within a week. I'll even pay out of my own pocket to add a few rooms onto it while you're pregnant. No problem."

"Dad!"

"No thank you," Gerri got out, amused and horrified at the same time.

"Have you met Graves? He's my other son. He's not as friendly as Micah but he's a good-looking man too."

"Dad, stop! You're being worse than Mom."

Angelo whirled on him, growling. "She's driving me nuts. Take a mate or I'll find one for you, just for some peace of mind. Do you know what it's like to hear her day after day, going on about it? She's blaming *me*! She thinks I wasn't a good enough example to you boys about how happy a man mated is."

They both suddenly stilled, turning their heads toward the front door. Gerri followed their gaze and the door opened. A tiny blonde woman walked in, three shopping bags clutched in one hand. She wore a summer dress, a big hat, and sunglasses.

"Hello! I'm home, loving family." She dropped the bags, took off the glasses, and set her purse on the table next to the door. "We are so honored to meet you! I'm Mandy." She smiled big, her blue eyes fixed on Gerri. She wobbled a little in the high heels strapped to her feet, as if she wasn't accustomed to wearing them.

"Oh damn," Micah muttered.

Mandy gasped. "Language! Shame on you. I raised you better, young man. Never in front of ladies." She kept coming, not stopping until she was in front of Gerri. Her eyes widened and she sniffed a few times. The color drained from her face.

"Yes, you're smelling Wen on her," Micah sighed. "Gerri is *not* my girlfriend, although she is human. She knows what we are so there's no need for this act. I really am guarding her for Wen. He got hurt, but he'll be coming to get her."

Gerri bit her bottom lip, then offered her hand. "It's nice to meet you."

Mandy slowly reached out and shook it gently, then let her go.

"I appreciate the trouble you went to though," Gerri added. "You have a beautiful home."

Mandy glared at Micah.

"What in the hell are on your feet?" Angelo stalked forward. "Are you trying to twist an ankle?" He just grabbed the much smaller woman and lifted her, carrying her to a chair. He gently deposited her into it, crouched, and lifted one of her shoes. "Buckles? They look like torture devises. I'm taking them off you."

"Explain this to me right now, Micah," his mother demanded.

"You assumed. Remember what they say about that?"

Angelo turned his head and snarled, flashing fangs. "Don't call your mother an ass. She was hopeful. We both were."

Micah stepped next to Gerri. "Meet my crazy parents."

Gerri had a feeling it was going to be a very interesting stay. She hoped Wen came for her soon.

* * * * *

"Is the room okay?"

Gerri turned away from the closet where she had stored her suitcase to watch Micah enter her room through the open door from the hallway. "It's perfect."

"I'm sorry about downstairs."

She smiled. "They are actually really sweet."

"For crazy people?"

"They're nice. I have to admit your mom wasn't what I was expecting. Both you and your father seem kind of afraid of her. She's small for a Lycan. Was she turned?"

"No. Don't let her fool you. She might have been the runt of the pack but she can be scary at times. May I?" He waved at the edge of the bed.

She nodded and took a seat a few feet from him. There was a table and chair near the bank of window but it was a large room, so she kept close so they didn't have to raise their voices.

"I have to admit I'm really curious about one thing."

Micah arched his eyebrows. "What?"

"How does your mom normally dress?"

He chuckled. "She loves stealing my dad's shirts, which look like dresses on her. We're not as strict about modesty as humans, or as fashionable. His boxers are her bottoms. She hates shoes during the summer. In winter, it's always these chunky snow boots she tromps around in outside."

Gerri laughed. "I hope she wears more than just your dad's things in the winter."

"She does but she steals his jackets. He's got dozens of them. It's a scent thing. They're really in love."

"I could see that."

"I'm sorry for what my dad said about Wen."

She knew instantly what he meant. "That he wouldn't mate me? It's true. No need to apologize."

"And the pregnancy remark. I can't believe he brought that up."

She studied him. He looked upset. "Hey, don't worry about it. It was understandable to think that Wen wouldn't have purposely...well, you know. I do scent like him and there's only one way that happens. The condom breaking would explain it. Your parents don't know anything about the mission we were on, right?"

"No. We don't share Wen's business with our parents or the pack. I'm still sorry you were subjected to that. I should have just taken you to my cabin, but I figured you'd be more comfortable here. I didn't know my dad would try to bribe you either. I swear I'm not pathetic enough to need my parents to try to buy me a woman."

She took pity on him because he looked miserable. "I can one up you on that. Want to hear?"

He nodded. "Sure, but I find that hard to believe. Did your parents try to buy you a husband?"

"No, but my mom joined a pack that doesn't believe in taking mates or having monogamous relationships. She got mad when I wouldn't bend over and let them fuck me too. It's why I'm not in her life anymore. I took off before I was forced into it."

His jaw dropped open and his eyes widened.

"Your parents aren't so bad, Micah."

"I'm sorry, Gerri. Do you talk to her? See her?"

She shook her head. "I'm afraid if I call the pack, they'll tell me she's dead. I don't want to know. I like to imagine she's fine and things worked out the way she wanted them to. It kind of makes me a coward, but she's all I have as far as family goes."

"You think they'd kill her?"

"It's not that. She's human but they give her their blood since she hated aging. She's getting it from the ones she's sleeping with."

He cursed softly. "Doesn't she know how dangerous that is?"

"She knew. Wrinkles and gray hair were more frightening to her."

"What about your biological father?"

"My mom worked in an art gallery and he kept coming in, trying to sell paintings. I guess he was charming and attractive enough for her to fall for him. He moved in with her. She found out she was pregnant with me and he took off. He said he didn't want to have responsibilities. She tried to track him down to get child support but found out the name he'd been using wasn't real." She shrugged. "My mom had been adopted by an older couple, who'd died while she was in college. It was just her and I after Klentz died. I wished so many times she hadn't left the clan."

"Klentz was her mate, right?"

"Yes. I loved him so much. He never treated me as though I wasn't his real child. She could have mated another VampLycan if we'd stayed. I could have..."

"What? Don't stop, Gerri."

"It's stupid, but I always thought if I'd been able to stay, that Wen and I would have mated. I didn't know that his brother had died."

"He loves you, Gerri."

She looked at him knowingly. "It's not enough though, is it? Have you heard from him?"

"No. I talked to Graves though. You didn't ask, so I haven't said anything, but...Wen was ordered back to his clan. I've been asked to keep you with me until his scent fades and it's safe for you to resume your life. But I'm sure he'll get in contact with you soon."

God, that hurt. Wen had broken his word about staying with her, and she sincerely doubted he'd ever be back. Being together, knowing they couldn't have a future, was too painful for them both. "It's for the best if we never see each other again," she managed to get out. Tears filled her eyes.

Micah scooted closer and twisted, opening his arms. "Think of me like a brother right now. Come here."

She didn't need any more encouragement. She leaned forward and burst into tears. He held her tight, stroking her back.

* * * * *

229

Wen arrived home after dark. He went straight to Trayis's house and knocked. It surprised him when there wasn't an answer. He returned to his house and went to unlock the door. A note was pinned to the wood. He read the words.

Meeting with me at 2pm tomorrow. Go talk to your parents. That's an order. T

He was furious as he twisted the locks and entered his house. That's the last thing he needed after dealing with a plane full of humans, then waiting six hours for a repair to be done on the smaller plane that had flown him home. He sure as hell hadn't wanted to drive hours more from the human airport to reach his territory, so he'd coerced the pilot into flying him farther than planned. He'd had a headache by then, and controlling the man to land on a road four miles from home had taken a lot out of him.

All he could think about was Gerri. He knew Micah would keep her safe, but was she upset that he wasn't with her? It tore his guts out imagining her crying, or worse, what if she was mad enough to ditch her protection? Gerri had a temper. She could also be irrational. He flipped on lights and headed into his bedroom, stripping when he reached it.

He threw his clothes on the floor and turned on the shower, not even waiting for the water to grow warm. Hair sprouted out along his skin and he just shifted. A howl tore from his lips and he shook his body, sending water flying. The urge to shift back hit but he fought it. Otherwise he might destroy the tile walls around him by shoving his fists through them. He just wanted to call Gerri, hear her voice, make sure she was safe.

A noise had him spinning, his body going into a crouch.

230

The tall man who stepped into his bathroom frowned, then leaned against the wall.

"You okay? I heard the howling when I was walking up to your door."

He allowed himself to shift to skin and stood up. "What in the hell are you doing here, Tymber?"

"Making sure you made it home. We expected you to make better time."

"My bush pilot had to wait for a part."

"I hate when that happens. You look like shit—and you forgot to lock your door. I could have been someone your parents sent." Tymber grinned, his gaze running down Wen, then back up to his face. "Good thing you're not my type, since you're naked. Are you trying to make it easy for them? Ready to get some VampLycan pregnant yet?"

"Fuck off." Wen turned his back on the enforcer and reached for the soap. He dumped most of the bottle on himself, grabbed a washcloth and began to scrub.

"You're going to take off skin if you aren't careful. Do I piss you off that much? It was a joke. You were supposed to laugh."

"I'm not in the mood."

"I see that. Are you upset at Trayis for ordering you home, or did I already miss you having to chase away a woman your parents sent over here to wait for you on your doorstep?"

"Neither." Wen sniffed, then reached for more soap. He emptied the bottle, scrubbing harder.

Tymber pushed off from the wall and came closer, almost stepping into the shower with him. He lifted his arm, pulling up his shirt to expose the meaty skin just under his elbow.

Wen frowned, then looked at him questioningly.

"No amount of soap is going to help. Your eyes are black and you're as agitated as shit. It's the faint scent I'm picking up, isn't it? Human, but not the right one. I know Trayis had Sherry give you her blood, but you've recently been with Gerri. Bite me. It'll mask the scent of the human lawyer."

Wen growled.

"You could wait a day and hope it's completely gone by then, or you could get rid of it now. Your call."

"At least let me wrap a towel around my waist."

Tymber chuckled. "We work together. I've seen you naked a thousand damn times after we've shifted. I don't even notice unless it's to give you shit. You getting prudish spending time with humans?"

"The taste of blood makes us hard, regardless of the circumstances. I'm getting a towel."

Tymber laughed and backed up. "I'll meet you in the living room. Put some pants on. Somebody could walk in and that would be awkward. I didn't lock your door either."

Wen turned off the water and grabbed a towel. The headache just kept getting worse. He rubbed his skin dry as he entered his room, pulling on a pair of jeans from his dresser. Tymber waited in the living room, as promised.

"You sure about this? You don't have to offer me your blood."

Tymber nodded. "We're a family as enforcers, and we look out for each other. You'd do the same for me if I had one woman on my mind but carried the blood scent of another. How hurt were you? You seem completely healed."

"I was pretty fucked up. The Lycan pack fought like a swarm, probably learned that tactic from those fucking Vampires they were hanging with."

"How many bites?"

"I don't know. I didn't exactly count them."

"I'm guessing you needed a lot of blood." Tymber held out his arm again. "You'll smell like me instead but that shouldn't bother you."

Wen took a deep breath, then exhaled. "I do appreciate it. We should only bite each other for a life or death situation."

"Sanity counts. Stop stalling and do it already. I'd hate carrying someone's scent that bothered me."

Wen took his friend's arm, closed his eyes, and let his fangs come out. He didn't lick Tymber before he sank his fangs in. He just bit down. His heart pounded and adrenaline shot through his body. He let go as soon as he figured he'd taken enough and backed away.

Tymber licked his own arm, sealing it and starting the healing process. "You sure that was enough?"

Wen nodded. "Thanks, brother."

Tymber moved into his kitchen. "Hungry?" He opened the fridge. "I'll make you something."

Wen followed him and grabbed a few glasses out of the cabinet. "I got a ton of sandwich stuff. I bought it before I left, figuring I wouldn't want to go hunting or shopping when I came home. You're going to eat with me."

"I *am* a little hungry."

"Trayis has ordered me to talk to my parents."

"I know." Tymber set lunchmeat, cheese, mayo, and bread from the fridge on the counter. "I'm supposed to make sure you tell them you were with Gerri."

"Fuck. They won't take that well." Wen poured juice into two glasses.

Tymber met his gaze. "How is she? Did she ever get any bigger?"

Pain squeezed Wen's chest. "Not by much." Anger came next. "She lives in a shit apartment in a neighborhood that reeks of Vamps."

"She doesn't know?"

"She thinks brick walls and bars on the windows will protect her, even if they really want in. Sure, she made it harder for them, but they could still reach her."

Tymber dropped his gaze, putting together six sandwiches on the countertop. Wen got out two plates, then grabbed an unopened bag of chips from his pantry. They sat at the bar to eat a few minutes later.

Tymber was the first to speak. "I know there's going to be hell to pay but it's time you stood up to your parents. You've denied what you know is true long enough out of guilt and duty. You've finally sought out your little golden locks. She's your one, isn't she? Not just some crush you've had from boyhood."

234

Wen stared at the sandwiches on his plate. "Father is going to make me kill him. Mother will die too. What kind of fucking choice is that to make? They're my parents. Father's an elder. Trayis will have no choice but to punish or ban me from the clan."

Tymber didn't say a word, so Wen finally looked at him. He saw sadness in his eyes.

"I don't envy the situation you're in, Wen. But you're not the one who's done anything wrong, so there will be no repercussions from Trayis. Mandro and Elna had no right to do this to you. You are *not* your brother. It's cruel, what they've done. You're a good son. Everyone in this damn clan could see how much Gerri meant to you. You were her protector. We all figured you'd go after her the day she hit mating age and bring her back to the clan. Did you know Trayis kept track of her and Carol those first few years, so he could tell you exactly where she was?"

Wen didn't hide his surprise. "No."

Tymber nodded. "And were you aware that Klentz had spoken to Trayis about you mating his daughter?"

Wen tensed. "*No.*"

His friend smiled. "Klentz knew Mandro was set against it, and he worried your father would ask Trayis to pull rank by ordering you away from Gerri. You never listened to your father back then, but you were in training to become an enforcer. It was right after that bear attack, when your father punished you for saving her life. Klentz asked Trayis to never ban you from seeing Gerri. He knew how deep your feelings ran for her, and that they would only grow stronger as the two of you aged."

Wen closed his eyes. "He never said a word. Either of them."

235

"I overheard Klentz pleading with Trayis to never do that to you or her."

Wen opened his eyes. "What was Trayis's answer?"

"He said he'd never ask one of his clan to deny a mate, regardless of bloodlines or if it pissed off an elder."

Wen let that sink in.

"Klentz also brought up the possible consequences of you breeding children with a human. He knew Mandro would assume your children would be weak if they took after their mother, and he'd use that excuse to get our clan leader to side with him." Tymber grinned. "Want to know how Trayis responded to that?"

Wen nodded. It was a valid reason not to mate a human. The clan depended on him to breed strong youth for the next generation of enforcers.

"Trayis said it's not strength that makes a good VampLycan, but what is in their hearts. Any child born out of love as pure as what he saw in the two of you could only be destined for greatness. The ability to shift or not wasn't a concern for Trayis."

Wen felt tears fill his eyes. He looked away. "I'll speak to my parents. It's time I step out of Gerbin's shadow."

"Yes. It's about fucking time."

Chapter Fifteen

Gerri jerked awake. The room was still dark—and she sensed danger. A chill ran down her spine. She wanted to reach for the light on the bedside table but pure fear kept her frozen.

It only lasted a few heartbeats. She shoved at the covers, rolled out of bed, and launched herself into the nearest corner. Her fists came up as she spun around, prepared to fight whatever it was that woke her. It was so dark in the room that she couldn't make out much.

"Easy," a deep voice rumbled. "I'm not here to hurt you."

He was male. She didn't know who or what he was, but she guessed not human. She did adjust her head a little to track where his voice had come from. He was somewhere near the end of the bed, if she had to guess.

"You have good instincts, and I like that you were aware when I came in then protected your back. That's a great defensive spot. I can only come at you from the front."

Her mind went over possibilities. "I have permission to be here. You really don't want to mess with me." She swallowed, hoping Micah would realize she was in trouble and rush to her defense. It was tempting to scream, but the man in her room hadn't attacked her so far. He might if she called for help. "What do you want?"

"I was curious about you."

She went over what she knew so far. He'd said he wasn't there to hurt her. He could also see in the dark, since he knew she'd gone to a corner. "You're smelling a VampLycan. I'm guessing that you belong to this pack, picked up my scent, and came to investigate what the hell it was that caught your nose? Now you know. I'd like to point out that it's really rude, no matter what race you are, to sneak into a woman's bedroom in the middle of the night. Rethink it if you believe that just because I smell like one guy, I'm open to sex. You'd have to kill me, because I'll fight you—and then you'd die next. I'm protected."

He chuckled.

"I'm not joking."

"I know you aren't. You amuse me, is all. Forgive my response."

She relaxed a little since he stayed near the end of the bed, but didn't she unclench her hands. He was in for a fight if he did try to touch her. It wasn't one she could win, but she might manage to stay alive long enough for Micah or his parents to be alerted that they had someone else in their home. Hopefully they'd come.

She wished she could see. "You know I'm human. Will you turn on a light? I'm blind without one; you know that."

"I'll turn on the light. Ready?"

She nodded. Part of the darkness moved and came closer. He turned on the lamp next to the bed.

Gerri blinked, adjusting to the sudden brightness, then gawked as she stared at the nighttime intruder.

He hadn't changed all that much since the last time she'd seen him.

Shock held her still for a moment, but then she dropped her chin, her gaze lowering to the carpet between them, and she put her hands to her

238

sides. She stepped away from the wall and bowed slightly, staying in that position.

He came toward her and she noticed the black boots he wore, with black cargo pants. "Look at me, Gerri," he said.

She straightened and raised her chin. He wasn't as tall as Wen, but no one would ever call him short either. Trayis was about six feet four. She couldn't believe he was in Colorado.

He smiled. "Do you still paint on canvas?"

It wasn't a question she'd expected. "No."

"A shame. You had real talent as a child." He reached out and touched her hair. His smile widened. "It's as wild as ever. Your mother used to try so hard to restrain those curls, but they always burst out of the braids she wove."

Fear came next. "Is Wen okay?" What if he'd come to tell her something horrible? She couldn't understand why else the clan leader would be there.

"He's fine. I ordered him back to Alaska. Tymber sent me a text when Wen arrived home."

She breathed out a sigh of relief. Then the next guess on why Trayis would come to see her struck—and she took a step back, bumping the wall. "You're angry that I went on that mission with Wen, right?"

His mouth firmed into a grim line for long seconds. "Furious," he finally sighed. "He put you in danger."

"He didn't force me to go."

Trayis reached out his hand. Gerri hesitated then clasped it. He backed up, leading her toward the table and chairs by the windows. Memories from her childhood returned. Trayis used to take her on walks sometimes, asking her how the other children treated her. He'd always been kind to her, like some kind of uncle.

"Sit." He let her go.

Gerri took a seat across from him. Trayis put his hands on the table and leaned forward a little. "How is human life?"

She debated on how to answer, then decided to be honest. "Not that great."

"Is your mother well?"

"I don't know. We parted ways."

Trayis's shock showed on his face.

"She hooked up with a pack. Long story I don't want to go into, but I wasn't staying. She wasn't leaving."

"Do you have any children? I know you don't have a human man in your life, at least not anymore, judging by Wen's scent on you."

"It's just me."

"That will make things easier."

She leaned forward and crossed her arms on the edge of the table, staring at him. "Did you come to try to wipe my memories? It won't work long term. Klentz tested me."

"I remember that you inherited your mother's immunity to mind control, although you're not as strong as she was. The truth is lost to you, but you dream about it until you remember it's an actual memory. No, Gerri. I'm only here to talk to you."

She inwardly winced. "Did Wen break the rules by getting me involved in VampLycan politics? I've always kept clan secrets, lived under the radar, and never caused trouble. I'm not about to change any of that now. I give you my word, for what that's worth."

"Wen shouldn't have involved you. I'm angry with him about that, but I've never questioned your honor. You swore to keep quiet about everything you'd learned growing up. I never would have allowed you to leave home if I had doubts. You have a good heart, Gerri. I tried to talk your mother into staying, but she had her mind set. It's not my way to force people to live with us."

She breathed easier, relaxing. "I promise that I'll never talk about Washington. Is that why you came? To make sure I wouldn't say anything?"

"I'm here to offer you a choice."

That confused her. "What kind?"

"You were a child under your mother's care when you left the clan. She made decisions for you that I had no right to interfere with. You're an adult now. Would you like to rejoin the clan?"

His words nearly floored her. She hadn't expected him to make that offer in a million years.

"You can return to Alaska with me or go back to the life you built with humans."

"I don't understand. I'm human. I mean, I was only allowed to live with the clan because of Klentz."

"Bloodlines don't matter to me. I accepted you into our clan, Gerri. *You* never asked to leave, your mother did." He smiled. "I still consider you one of mine. You can come home if you want to. The house your parents raised you in still stands. We maintain it. The interior isn't quite the same, since we've had people stay there from time to time, but you could move right back in. I even have a job to offer you. It will involve human relations, since you have more experience dealing with them than anyone else in the clan. You've lived amongst them for fifteen years. I'll have you handle phone calls and such, but you won't be going on more dangerous missions if you accept. I want you safe inside our territory."

Tears filled her eyes. There had been so many times when she'd wished more than anything that she could go back to the life she'd once had. It wouldn't be the same though, since she no longer had family there.

Then there was Wen. His parents would flip. Fear filled her—they wanted her dead.

Trayis seemed to guess her thoughts, or maybe he picked up her scent changing with her emotions. "There will be difficult things to deal with, but you'll be under my protection. No one would dare harm you. It will also keep you close to Wen."

She noticed that the brown in Trayis's irises had turned more golden, but then some black bled through. Whatever he was thinking, he was feeling various emotions too. She couldn't smell them the way he could but VampLycans showed them in their eyes. He wasn't trying to mask them.

"That's complicated," she finally whispered.

"I'm more than aware, Gerri. I don't get involved between parents and their children, but Wen is also my enforcer and friend." His eyes turned totally black.

"You're angry with his parents," she guessed.

"Furious. It's fucked up to expect a son to replace the one they lost. They've done their best to mold Wen into a version of Gerbin. I've talked to Mandro and Elna many times, but they refuse to hear me. Mandro is arrogant. Elna is insane. Neither of them seem to be able to see or care what they're doing to their son. And Wen was always eager to please, since they made it clear who their favorite child was. It did a number on him. I may not have young of my own, but I'd never make them feel as if they were worth less than a sibling. I'd hoped he'd defy them and come after you one day. It finally happened."

"He's not going to mate me, Trayis. He just wanted to spend time with me. We were kids when we parted and there was so much left unsaid."

"Is the bond still there between the two of you? Be honest with me."

She nodded. "He fought not to bite me. He said his parents would kill me."

"What do you feel toward *him*?"

"I love him. I always have, and I always will." There was no reason to lie to Trayis.

243

"Is he your mate in your heart, Gerri?"

She nodded again.

"Then the choice has been made. We leave first thing in the morning. I'll ask my brother to send Micah to pack the human possessions you left behind in whatever dwelling you had and fly them to you later."

"It's not that simple."

"What's the problem?"

"I called to check on him and Sherry answered the phone. They were lovers. He was with *her* but sent *me* away with Micah." It still hurt.

"I sent Sherry to Wen, Gerri, because I didn't know he had his cousins nearby. I couldn't send a VampLycan into that city to back him up. Fucking security cameras and cell phones are going to be the death of us. Are you aware that Wen's been arrested twice in the past?" Trayis sighed. "Wen couldn't control multiple minds at once so he had to allow himself to be taken into custody. The police have to turn off the cameras in their interview rooms when an attorney consults with her client. It meant Wen could mind control the officers without it being recorded when she'd have them escort her in, spin a story, and order them to destroy any evidence they had. Sherry works in that capacity for me."

"I knew that."

"Wen had no idea that I'd sent her. He didn't ask her to be there. I can also assure you that he has no feelings for her."

"You don't know that."

244

"I do. I've read his mission reports and talked to him at length when he's had dealings with her. It was just sex and nothing more to him. You're his heart, Gerri. Come home."

She reached across the table but hesitated before touching him, remembering that VampLycans didn't just do that.

Trayis lifted his hand and took hers, clasping it. "You always have permission from this moment on. Consider me your family now, Gerri. I will take the place of Klentz as your father figure and protector in the clan."

Trayis was full of surprises. He was pretty much stating he'd just adopted her. "Thank you. I'm honored."

He grinned, his eyes turning golden, reminding her of an amused cat. "But?"

"I don't know if I can go back. Wen won't be happy if I return to live with the clan because his parents are probably going to try to kill me."

"It's time to shake things up, Gerri." He winked. "You always had courage. Let me help you claim your mate. It's time for you to come home."

Tears flooded her eyes. "I want to so much. Thank you."

He squeezed her hand. "You and Wen deserve to be happy. I couldn't do anything in the past to stop you from being separated, but that time is gone. Now it's about building the future you two were meant to have together." He leaned in. "And I don't give a damn if your children can shift or not. We have way too many boys being born. I'll be thrilled if you birth some girls. If mind over matter exists, give it a shot. Think 'girl' when you and Wen try to get pregnant. That's all I ask."

245

Gerri recovered from the astonishment fast. "I'll try my best."

"Raise them just like you were. Did I ever tell you that you're the only girl child who never gave me headaches?" He let her hand go and rose to his feet. "Try to get some sleep. Things will work out. Wen won't be able to deny his instincts once he's around you day after day. He's in deep shit for putting you in danger, so I've decided to punish him by making him work with me in my office." A slow grin spread across his face. "He'll get the desk right next to yours. Sweet dreams. I'll see you early in the morning."

He crossed the room, but paused by the door, glancing at her over his shoulder. "Worst case scenario, if he's really stubborn, he'll break when he goes into heat."

Trayis seemed to be waiting for a response.

"Um, okay."

He turned to her fully and leaned against the door, a grin on his face. "Klentz never told you?"

She shook her head. "No."

"You had barely turned fifteen when he was killed. I guess he wouldn't have had that talk with you yet, and your mother always tried to shield you too much. VampLycans go into heat once a year. Wen is just a little older than you are. He started feeling the heat when he turned fifteen." His grin widened. "Klentz caught Wen with his claws embedded into a tree, staring at your bedroom window one night. You were too young for Wen to touch, but his instincts demanded he remain close to you. He'd damn near destroyed that tree, clinging to it for three days until the heat let up. As an adult, it lasts longer—and you're not too young to

246

stay away from this time. He'll go into heat and nothing will stop him from going to you."

She bit her lip. "What if he picks someone else?"

The golden gleam returned to Trayis's eyes. "He'd have to go far away and pretend whoever he fucked was *you* to be able to achieve sexual release. Even that would be tough to do, since any other woman's scent would put him off. He knows for certain now that you're his mate, if he had the urge to bite you. I'm not letting him leave the clan. You'll end up with Wen tearing off your clothes and claiming you. Count on it." He left her room, closing the door quietly behind him.

She stayed seated in the chair and sighed. She hoped Trayis was right about all of it. That things would work out and Wen would claim her. A warm sensation settled in her stomach, thinking about having girl babies with Wen. Real hope that she might be able to build a life with the VampLycan she loved flared.

"Please let this work out," she whispered.

* * * * *

Wen knocked on his parents' door. Their lights were on, despite the late hour. He was certain they'd waited up for him. As an elder, his father would be aware of his comings and goings. The door jerked open and the smell of food filled the air. His father smiled. "Finally. I've never eaten this late in my life. Get in here. Did you rip that Vampire apart?"

"Yes. Horton is no longer." He stepped inside and spotted his mother.

247

She came out of the kitchen with her hands on her hips. "The roast is probably dry. I thought you'd be home hours ago. Come in and take a seat at the table."

He sighed, doing her bidding.

An unfamiliar scent hit him and he growled, his gaze darting to the hallway that led to the bedrooms. A tall woman stalked out of the darkness. She was a beauty, with long black hair, a dress that hugged her body in all the right places, and a flirtatious smile on her lips.

His father took a seat at the head of the table. "Come join us, Quilla. This is the son we told you so much about."

The VampLycan woman took a seat across from Wen, smiling. "Hello."

She had a deep, throaty voice, and her dark gaze raked over his chest and face, her approval obvious. "You are as handsome as they promised. Your parents have told me all about your accomplishments."

Wen wasn't surprised. They did this to him almost every damn time he returned home from a mission. "I apologize to you for their deception. I'm not looking for a mate."

The woman didn't appear surprised. "They mentioned you are resistant."

He tensed more, not liking her reaction. Most of the women they brought to him had been under the impression he was lonely and ready to settle down. "To say the least. They shouldn't have brought you here. What clan are you from?"

"Crocker's, and yes, I've heard the experiences other women have had, who your parents have invited to meet you. I'm different. I enjoy my independence." She winked. "I don't want to change clans but I'm not opposed to having a child. I'm seventy-two years old. I'd like to have one while I'm still young enough to enjoy them. I've never found my true mate. I might consider settling for you if we get along well."

"Don't look at me to be the sperm donor. I'd never settle for a loveless mating."

"Wen!" his father snarled.

His mother came storming into the room holding a large serving dish. She slammed it on the table. "We found you a breeder, and you will fuck her until she's with child!"

He seethed. "No."

His father snarled again and glared at him, his eyes turning black. "You will give us that grandchild your mother wants. Do your duty!"

"We've already decided custody arrangements," his mother added. "You won't be bothered. Just breed her until she's pregnant. Then your duty to me will be done." She spun, going into the kitchen to gather more prepared food. "Start tonight, Wen. Don't disappoint me. Quilla will go home with you."

His claws grew from his fingers, his rage increasing. They made it sound as if he would have no part in raising this child they demanded. He slowly stood. "*No!*"

His father shot out of his chair. "Your mother has spoken! It has been decided. You refuse to take a mate, so we are meeting you halfway. Breed her!"

Wen felt hair sprouting along his skin and face, his fangs elongating. "I said no! You want a child so bad? You breed your mate and let her birth you another son!"

Glass crashed in the kitchen and his mother ran out, gasping. "Wen!"

He turned his gaze on her. "You heard me. I'm done. No more women, no more parading them in front of me, and no breeders. I decide who I mate, and when I have a child, it is mine to raise. Not *yours*."

"Gerbin would do it for us!" Tears filled his mother's eyes.

"I'm not him!" Wen roared. "*He's dead!*"

His father instantly attacked, and pain shot up Wen's ribs.

He acted on instinct, shoving his father back. They were evenly matched in size, but Wen had a lot more fighting experience. He struck out, ripping into his father's arms, doing damage to muscle.

His mother screamed and Wen jumped back. His father appeared stunned as he sank the floor, blood running down both injured arms, which hung limply at his sides.

His mother rushed to her mate, throwing her body over his, and turned black eyes on Wen. Hair sprouted along her features, her fangs flashing as her mouth elongated. She was shifting.

"Don't make me incapacitate you too, Mother. Make no mistake—I will if you come at me." It tore him up, seeing his parents that way, knowing they must hate him at that moment. No child should ever injure their own father or threaten their mother. No child should ever be forced to.

Sadness came next. "I'm not Gerbin," he rasped. "I will *never* be my brother, and no child can ever replace him. Not mine and not one you might have together. He's gone forever. Accept that! Finally deal with it."

He glanced at Quilla. She had leapt out of the way of the fighting, standing in the living room. "Go home. Find another sperm donor for your child. I wish you luck with that."

He walked to the front door, half expecting his mother to attack his back. She didn't.

Wen fled, slamming the door behind him. He made it about ten feet from the bottom of the porch before motion from his left brought him to a halt.

Tymber grimly regarded him from where he leaned against the house, arms crossed over his chest. He would have been able to hear everything if he'd been there for a while.

His friend spoke first. "You had no choice. I'm glad you finally stood up to them. Go home. I'll stay here to make sure your father doesn't need a healer. I can hear your parents talking. He still lives."

Wen opened his mouth but then realized he didn't know what to say. His family life had been strained before, and now it was destroyed. His parents would never forgive him, but then, he wasn't so sure he could forgive them either.

He locked himself inside his cabin and took a shower. His father's blood on his hands made him feel sick. Tears came as he stood under the spray. He wanted Gerri but it would never be safe to bring her to the clan. His parents would be spiteful for certain now. They wouldn't just harm her because she was human, but to get revenge for his defiance.

251

He had done the right thing though. It was clear they'd planned to mold his child the way they had him in the years since his brother had died. He'd never allow that to happen.

The only way he could claim Gerri as his mate was to leave the clan and break his allegiance to Trayis. Honor vs. his heart. It was the worst decision a VampLycan could have to make. "Fuck."

Chapter Sixteen

Gerri missed Micah's skills in the worst way as the bush pilot swept down from the sky at an alarming speed. She grabbed at the seat belt for dear life, expecting them to crash at any moment. Her eyes were tightly closed, refusing to witness the impact. The wheels hit the ground, they bounced back into the air, and her stomach seemed to hit the roof. The wheels landed again but this time they weren't thrown back into the air. The engines droned louder.

The crazy pilot laughed. "I knew I could do it."

Gerri peeked an eye open, realizing they were slowing. It was an old road they'd landed on, two lanes in an area cleared of trees. She hoped a car or truck didn't show up ahead of them to cause a head-on collision. The plane came to a stop and she opened her other eye.

Trayis turned to the pilot next to him, his eyes glowing. He lifted his hand, reached back to Gerri, and shielded her from seeing him. She sighed and held still.

"You did well with this emergency landing. The plane is no longer experiencing engine troubles. We shall get out, you'll go deliver your supplies, and not remember having any passengers or where you've been with us." Trayis paused. "And you have a strong desire to take more lessons from an instructor. I realize you have your license but do it. You wish to be an even better pilot."

"I do," the pilot stated.

Trayis pulled his hand away from Gerri's face and he rolled his brown eyes when she looked at him. He mouthed one word. "Scary."

She glanced at the pilot. He was smiling, seemingly in his own little world, staring out the front of the plane. She nodded, looking at Trayis again. "No shit," she breathed.

Trayis opened the door and helped her out. Her backpack wasn't stored in the side compartment but instead sat on the seat next to her. She slid on the straps and followed Trayis away from the road. The plane began to roll forward.

"Where did you find that guy?"

"I just grabbed him from the airport. He was going on a supply run to some resort in this area. My mistake."

The plane took off down the road and Gerri looked both ways. "So is someone picking us up?" She watched the small plane lift off the road, climbing into the sky.

"Yes. This isn't a public road." He pulled out his cell phone, calling someone. "We're here. You know what to do." He hung up. "It should be about twenty minutes."

"Why are we so far from your territory, since that pilot won't remember where he dropped us anyway?"

"This was the longest straightaway and where the road is the least damaged by winters. It used to run to a tiny town that died out five years ago."

"Not the one that the Vampires took out?"

"No. There was a hunting lodge some humans opened, even put in some tourist stores, a restaurant, and a gas station. Some corporation thought they could make a bundle so they built it. It was too close to our territory."

"What does that mean?"

He grinned. "Let's just say we made sure their guests never found game and wouldn't be returning. The first month they were open, we got groups of trespassers on our border. I refused to allow our clan to be shot at by idiots. They didn't turn a profit in the two years it was open and we bought it from them at a discounted price."

She was amused. "That's kind of evil but brilliant."

"I do what I must for the protection of my clan. They should have opened one of those nature lover retreats. Instead they brought guns." He shook his head. "Mistake."

Gerri took off her backpack and stretched. She was tired of sitting after two flights. Not that she could complain about the first one. "Do you always fly first class when you travel on human transportation?"

He chuckled. "I don't fit into coach."

She glanced at his big body and realized he was right. "I didn't know you ever left Alaska."

"I go visit my brother every five or ten years. He can't come to me."

"Why not?"

"He's mated, with two sons. His need to keep his family safe won't allow him to be apart from them. He'd never trust humans to fly his mate or children this distance. It's easiest to use their airlines when available, plus a hell of a lot cheaper. Do you know what it costs to hire a private jet?"

"No clue."

"It's outrageous."

She let the matter drop. "Were you visiting him when I got there?"

He met her gaze and held it. "No. I came just for you. I'll visit with my brother again soon."

"You could have just called and asked me to come."

He grinned. "That was a conversation we needed to have face to face. I doubt you'd be here otherwise."

She glanced away. He was probably right.

"It will work out, Gerri."

She stared at him, remembering her whispered words the night before after he'd left her room. He must have heard them. "I hope so."

"You'd be miserable without Wen. This way, regardless of the difficulties the next few days or weeks may bring, he'll be close. Instincts won't be denied. You're back where you belong." He reached up and tapped his temple. "Think like a VampLycan. You're clan."

She wasn't a VampLycan though. She kept that to herself. He was more than aware.

Trayis backed away. "I'll be right back. I have to take a leak."

"Me too. I'll meet you back here in a few." She crossed the street and went in the opposite direction. The scents and sounds from the trees made her smile as she found a spot to squat to relieve her bladder. There

256

were no traffic noises, no car alarms, no sirens. Just birds and the rustling of the wind through the treetops.

Trayis waited for her back at the side of the road. He sniffed, motioning for her to come closer. "Bears are in the area. Stick close."

"Yeah. I'm home."

He chuckled. "You won't be taking any strolls alone and we cleared the area around our homes after you were attacked. Some things have changed."

"Good to know."

A short time passed before a black SUV with tinted windows pulled up, stopping next to them. She couldn't make out the driver until he opened the door. She instantly recognized him. He hadn't changed at all, which shouldn't have surprised her. VampLycans didn't age the way humans did. It could have been days since she'd last seen him instead of fifteen years.

"Hi, Yern."

He rounded the SUV and stared at her. His gaze lowered to her chest. "You've got boobs."

She glanced down at the tank top she wore, noticing that it did reveal some cleavage. She grinned and looked up at him. "I do."

Trayis sighed. "That's the first thing you've got to say to your clansman after all these years? Tell me again why you're an enforcer?"

Yern laughed. "But she's got boobs. Big ones. She used to be flat as a board."

Trayis rolled his eyes heavenward and shook his head. "Why me?"

Yern came toward her and opened his arms. "Give me a hug."

She met him halfway and gasped when the big guy grabbed her and lifted her right off her feet. He gave her a bear hug, almost crushing her.

"Gently," Trayis snapped. "Don't break her."

Yern eased his hold a tiny bit. "It's good to have you home. We resume lessons tomorrow, Gerri. I doubt those stupid humans taught you any survival skills." He put her down then cupped her face, leaning down to study her features.

"Looking for wrinkles?" They had always teased each other.

He cracked a smile. "You look good, baby. Just more mature. I like the differences." His gaze lowered. "Especially the boobs."

Yern suddenly snarled, jerking away and releasing her. Trayis had a grip on the back of his neck. "Wen would kill you, so don't even think about it."

"I'm not flirting with her. She knows."

"It's okay," Gerri laughed. "It's an old joke between us."

Trayis let him go and scowled. "I don't think Wen would find that kind of talk funny."

Yern rubbed his neck. "Ouch. I used to tell her if she was ever attacked by a male to flash her boobs at him, but she didn't have any." He smiled. "Now she does." His gaze turned to Gerri and he put his hands in front of his chest, making a motion as if to tear open his shirt. He winked. "Would totally work now."

"You think that would actually stop a man from killing her?"

258

Yern nodded at Trayis. "He'd want to fuck her instead, and he'd lower his guard by trying to get her clothes off. That's when she could kill him. Gerri's always been small. She has to outthink her opponent since she doesn't have claws."

"Spoken like an unmated man. Just take us home. I'm tired. I know Gerri is too." Trayis opened the passenger door and sat. "Get in."

Gerri climbed in the back after grabbing her backpack. They left the road for a dirt trail after a few miles. She had to put on her belt to avoid being tossed around since there were lots of potholes and uneven ground. That was one thing she hadn't missed about her old home. VampLycans didn't make it easy to travel around their territory.

Yern kept glancing at her in the rearview mirror and smiling. "It's good to have you back, baby."

"Stop calling her that," Trayis sighed. "Wen will get angry."

"He knows we call her that. She was so little and cute. Still is." Yern paused. "So does the wind still blow in Wen's direction? You smell like him." His gaze caught hers in the mirror again. "I take it that you're still feel attracted to him as much as you used to?"

"Yes."

"They are mates. He just hasn't claimed her yet," Trayis added.

"Dumbass," Yern muttered. "I know his parents are mental after what they suffered but coddling them hasn't helped any. I told him as much dozens of times. We're VampLycans, not humans." His gaze met Gerri's again. "No offense."

"None taken."

"You don't act like a human. Never did. You're just a short, non-shifting VampLycan who smells human. Only right now, you smell like Wen. Guess I should have guessed you were his, even if you haven't exchanged blood yet, since you're obviously letting him between your thighs. Bet he was happy as shit about that. It was no secret how desperately he wanted you as a youth. You'd walk by and he'd get a hard-on. Please tell me he lasted more than ten seconds. That man wanted you so bad, he might have shot off before he even unzipped if you were naked."

"Shut up," Trayis barked. "You sound like a youth yourself."

Gerri laughed. "He didn't embarrass himself when he got me in bed."

The clan leader turned in his seat to look at her but he smiled. "Don't encourage him." He reached over and slapped Yern with the back of his hand on the side of his arm. "Stop looking for something to tease Wen over. He's got it tough enough right now without you adding shit."

The sight of her old home came into view and Gerri unbuckled her belt, leaning forward to get a better look at it. Memories of her childhood flashed through her mind, and with them came sadness.

Yern parked and both men in front got out. Trayis opened her door and inhaled. "Klentz was a good man."

She blinked back tears. "He was."

"This is your home again." Trayis took her backpack. "I had it cleaned this morning, since we haven't had visitors staying here in about a month. Food has been put in the fridge." He led the way.

She followed with Yern at her side. More memories surfaced. She'd been so happy being raised in this cabin. She hesitated when they reached the front door, staring at it. Trayis opened it wide and stepped inside first.

Yern waited for her, so she moved forward. The interior had been painted and the furniture had been upgraded. The coffee table was the only piece she recognized, and she was touched that it was still there. Trayis followed her gaze.

"I know Klentz carved the dolphin-shaped legs for your mother. We kept it." Trayis put her bag down. "Gerri?"

She gave him her full attention.

"You stay inside for right now. I plan to inform the clan first thing tomorrow that you're back with us. Most will recognize you but we have youths who won't. This isn't a remote home and you'd run into clansmen. Wen's scent is still with you but I don't want some overzealous teen to think they're protecting the clan by grabbing you. They wouldn't mean to hurt you, but I won't risk you being bruised up or hauled in. Yern will be outside on guard duty. His brothers will switch shifts with him. You're to have round-the-clock protection."

"Wen's parents?" She didn't fear anyone else in the clan.

"They are unstable." Trayis stepped closer. "Wen will deal with them, or I will. One way or another, this is a temporary solution. I refuse to have you in danger with our clan."

"Thank you."

"It's good to have you back where you belong. Now I have to go meet with Wen."

Her heart sped up. "Does he know I'm here?"

Trayis shook his head. "I plan to go home and shower, change my clothes, before I see him. He'll find out tomorrow with the rest of the clan. I want to give him more time to think about all the horrible things that could happen to you in the human world." Golden streaks flared in his brown eyes and that mischievous look returned.

"You're going to give him some shit," Yern chuckled. "No fair."

"That's why I'm clan leader and you're an enforcer." Trayis winked at Gerri. "Stay inside. Promise? Tomorrow morning I'll come for you and hold that clan meeting. We'll hold it around nine."

"You have my word. I'll eat and then sleep. I didn't get more than a few hours last night."

Trayis left and she faced Yern. "Are you hungry?"

"No, but thanks. I'm going to go outside. Do you need anything before I leave?"

"You can stay in here."

"It's against orders. I'm to patrol outside, and hell, when Wen does find out you arrived today, he'll try to kick my ass if I spent the night alone with you." His gaze lowered and he shook his head. "You have boobs. I'm so not getting over that. I was sure you'd be flat as a pancake."

She laughed. "Fine. If you get hungry or don't want to piss on a tree, I'll leave the door unlocked. I can still do that here, can't I?"

"Yeah. No one is going to hurt you."

"Trayis wouldn't tell me the truth so I didn't bother to ask him. Will my being here cause him any trouble?"

Yern shook his head. "You're clan, Gerri. Always have been. I know some of the adults were assholes about not trusting you when you were a child, but you never betrayed us." His expression tensed. "We have bigger things to worry about these days."

"Like what?"

"Whatever underhanded thing Decker will do. You helped Wen on his mission, so I know you're aware that the son of a bitch sent a nest to attack his old clan. Some worry he'll expose us to humans next and send them here."

"He's still the boogeyman."

Yern nodded. "Pure evil. We all long for the day he dies. We're finally at peace with his old clan and united though. They visit us and we visit them."

She thought about her house. "Where will they stay if they come to visit, now that I'm here?"

"We have a few other cabins we built. This home was only used since no one lived here." He reached out and touched her cheek. "Now someone does."

He turned, closing the front door closed behind him.

Gerri made a slow circle, taking in the large room. It was good to be home.

* * * * *

Wen went over every detail of what had taken place in Washington. Trayis had called in a few of the enforcers to be present at the meeting.

He'd been relieved that no one questioned it when he'd skipped over his private time with Gerri. He wasn't about to share those moments with his clan.

Trayis had food brought in and they ate dinner together as they discussion the mission.

"Why do you smell like Tymber?" one of the enforcers asked.

Wen opened his mouth to respond but his friend spoke first.

"Because he was injured still when he arrived. You've met our human lawyer. There's not much meat on her bones. Wen didn't want to take too much blood. I gave him some of mine. If you have a problem with that, or want to give me shit over it, I promise to never let you bite me if you're hurt in battle."

Kavler grinned. "Where'd he bite you?"

Tymber lifted his middle finger. "Right here."

"I'll call this meeting to an end, since it's obvious we're all relieved the threat has been taken care of. I'll share the details with the other clans." Trayis smiled though. "Go. Wen, you stay. The clans might have questions for you."

Everyone left, leaving him alone with his clan leader. Trayis didn't reach for his phone though, instead leaning back in his chair.

Wen regarded him with a frown. "I thought you were contacting the other clans."

"No need. They know the highlights I'd gotten from Graves and then you over the phone. Horton is dead. That's all that matters. I wanted to talk about your parents. No one else needed to know that."

264

"My father attacked me first. I slashed his arms to prevent him from doing me harm."

"I figured. He's healed. I saw your father before the meeting. He wants me to punish you for attacking an elder."

Wen couldn't say he was shocked. "What's my punishment?"

"Having Mandro as a father. I told him he was lucky you didn't take his arms off for attacking *you*. What he didn't tell me was what prompted the fight. It had to be bad, since you normally tolerate a lot of shit from him."

"They found a woman from Crocker's clan willing to breed a child with me, and she didn't want a mate."

"Fuck."

"I guess they figured I'd do it, have nothing to do with my own child, and they could help her raise it." Anger filled him again at the thought. "I said no, and all hell broke loose. Didn't Tymber report that to you? He was outside."

"His orders were to stick close to you, not tattle. I figured your parents would pull some shit and I wasn't around to deal with it. I asked him to."

"Where were you?" Wen instantly regretted the question. It wasn't his place to ask. "I apologize."

"No problem. I was with a woman."

"Oh." That was news. Trayis avoided women unless he was in heat. He usually had a Lycan brought in to stay with him, and then the woman would leave when his heat had passed. It was well known he avoided

VampLycans after some incident in the past. "Did you find your mate while I was gone?"

"No. It was just a one-night thing." Trayis smiled. "She's really cute too."

"I'm glad. You need to do something to relieve all the stress you deal with on a daily basis."

"That's what I'm trying to do. Mandro and I had words about you. I told him to leave you alone, reminded him that you are no longer a boy but a man. You're also one of my enforcers. Even as an elder, he has no right to issue you orders. They are there to give advice, not manipulate the lives of the clan."

"I bet he didn't take that well."

"No, he didn't. I told him if he didn't like it, that he was welcome to leave the clan to join another. I ordered him to leave you the fuck alone and told him that he wasn't permitted to interfere with your life anymore. That goes for his mate too. He's fucking with my enforcer, and I won't have that kind of tension in my clan."

That stunned Wen. He didn't even know what to say.

"I made it clear that their actions have made you reckless with your duties. That gives me the right to step in. You put Gerri in danger just to spend time with her because they forbid you to."

A sick feeling settled in Wen's stomach. "Did you tell my father I was with her?"

Trayis nodded. "I did. I also made it clear that I'd be thrilled if you mated her."

266

Wen shifted in his seat. "I'm sure he had plenty to say to that."

"He did. He started in with that bullshit about weak bloodlines clouding the next generation. I told him that wasn't something I considered a problem. He called me incompetent to lead our people, if I felt that way. And I told him he was more than welcome to challenge me."

Wen stopped breathing, staring at his clan leader.

"He immediately backed down."

Wen sucked in a sharp breath. "You would have killed him if he'd attacked."

"You're a good man, Wen. You have honor. So do I. I can't say the same for Mandro since your brother's death. His mind is the only thing clouded and incompetent. One of us has to deal with him." Trayis stood. "You volunteered for a very dangerous mission to be with the woman you want. That not only put your ass on the line, but Gerri's. I'm done waiting for you to stand up to them. I'm forcing the issue to a close, one way or another. I refuse to lose you. That weakens the clan. But you're miserable and a danger to yourself because of their demands. Fix this. I don't care how. Do you understand?"

Wen stood. "I do."

"Do you have a problem with anything I've said?"

"No. You're right."

Trayis got to his feet and rounded his desk. "He's an elder but that doesn't make him infallible, Wen. I'm considering it a family matter between the two of you, however this ends."

Wen stared deeply into his eyes. "You're giving me permission to kill him?"

"I'm telling you this can't go on any longer. Stand your ground. Make it stick. If he won't allow it, that's his choice. Not yours. I won't lose you." Trayis reached around him and gripped the back of his neck, holding tight. "You've been an amazing son to them, tried your best to make them happy, but you are not Gerbin. It's time you let them suffer the pain and reality of his loss without trying to soften the blow. However they handle that is on their shoulders, not yours. I need you, Wen. *You*. Be who you are. No more living in the shadow of death."

Wen understood.

"It's been a rough few days for you. Yesterday you were severely injured, and while I'm sure you're mostly healed, your strength isn't at its peak. I don't want you to deal with your parents tonight. Tomorrow is soon enough. Tymber is waiting for you outside. His orders are to make certain you get rest tonight and that no one disturbs you."

"Thank you."

"You're my friend, you're my enforcer, and I consider you to be like a brother. I'm done watching you suffer. Tomorrow is a new day." Trayis released him. "Now go. I do have phone calls to make."

Chapter Seventeen

Gerri jerked awake when the master bedroom door slammed into the wall. She'd closed it just in case Yern entered the house to eat or use the guest bathroom, which happened to be just a door down. The outline of a big man framed the doorway. She'd left the living room lights on but they were down the hall a bit so she couldn't make out much of whoever stood there.

"Gerri?"

She'd recognized that growl anywhere. "Wen?"

"What in the hell are you doing here?" He took a few steps closer, then halted.

"Trayis brought me."

He just stood motionless. She shoved off the covers and scooted to the edge of the mattress, then flipped on the lamp next to the bed. Wen was staring at her with a furious expression on his face and his eyes were dark. The color hadn't quite reached black but close.

"That sneaky bastard," he finally muttered.

"He was going to tell you tomorrow, along with the rest of the clan. He invited me back. I accepted." Was he angry that she was there, or just angry that Trayis hadn't told him yet? She climbed out of bed but didn't approach him. "He said I'm still clan and gave me the option of returning." She straightened her shoulders and prepared to do battle with him if he ordered her to leave.

He didn't start a fight. He just stood there staring at her. He didn't look happy to see her though. That hurt.

"I wanted to come back. This is where I was raised. Living with humans sucked ass, Wen. I know I'll face some problems with the clan until some of them adjust to me again but at least I'm not living behind bars on my windows. I don't have to worry about being mugged or murdered on a daily basis. I have a job here. Trayis gave me one. You got me fired from the last one I had, remember? I told you it's not easy for me to find work since I never graduated high school and I sure as hell couldn't afford college."

He blinked but said nothing.

"It doesn't mean I expect anything from you, if that's what you're worried about. You made it clear you couldn't mate me. Fine. But I'm still going to live here. We can avoid each other if that's what you want." She remembered then that Trayis was going to force Wen to take a desk next to hers in his office. "Say something."

He didn't.

Now she was getting angry. "What are you doing here anyway? In my house?"

"Trayis didn't want me to get into another fight with my father so he had Tymber escort me to a guest house. *This* one. He set us up to be here together. I came inside and picked up your scent."

"You got into a fight with your dad?"

He closed his eyes and took a deep breath, blowing it out. He turned, lifted his hand, and ran it though his hair. "That sneaky bastard," he said again.

270

Her anger drained, only to be replaced by amusement. "Your dad or Trayis?"

He turned back to her and actually smiled. "Trayis." He took a few steps closer and his attention focused on her body. She wore a nightshirt that hit her thighs.

"Eyes up here and off my legs. You didn't answer me. You got into a fight with your dad?"

He held her gaze. "Remember the homecomings I told you about?"

She did—and jealousy instantly rose. "Some woman was waiting in your bed?"

"At their home. They always insist that I eat dinner with them on the days I return, no matter how late the hour." His expression hardened into a grimace. "Gerbin always did that."

She closed the distance and wrapped her arms around his waist, pressing against his chest. "I'm sorry. You're not him, and that's so fucked up."

He stiffened but then his arms came up, loosely hugging her. He relaxed and pulled her closer. "I'm glad you're here."

She kept her head tucked down, cheek pressed against his shirt. "I'm kind of upset with you but I'm so happy you're healed. You are, aren't you? I didn't see any bandages, and that T-shirt you're sporting is pretty tight." She ran her fingers along his back, feeling only warmth and smoothness under the soft cotton of his shirt.

"I meant to come to you after that fight but I was injured. Micah took good care of you, didn't he?"

271

"Micah was great. That's not why I'm upset." It was easier not looking at him while they talked. "Sherry."

His body turned rigid against her once more.

"Yes, I know she gave you blood. I was worried sick when Micah said you were injured so he let me use his phone to call you. She answered while you were in the shower. She assumed I was Stellia. I didn't correct her."

Wen let her go with one arm. His fingers slid into her hair and gave it a tug that forced her head up. She looked into his eyes then. He frowned.

"I didn't fuck her, Gerri. It wasn't like that. Hell, I don't even remember drinking her blood. I had passed out from blood loss at that point. Graves said my fangs were out so they just shoved her arm in my mouth. Instinct took over to feed, since I was so hurt. I *am* part Vampire. I never break my word. It's over between her and I."

She believed him. "It sounded like she was in your room while you were in the shower because she talked to you and you answered." She paused. "And she called you 'babe'. That sounds pretty intimate."

His eyes turned black and he growled. Gerri gasped when he suddenly lifted her off her feet. He strode over to the bed and threw them both on it. Wen nearly crushed her under his body but he adjusted fast, using his arms and legs to pin her down as he lifted his chest so she could breathe. Their faces were inches apart. He wiggled his hips against her legs and she spread them until his lower body fit between her thighs.

"I didn't fuck her, Gerri," he snarled. "I washed off the blood and she was in Micah's room. So was I. That's where Graves took us. I'd taken too much blood from her so she was recovering on the bed, fully clothed, so she didn't faint."

She wiggled and freed her arms enough to touch his face. Hair had sprouted on his cheeks. "Okay. I trust you. Do you need to shift?"

He seemed to calm enough to get himself back under control. The excess hair went away, his eye color returned to blue, but the fangs in his mouth remained. "No. I went for a run with Tymber before I came here. I'm just pissed. I'd never break my word to you."

"I was jealous," she admitted. "I really hate her. How sad is that? I haven't even met her and yeah, I want to strangle her for calling you babe and being anywhere near you when you were in the shower. Did she get to see you naked and wet?"

His expression softened. "Doubtful. She paled every time she sat up on the bed from blood loss. I don't even know how she managed to make it inside the hotel and up to the room in that condition. I was too out of it to remember that part myself. I had to ask Graves how he got me to the room."

She stopped caressing his face and lowered her hands to his shoulders, resting them there. "Are you upset that I'm here? I don't want to go back to my old apartment or to that life. I know you can't mate me but I want to be close to you. We could be lovers. I thought about that. We'll use condoms and shower after we're together. That way your scent won't linger on me. We'll have to be careful about not touching when we're not in this room, since contact can be smelled on our clothing if we hug."

"I don't want to sneak around with you."

273

"Oh." His words hurt but she wasn't surprised. He'd made it clear about his parents and how they would react if they found out.

"I don't plan to hide that you're mine any longer."

Gerri gaped at him, stunned yet hopeful. "What are you saying?"

"Do you honestly believe you could live this close to me and I would be able to stay away? Trayis knew that when he brought you to the clan. There's no fucking way I'd be able to sleep knowing you were alone in a bed I could so easily share with you. I'd go insane within days worrying about you, wondering if other men were considering pursuing you. Fuck that. You're mine, G.L. You're here and you're staying. I'm headstrong, sometimes do stupid shit, but I'm not a total moron."

She smiled. "You can occasionally be a bit of a bonehead."

"True but not about you or this. Trayis has left me with no choice."

His last words almost made her want to flinch. "Do you resent that? Or me?"

"No. He's right. I haven't been happy because you weren't in my life. I've tried my best to do right by my parents but it's time to claim you." His gaze slid to her shoulder, then studied her eyes. "I'm going to get off you, we'll strip, and then I'm going to bite you. Are you ready to become my mate?"

"I've always been ready."

He smiled. "Me too. You're going to have to drink from me."

"I know how it goes."

He lifted up and climbed off the bed, yanking at his boots. "Get undressed."

274

She didn't have to be told twice. After so many lonely years, Wen would finally be her mate. Her deepest fantasy was about to happen.

She was able to get naked faster than him, since she only had to toss off the nightshirt and get rid of her undies. Wen didn't say a word as he pulled his T-shirt over his head then unfastened his jeans, pushing them down his long legs.

"You sure about this, G.L.? There's no going back once we bond."

"I've never been more certain of anything in my life." He was her heart and always had been, for as long as he'd been a part of her life.

"Nervous?"

"A little. I'm not a fan of pain and you've got some awfully big fangs." She smiled though, teasing him a bit. "Of course, everything on you is big." She openly admired his stiff cock when he straightened. "You look excited."

He chuckled. "I am. I'll bite while you climax. It will distract you. I promise." He took a step closer.

She held up her hand. "Wait."

He froze. "What?"

"I don't have fangs. Don't we exchange blood at the same time in a mating ritual? How do you want to do that?"

"We'll figure it out." He moved fast, wrapped his arm around her waist and hoisted her off her feet. He turned and they landed on the bed side by side, against each other. "Step one. Get her naked in a bed." Amusement teased his voice and showed in his glowing blue eyes.

She laughed.

He rolled on top of her, adjusting until once again his hips were between her thighs. This time clothing didn't separate their skin. "Step two, pin her down so she can't get away."

"I can't wait for step three. Did they teach this to you as a young VampLycan?"

"Blame Angelo. He's Micah and Graves's father. He claimed his mate in the woods while he was walking her home to her parents after a pack event. They got into an argument and she threatened to date other Lycans because some women had been flirting with him. He lost his mind, since he knew she was his. Took her to the ground, seduced her, and that's how it went down." He laughed. "It wouldn't have been so bad except it had rained earlier that day. She was kind of pissed about having to tell her parents they were mated while both of them looked as if they'd been mud wrestling. Their clothes were ripped up too. He nagged us boys to never make that mistake."

"I met them." Gerri laughed too. "I can't imagine Angelo doing that to Mandy. She's so tiny."

"She had more clothes left on her than he did, from what I heard. Don't let her size fool you. She's pretty strong and had wanted to mate Angelo for a while. He's two years older than her and didn't want to take her the day she turned eighteen. He wanted her to have at least a year to enjoy being an adult before she started having his cubs. One of the downsides to being full Lycan is the males get the urge to impregnate their mate right away." He frowned all of a sudden. "You met them? How?"

276

"I'll tell you later. Right now…" She ran her hands over his arms. "I have this super-hot guy on top of me with some sexy fangs. Don't be a tease, honeybun."

He growled, his eyes glowing brighter. She didn't look away from him, knowing he wasn't trying to control her mind. He was just seriously turned on. So was she. He kissed her, his mouth taking full possession. Gerri moaned, meeting his passion.

The scent of him filled her nose and she knew his pheromones were filling the room. Wen smelled like pure sin and sex. She wrapped her legs around his hips and ground her pussy against him. He broke the kiss and tried to lower down her body.

She fisted his hair to keep him in place and shook her head. "I'm ready and wet. Feel me?"

"I want to taste you."

"Later. We have forever for that."

"I don't want to rush this."

"Are you kidding? I've always wanted you. Fuck me and bite me, Wen. Now."

He grinned. "So bossy."

"Get used to it, honeybun."

A deep laugh blasted out of him. "Promise to never call me that in front of anyone else."

"But I want to lick you and savor everything about you. Honeybuns are my favorite. I always crave them."

He lowered his face, brushing hot, sensual kisses along her throat. His fangs came into play, lightly biting her. "You drive me insane in the best way."

She lifted her legs higher, digging her heels into his ass, trying to urge him to enter her. "Fuck me," she moaned.

He nipped her hard, then twisted his body a little, arched his back, and reached down. She knew what he was doing and helped by holding still when he gripped his shaft, rose up a little, and guided the head of his cock to her pussy. He groaned deep as he slid in a bit. He released himself and then used his upper arms to cage her under him tighter.

"Yes," she urged. "Do it."

"I'm not going to last long," he warned.

"Me either." She bucked her hips. "Stop teasing."

"Gentle or rough?"

The words came out snarled but she understood. "Don't hold back. Take me."

Gerri moaned louder as Wen thrust into her deeply. His cock felt big, thick, and incredibly hard. He didn't try to kiss her mouth but stayed at her neck, licking and lightly biting. She clung to him as he powered into her. Between the sensation of him physically inside her and the way he smelled so incredible, she felt nearly overwhelmed with pleasure.

"Oh God," she cried out, knowing she hadn't lied about coming fast. Ecstasy built as he pounded into her. Wen sank his fangs into her throat, the sharp jolt of pain sending her over the edge. She almost screamed but didn't have the breath to do it. She threw her head back, her mind blown from the power of her orgasm.

Wen didn't slow, only fucked her harder, making animalistic sounds as he clamped his mouth tighter onto her throat. He lifted one arm and shoved his hand near her mouth. It was wet, and she realized what he'd done. The soft, meaty area of his palm bleed. He must have used a claw to tear it open. She closed her mouth around it, drinking.

Wen groaned, and she felt him coming inside her. He shook from the force of his release, riding her until the last tremors shook his body. They both drank, locked together. Wen released her throat first, running his tongue over the bite a few times. He pulled his hand back and kissed her, the taste of blood on their lips.

"My mate."

"My mate," she repeated.

"I'm never going to let you go, G.L."

"I'm counting on it."

He slowly began to move inside her again, and she moaned. "What are you doing?"

"No rest for the wicked. Do you want to know how I'm feeling? I'm inside my mate. I'm going to be here for a while."

The blood she drank suddenly hit her system. Adrenaline and heat made her claw at him, desperate to hold him tighter. "Please!"

"Get used to the blood highs, my sexy little powerhouse. It's going to be a long night but I'll let you get some rest in between."

"Shut up and make me come again."

He laughed. "Bossy mate."

"Tease."

Chapter Eighteen

Wen answered the door when the knock came. He jerked it open, not surprised to see who stood there. "Morning, you devious asshole."

Trayis loudly inhaled and then had the nerve to grin. "I knew you'd mate Gerri. Are you able to step aside to let me in or are you going to be an overprotective ass about letting even safe males around your new mate?"

Wen backed up. "She's still getting ready and should be out soon. Come in."

"Have you shared the news with anyone yet?"

"No. We woke up, I made breakfast with her, and then we showered, since you told her you were coming at this hour. All that long hair of hers takes forever to towel dry enough so she doesn't have a soaked shirt on her back. At least that's what she said when I asked why it was taking her so long in the bathroom." Wen closed the door and faced the man standing just inside the house. "I figure I can announce it when you let everyone know Gerri is back with the clan. Or they'll smell it if we get close to them."

Trayis sniffed again and grinned. "Your scent is mixed with hers pretty strongly. Is she okay?"

"I'd never hurt her."

"She's not a large woman and you took a lot of her blood."

"I gave her a lot of mine back."

"No side effects? Weakness this morning?"

"She's fine. Are you looking for a reason to delay this meeting?"

"No. It's new for me to play an actual father role. I verbally adopted her." He winked. "I imagine that would be a question I'd ask someone who'd just claimed my daughter."

Wen frowned, not liking that. "Why would you do that?"

"Because Mandro can be an asshole and a problem as an elder. Some may side with him. It's an extra layer of protection for her against your father. Gerri is no longer just a human with clan standing that you took as a mate. Let him try to claim now that my daughter would make weak offspring with his precious only son."

Understanding hit, and Wen had to keep his jaw from falling open.

Trayis smiled wider.

"Insulting a clan leader is punishable."

The humor left Trayis's face. "Damn straight it is. I want you both happy, Wen. You and Gerri belong together. You always have. I'm tired of parents getting in the way. Hers. Yours. My priority is a happy clan."

"She didn't tell me you'd adopted her."

"Did you two really talk all that much last night?"

Wen shook his head. "No."

"I didn't think so. She probably doesn't realize the full extent of being put under my protection. At least you look as if you might have gotten a few hours of sleep."

"She's human. I didn't want to wear her out by keeping her up all night."

Trayis reached out and gripped his shoulder. "She'll get stronger the more you exchange blood."

"She's no weakling."

"I'm aware." Trayis released him and his head turned.

Wen sensed Gerri coming and smiled at the sight of her. "There's my beautiful mate."

She hesitated upon seeing Trayis, then bowed. "Trayis."

"Enough with that shit, Gerri."

Wen didn't like Trayis's tone and growled.

Trayis snarled back.

Gerri was between them faster than he thought she could move. "Is it time to go? No fighting in the living room. I'd forgotten how much testosterone you VampLycans ooze. I'm not even sure what you both are upset about."

"Wen doesn't like me giving his mate an order."

"I don't," Wen agreed. "She was being respectful."

"Her status in the clan has changed regardless of you mating her. She no longer bows to me because she's family." Trayis lowered his gaze to Gerri and his tone softened. "Okay?"

"Yes. I'm just used to doing it."

"No longer," Trayis repeated. "Let's go. I told the clan we'd meet outside my office. Everyone has been ordered to be there."

Wen kept close to Gerri as they walked through the woods. A few other VampLycans joined up with them. He caught their surprised looks at seeing Gerri—then outright shock when their sense of smell kicked in as they got close enough to them. He held their gazes, daring anyone to give him any shit. None did. Instead, they all smiled at him and he saw genuine happiness in their expressions.

Though relieved, it also saddened him when he realized why he'd automatically expected opposition. His parents had darkened his outlook on mating humans so deeply, he'd projected those negative feelings on the rest of the clan. The truth was there every time another VampLycan joined them on their walk and their reactions continued to be so positive. No one spoke though, because Trayis remained silent.

They finally reached the office. It was a large barn-like structure. Nearly eighty VampLycans waited outside. Wen noticed that Gerri's grip on his hand tightened when heads turned and it seemed everyone was staring at them. He pulled her even closer, their bodies bumping together with each step. He searched for his parents and found them near the office door.

Mandro's eyes turned black with rage when he spotted them. His mother clutched at his father with a look of horror etched on her face. Wen felt dread. They obviously remembered Gerri. She had changed over the years but not enough to confuse them regarding her identity. They would cause a scene.

His father didn't even wait for Trayis and them to reach the front of the building. He pulled away from his mate and threw up his arm, pointing at Gerri. "What is the meaning of this?"

Wen halted with Gerri next to him. He pulled her flush to his side but prepared to leap forward if his father attempted to get close to her. He wouldn't allow it.

284

Trayis stepped between his father and Gerri, probably blocking his dad from even seeing her.

"The meaning of what, Mandro?" Trayis's voice boomed in the silence. "Everyone here who is an adult will remember Gerri. She's returned to her clan. For the youths gathered, I'm certain you've been told about Klentz mating to the human Carol, and that she had a daughter named Gerri. This is her. Her mother left our clan to return to the human world. Gerri was a youth who was forced to leave at her mother's demand. She's returned to her home, now that she's an adult, and has finally mated to Wen. They are true mates. That calls for a celebration."

"No!" Wen's mother screeched.

Wen tugged Gerri behind him and let her go. Two VampLycans flanked him from behind and he glanced back. Tymber and his brother Yern were there, taking protective stances inches from Gerri. The look in their eyes told him they'd keep her safe. He stepped up next to Trayis just as his mother dodged around his father.

"I won't allow it," his mother shrieked. Her claws flew out and hair sprouted along her skin. "She's not mating my son!"

Mandro grabbed her around the waist and jerked her into his arms. "You can't attack her. Calm."

She fought him, trying to break free. "I can! Not a human, not with *my* son! Never! I'll kill her first!"

"Enough!" Trayis thundered.

Wen winced, pain shooting through his ear from the volume of his clan leader's shout so close to him. Other clansmen had the same reaction, some of them even throwing their hands up to cover their ears. Wen's mother stilled in his father's arms.

"Is it true?" Mandro snarled. "You mated her?" His black eyes locked on Wen.

"Gerri is my mate. She was always mine. You've known it since we were kids. I'm not Gerbin, nor will I ever be."

Mandro took a step forward, must have remembered that he held his mate, and growled. He lowered Elna until her feet touched the ground but kept his arm around her waist. "I forbid it!"

"It's done." Wen approached his parents. "Trust your noses if you don't want to hear the words. Gerri *is* my true mate. She will be the mother of my young one day."

"You can't forbid it." Trayis stood next to Wen. "He's not your child anymore. He's my enforcer."

"She's human. They are weak!" Mandro hissed. "She can't birth the next generation of our bloodline."

"I've adopted her as my daughter. Think carefully before you say those words again." Trayis glanced around. "I had hoped to announce it with a bit more tact, but there it is. Klentz was a good friend to me, and I swore I'd look out for his daughter as if she were my own if anything ever happened to him. What better way than to adopt her myself?" He glared at Mandro. "She's always been a part of our clan, but she's also family. Understood?"

Wen felt pain as his parents both paled and he took in their reactions. His father stumbled back, dragging his mother with him. His mouth opened, closed, then opened again…but no words left his father's lips.

A small hand pressed against his spine and he reached back for his mate. He knew it was Gerri. She leaned against his side and he was glad she was there. He put his arm around her, hugging her.

His father spun, lifted his mate into his arms, and stormed off into the woods. Wen watched them go.

Trayis turned his head to speak directly to Wen. "They must face this head on. Adapt or not. That's their choice, not yours."

He knew his leader was right. He hated that the clan had witnessed the tense scene though. His parents were too proud. It hadn't been their best moment.

Trayis strode over to the office door and smiled. "Who said clan meetings are boring?"

A few people laughed.

"Gerri is back and Wen is mated. As I was saying, that calls for a celebration. For those of you who haven't met Gerri, introduce yourself to her today. She was raised with us, so there are no secrets. They need a few days to bond so we'll hold a clan lunch feast on Saturday. We'll also be inviting some of the other clans. They have reason to celebrate too. Wen took care of the last Vampire who attacked the human town and Lorn's clan. That threat is over."

Wen saw smiles break out amongst the assembled clan. Trayis walked around, taking questions. Some of his friends wanted to see Gerri again and youths came forward to meet her. He kept her at his side but his gaze continued to roam, and he hoped his parents didn't return.

Gerri felt exhausted by the time Wen led her back home. It had been nice to see familiar faces. The children had wanted to touch her hair, her skin, and ask her about the human world. The most uncomfortable questions had been those about her mother.

"You did really well."

"Except the lying."

Wen opened the front door, sniffed, and then motioned her in. She guessed why he did it. His parents had taken off from the meeting and not come back. Neither of them had been thrilled upon learning of their mating. Not that she'd thought they'd take it well. But no blood had been spilled, so there was a plus side.

"You said your mother was living with a pack in California. How was that a lie?" He closed the door and twisted the bolts.

She frowned. "Because there's a real possibility that she's not still alive. Why did you bolt the door?"

"My parents. It's a habit I've formed thanks to them. I don't want them walking in here."

"Do you think they'll come after me?"

Wen hesitated. "It would be stupid."

"But you think they would? Just answer."

He shrugged. "They aren't the same as they used to be. I never know what they're capable of now. I won't risk it. I checked all the windows this morning. They are secured. They'd have to kick in a door or break glass to get in."

Damn. She hated that he was on high alert from his parents. It wasn't necessarily her fault but it had to suck for him. She walked over and hugged his waist, closed her eyes, and rested her cheek against his chest. "I love you."

He held her tight. "I love you too. You're not responsible for their actions."

"I know that. You aren't either."

He said nothing, so she opened her eyes and looked up at him. The tortured expression on his face made her chest ache.

"People can get broken inside when someone they love dies. They either bounce back or they allow it to eat them up. I saw that with my mother. The loss of her mate changed her."

"I'll just never understand why I wasn't enough for them."

"Please don't think that way. I've gone that route and it takes you nowhere good. I talked to my mother until I was blue in the face and begged her to get her life together. I was her daughter, and she should have loved me enough to try to hang in there. That didn't happen. She was slowly spiraling deeper into screwing up her life *and* mine. I couldn't snap her out of it. I told you that she drank and I suspected she was doing drugs. The pack she got involved with was my wakeup call that she was hell-bent on destruction. That one asshole attacked me but she took their side. It's not like I just disappeared on her without warning. I begged her to leave with me but she refused to go."

Wen rubbed her back. "I'm sorry."

"It was cut ties or let her drown me in that murk with her, Wen. She failed me. Not the other way around. Your parents have done the same to you. You're an amazing son if they never figured that out. Don't ever allow them to make you feel like less. It pisses me off."

A faint smile curved his lips. "I'm pissed at your mother."

"Me too but I'm not going to let that eat at me. We have shitty parents. That's okay, because now we have each other."

"Don't you want to contact Carol to tell her we mated?"

"No."

"Perhaps she left the pack and got her life in order."

"Then I wouldn't know how to find her anyway. Her boyfriend didn't allow her to have her own phone. He was a controlling jerk. It's better this way. I made my peace with losing my mom the day she chose that pack over me. Besides, I like to imagine she actually turned into a Lycan from the blood she was drinking and ran off with some hot newbie who couldn't stand the pack he'd joined." She smiled. "They're mated in my fantasy and she's happy. Maybe even had a few more pups."

"You're breaking my heart, G.L."

"It's called hope. I used to fantasize about you too." She slid her hands up his chest and curled her fingers around the back of his neck. "And here we are."

He grinned. "Alone in your cabin."

"We should decide which place we're going to live in."

"I don't give a shit as long as we're in the same bed."

She laughed. "Speaking of, how about we go test out the mattress springs again?"

"First you need to eat. It's past lunch and your stomach is grumbling."

"Sex, then food."

"Food, then sex."

"Is everything going to be an argument with you, Wen?"

He ran his hands down to her ass and cupped both cheeks with his large hands, lifting her. "I'm your mate. I want to take care of you."

She wrapped around him. "It's our honeymoon. I want lots of sex. We have years to make up for."

He walked into the kitchen and shelved her butt on the counter. "Food first." He leaned in and nipped her bottom lip. "I wouldn't want you fainting on me. Besides, I want to impress you with my cooking skills."

"I'm more interested in what you can do in a bedroom right now."

He let her go and backed away. "How about a compromise?"

"I'm listening."

"I'll cook you something but we can eat it naked in bed."

She grinned. "Deal. Just don't make it too hot. I want to eat stuff off your bod."

He growled. "Tease."

"You're the one insisting on lunch first."

He yanked open the fridge. "I see lots of sandwich stuff. That will be faster than cooking a meal."

She slid off the counter as Wen rummaged in the storage drawers of the fridge. He held a lot of things when he rose up and turned. His mouth fell open when Gerri gripped the neck of her shirt and yanked it down, flashing him her breasts.

"What are you doing?"

"One of my training instructors recently reminded me to flash my boobs if I was about to be attacked. He said a man would want to fuck me instead. Was he right?"

Wen growled, his gaze locked on her breasts.

She backed away. "Come on, boy. Good doggy. Follow me."

Wen turned and just dumped everything back into the fridge. He growled again, slamming the fridge shut as he faced her again. "Are you really doing this, G.L.?"

She laughed. "Let's play with a bone. Got a big one hidden somewhere in your pants?"

He lunged and she twisted away, running for the bedroom.

Wen caught her before she reached the door and buried his face in her neck as he lifted her. He inhaled deeply. One of his arms was wrapped around her waist and he snaked his other up to cup her breast, gently squeezing it. "You smell so damn good." He carried her in front of him to the bedroom. "I'm trying to be a caring mate."

"Am I making it hard for you? Pun intended."

"Very hard."

He lifted her a little higher, released her breast and turned her in his arms. "I missed you so fucking much. I was dying inside without you."

She cupped his face and kissed him. He flopped them on the bed, twisting as they fell so she landed on top of him. She straddled his lap and

292

sat up. "I was dying inside too. Now it's about life and enjoying every moment of it together." She scooted down on him and unfastened his jeans. "And I am hungry—but I want to taste *you*."

"You are so damn sexy."

"So are you, honeybun. Now lift your hips and help me shove these down. You weigh a ton."

He arched his hips of the bed a few inches. "Mean mate."

"Say that when I'm licking you to death."

"My sexy, perfect mate."

"That's better." She got his jeans down enough to free his cock. He hadn't put on underwear. "Lower back down. Perfect. Never change, Wen." She shoved her hair to one side to get it out of the way and scooted back a little more so she could reach him with her mouth.

"I always fantasized about your mouth wrapped around me," Wen groaned.

"Dreams really do come true when we're together." She opened her mouth and gently gripped the thick shaft of his cock, running her tongue along the crown. She loved the low growls that erupted from him as she got to know her mate's taste.

Gerri used her mouth on Wen but lifted her gaze to stare up at him. He threw his head back, mouth open and fangs showing as she brought him pleasure. His hands fisted the bedding but he released it fast when his claws slid out. The animalistic noises he made turned her on. Everything about him did.

"I can't hold back," he snarled.

She moved her mouth over him faster, taking him deeper. His entire body tensed but he suddenly bucked his hips, dislodging her. He sat up, grabbed her, and flipped her onto her back.

"Why did you do that?"

He slid off the bed, grabbed her ankle, and jerked her down the mattress. He rolled her and put her on her knees in front of him, pressing her forward so she was bent over the bed. He shoved down her pants and panties.

"I need to be inside you when I come," he growled.

Gerri moaned his name as he slowly entered her. She clawed the bed, knowing she couldn't shred the bedding the way Wen could. He paused when he was fully seated inside her. A heartbeat later he was moving fast and deep, fucking her as if their lives depended on it.

He fisted her hair, pulling it out of the way, and he bit her. The pain and pleasure sent her over the edge fast. She cried out his name, knowing he got off at the same time she did.

They were both panting when he eased his fangs out of her and licked her neck. She lie there, feeling boneless. "I don't know what that was but I'm not complaining."

"Fucking Lycan side," he grumbled. "I thought, 'I'm going to blow, but what if that's the semen that could get my mate pregnant?' That's how you ended up in this position. Got any doggy jokes now, golden locks?"

Gerri started laughing. Being mated to a VampLycan would never be boring.

Chapter Nineteen

Wen wasn't happy about being called to Trayis's home late at night. He and Gerri had been sharing a bath, their first as mates, after he'd finally gotten her to eat. She walked beside him, holding his hand as he paused at the front door and knocked.

Trayis answered it. "Come in."

"What's wrong? What have my parents done? That's it, right?"

Gerri tightened her hold on him and shot him a worried look. He hated that his parents were a danger to her. He wanted her to feel safe as his mate. Trayis gestured them to take a seat on the couch.

Wen led her inside but didn't want to sit down. "Just tell it to us straight. What have they done?"

Trayis closed the door and leaned against it. "They informed me that they no longer wish to be part of my clan."

Wen had to lock his knees to keep from falling on his ass. He was that stunned. "What?"

"They wanted my permission to leave. I'd never force someone to stay. I made some calls. I didn't want to ask Lorn to take them in. He's got enough shit to deal with as far as troubled VampLycans go. Velder and Crocker both offered to accept them. They've decided to move into Crocker's territory. It seems they've made some friends there."

"That's where most of the women came from that they tried to throw at me." Wen was still reeling. "I'll talk to them."

"They're already gone, Wen. I guess they left the meeting, packed their belongings into their truck, and just wanted official permission to leave. I watched them drive away myself and had one of the enforcers follow them out of our territory." Trayis moved closer. "I'm sorry, but this is probably for the best. They each gave their word that they wouldn't attempt to harm Gerri or any children you had."

Gerri tugged on his hand and practically pulled him to the couch. She gave him a shove until he heavily sat. She climbed onto his lap and put her arms around him. "I'm so sorry."

Trayis took a seat in a chair near them, watching Wen with concern. "I didn't see this coming either."

Wen had never guessed they'd leave the clan. "At least I didn't have to kill anyone."

"There's one more thing I need to tell you." Trayis hesitated, his expression grim.

"Just say it." Wen braced for more emotional shocks.

"Man, it's so screwed up, I don't even know how to break it to you."

"Wen is strong," Gerri murmured. "I'm with him. Tell us. Whatever it is, we'll get through it together."

Trayis glanced at Gerri, then held Wen's gaze. "They came to tell me they wanted to leave. I told them I'd make those calls, which I did, and then I went to their house to let them know which clans they could live with. Your father told me they'd go to Crocker's territory, but...then your mother thanked me—for letting them know that *you* had died. She turned to your father and said they had nothing left here, now that both of their sons were lost to them forever."

Wen closed his eyes, fighting to remember how to breathe.

His mate held on to him tighter and he forced his lungs to work.

"Elna's totally fucking lost it," Trayis muttered. "And Mandro was going right along with it, assuring her they could have more children. He said it would be like when they'd first mated. I'm so sorry, Wen. I had to tell you in case you tried to contact them. That's how they're playing this now."

He nodded. "I'm dead to them."

"Oh, Wen. I'm so sorry."

He held on tight to his mate. "Don't cry, Gerri." He reached up and wiped at her tears. "I remember what you said about your mother and how you had to walk away from her. You survived that. I'm so proud that you're a survivor. So am I. You're the only family I need."

It hurt a hell of a lot, but in a way, his parents had lost him years ago when his older brother had died. He'd stopped being Wen to them and became a replacement for Gerbin. His gaze met Trayis's next. "It's for the best."

"It is," Trayis stated firmly. "Do you want me to adopt you too?"

The offer was a huge honor. He thought about it for half a minute. A laugh burst out of Wen. "Hell no. That would make my mate my sister."

Trayis sat up straighter but then amusement sparked in his eyes. "I didn't think about that. You're my son-in-mate. Just don't call me daddy. That would be weird."

"So fucking weird," Tymber stated from the hallway. "Kinky too."

Wen turned his head, staring at his friend. "I didn't know you were here."

"We weren't sure how you'd react, so I wanted to be close in case you wanted to beat on someone." Tymber sat on the coffee table. "Sorry your parents are fuckheads. The good news is that they won't be screwing with you, your mate, or the kids you have. No more unwelcome random bitches in your bed either. Just the hot little number on your lap." Tymber winked at Gerri.

Wen snarled at him. "Don't flirt with my mate."

"I think Tymber was looking forward to you kicking his ass around my yard if you needed to get out your frustrations and is still trying to make that happen." Trayis stood. "Anyone want a drink? I know I could sure use one."

All three of them said yes.

Gerri reached up and ran her thumb over Wen's lip. "Are you okay?"

"I am. It's actually a relief," he admitted.

"Really?" She didn't look convinced.

"I thought it would end in bloodshed. It didn't. I'm disowned. I can live with that. Best of all, I don't have to worry about them coming after you."

"I feel guilty."

"What did you tell me about it not being my fault that they're this way?"

Gerri smiled. "True."

"There are no regrets when it comes to us. I love you, G.L."

"I love you too, honey b—"

Wen lunged and kissed her lips to mute her. She laughed against his mouth and he pulled back, winking. "Only when we are alone."

Tymber leaned forward. "Honey what?"

"Forget about it." Wen shot him a warning look.

Trayis returned carrying beers. "Honey butt?"

"Maybe honey badass?" Tymber paused. "Honey badger? He can be kind of grumpy and mean. Come on, Gerri. Finish that endearment."

"Fine."

Wen tensed but she turned her head and winked at him, then faced his two friends.

"I was saying I love you too, honey, but I lust for you as well. Wen is my everything."

Tymber opened his beer. "I'm calling bullshit. Honey bee? His punches do kind of sting when he lands them."

"Here's to the mated couple." Trayis held up his beer. "Cheers to you two. The start of your mating was a bit rough but it's all good from here."

Wen opened the beer and lifted it. "To happiness."

Gerri clinked her can against his. "To love and lust."

"I'm going to figure out what you call him," Tymber promised. "Honey beehive? Because you don't fuck with those."

"Drink your beer and shut up," Trayis ordered.

They all took a sip at the same time. A phone rang and Trayis reached for his back pocket. His smile faded when he glanced at the screen, and he answered it. Then he was on his feet and down the hallway so fast, it was hard to see him.

Wen tensed, hoping it wasn't something about his parents. He hoped his troubles were over with them. The door down the hallway closed, so he couldn't hear a thing being said.

Trayis returned a minute later. This time, he appeared highly amused.

"What is it?" Tymber stood.

Wen stayed where he was. He had his mate on his lap and had no intention of moving her. She was right where she belonged. "Want to share what's so funny?"

Trayis glanced at his enforcers. "That was Lord Aveoth. He heard from Decker. The bastard wants to make a deal with him to come home. I'm guessing the Vamp Council gave him the boot." He grinned. "You did it, Wen and Gerri. I'm guessing Horton must have done or said something that messed up their little alliance."

Wen laughed, his night suddenly getting a hell of a lot better. "We do make a hell of a team."

Gerri tugged on his shirt. "Why is everyone so happy that Decker, a.k.a the boogeyman, wants to return to Alaska? Isn't that a bad thing?"

"No, G.L. It's fantastic. Lord Aveoth is going to kill that bastard."

She slowly smiled at Wen. "Never mess with a fur bat."

Tymber choked on his beer. "Did you just call Lord Aveoth a fur bat?"

Wen downed his beer and set it on the side table. He lifted Gerri. "That was your imagination. My mate would never do that. I'm taking her home. Good night."

Gerri clung to him. "Night. We're going home to do that whole love-and-lust thing."

Trayis opened the door for them. "Think girl!"

Wen carried her outside, heading toward her cabin. "What in the hell does that mean?"

She buried her face against his neck. "He wants us to have lots of sex."

"That's a weird way to put it."

She laughed. "He's a VampLycan. What do you expect? You're all kind of crazy."

He growled low at her, knowing she was playing with him. She could always make him laugh. "Seriously, what does 'think girl' mean?"

She threaded her fingers through his hair and tugged his ear closer. "He wants us to have some girl babies for the clan."

Wen came to a stop and stared into her eyes. "For real?"

"Yes. He believes mind over matter might work. So we have to think the word 'girl' every time we have sex. It's going to be easier for you than me, since I *am* one. Me on the other hand...I guess you're going to have to do things that make me totally mindless so I don't accidently think anything with the word 'boy' in there. Like, 'boy, is he good at that'. Are you up for the challenge, mate?"

He began walking again. "Accepted. Step one. Get her naked in a bed."

Gerri threw her head back and laughed. "But I'd totally do you in the mud, honeybun."

He stopped, sniffed, his gaze roaming the dark. "We're alone. I'm not scenting anyone nearby. How do you feel about dirt?"

She grabbed his face and kissed him. "I'd love to get dirty with you. Anywhere, anytime."

He left the path and hunted for a nice soft spot to make love to his mate. "You're about to be eaten by the big bad wolf, golden locks."

"You never get your fairy tales right," she teased. "That's the three bears."

"I got my fairy tale ending. That's all that matters. I have you."

Made in the USA
Lexington, KY
19 June 2017